THE LADY AND THE LAWMAN

Temptation pulled at Brannigan with a force and intensity that caught him off guard. Slipping his hands around Kate's slender waist, he bent down and whispered in her ear. "Need any help?"

"Brannigan!" His name was a shocked whisper on Kate's lips.

The silk of her gown flowed like liquid beneath his fingers and he couldn't resist caressing her back. He drew her closer, preventing her instinctive withdrawal.

"Brannigan." Kate's soft whisper invited, tempted, begged.

He complied. It was beyond him to refuse, especially when refusing was the last thing on his mind.

Her lips drew him with the same intensity that a flame draws the moth. He couldn't have stopped himself from taking her lips with his, not even if his life had depended on it. He took her lips hungrily, savoring the taste and feel of her mouth beneath his. But it wasn't enough.

She smelled of wildflowers, and sweetness and pure woman. He teased her lips with his and as he dragged his hands up to her cheeks, Kate curled her fingers around the edge of his leather vest. Her fingernails skimmed his chest and he sucked in his breath.

No other woman had ever made him feel like this with only her kiss. But with Kate it was far more than a kiss; it was a melding of two spirits, closer and closer together until they raged to become one. As he drew his mouth downward along the slim column of her throat, he pressed closer into her, his leg sliding intimately between hers.

He wanted her. Oh, how he wanted her . . .

Other Zebra Books by Joyce Adams

**REBEL MINE
GAMBLER'S LADY
MOONLIGHT MASQUERADE**

LOVING KATE

JOYCE ADAMS

ZEBRA BOOKS
KENSINGTON PUBLISHING CORP.

ZEBRA BOOKS are published by

Kensington Publishing Corp.
850 Third Avenue
New York, NY 10022

Zebra and the Z logo Reg. U.S. Pat. & TM Off. The Lovegram logo is a trademark of Kensington Publishing Corp.

First Printing: November, 1995

Printed in the United States of America

To Sueann Snow— my sounding board, shoulder, and friend. Thank you for teaching me the meaning of true friendship. And for going above and beyond the call of duty in your willingness to brave the wind and cold to ride a camel for research.

Prologue

Boston

"I absolutely forbid it!" William Danville decreed with the slam of his fist on the oak table.

"Papa, we're going to marry with or without your blessing," Kate stated defiantly, tossing her head and sending her copper curls bouncing.

"Not in Boston, you won't."

"Then we'll marry elsewhere."

"Do so, and I'll disinherit you."

She swallowed down her hurt and disappointment. Oh, how she'd hoped it wouldn't come to this. She'd dreamed of a wedding here in Boston with her father present, but now it looked as if Richard was right, they'd have to elope to his hometown of Deadrange, Nevada and start fresh.

"Papa?" Kate laid a hand on her father's forearm in an attempt to cajole him. She had to try one more time. "Perhaps—"

"Richard doesn't love you. All that no account loves is my money."

Money— it always came down to money with her father in everything. She swung away before he could witness the threat of tears his words had brought. She should be used to his beliefs by now. Leastwise one would think so.

She took a step towards the stairs. Her father wouldn't change his mind once it was made up. She had much to do before heading west.

"Good night, Kate," her father called after her.

"Good night," she answered in a choked voice. *Goodbye, Papa,* she added silently.

The next morning, William Danville paused at the foot of the stairs, resting one hand on the polished oak banister. With a weary sigh, he slowly mounted the stairs.

What was he going to do about Kate? She was too independent, spoiled, and headstrong for her own good. And she was bound and determined that she was in love.

He stopped outside her door, his footsteps heavy. He hated hurting his daughter more than anything in this world, likely the reason he gave her almost anything she asked for. Almost, but not this time. This time he had to stop her from her foolish notion of marrying. What he was about to do would save her a lot more hurt later, he assured himself, she'd forgive him.

He had to make her see reason about Richard Hale. Patting the parchment paper inside his breast pocket, he sighed deeply. She wasn't going to like what he had to show her. Tucked inside lay proof that her young man was nothing more than a liar and a thief.

"Kate?" He rapped softly on her bedroom door.

After waiting several moments for a response, he lowered his voice to his best negotiating banker tone. "Now, Kate."

Still no answer.

"Dammit, Katherine Marie, you've sulked long enough. Open this door."

Frustrated by her obstinate behavior, he turned the knob. The door swung inward on well-oiled hinges to reveal the unslept-in bed and a folded note atop the pillow. Across the room, the sheer curtains billowed in the breeze from the open window.

She was gone.

"Oh dammit, Kate, why do you always have to go off and borrow trouble?" he whispered.

One

Trouble was brewing.

Marshal Lucas Brannigan could feel it seeping through the hot Nevada air. Shading his eyes against the blazing summer sun, he pushed his black Stetson further back on his head and scanned the barren countryside.

Nothing.

It seemed as if not even a horsefly was moving, and that was part of the problem. No stagecoach, no riders, not even a cloud of dust rose on the horizon. The ten o'clock stage was over four hours late, and not even in sight.

Damn, he swore, pulling his hat lower against the sun's glare. In spite of the heat, he felt his skin turning cool— a sure sign of trouble.

Hell and damnation, trouble was definitely brewing.

Shouldn't they have arrived in Deadrange by now?

Kate Danville withdrew a lace-edged handkerchief from her reticule and dabbed at the perspiration trickling down the velvet-trimmed neckline of her lavender traveling gown. Beneath her aching derriere, the high-backed leather seat swayed back and forth. She swore the damned stage hadn't stopped rocking and swaying in the last week.

A rivulet of perspiration ran lower, threatening to pool between her breasts, and she swiped at the moisture. *Ladies never perspire,* the hated words of her finishing school instructor flogged her.

Not that Mrs. Parker had ever succeeded in making a true and proper lady out of her, claiming more times than she could recall that it only went skin deep on Kate. She dabbed at her neck again. Perspire— hell, she was sweating. Profusely at that.

Kate mopped the damp lace across her cheeks and forehead, blowing a stray copper curl away from her eye. If Richard were to see her now, he would likely walk right past her. She was a far sight from the perfectly coiffed lady who had boarded the stage so long ago.

A lady is always perfectly presented, another one of Mrs. Parker's well-learned rules rose up to taunt her. Right now Kate didn't feel much like a lady— inside or outside.

Irritated, she glanced at the two remaining passengers. The monotonous clackety-clack of the Concord stagecoach wheels had lulled them to sleep. The possibility of it was beyond her.

Kate wiggled on the hard seat, trying to find a reasonably comfortable position sandwiched between the ample form of Mrs. Madison on her left and the door jutting into her right side. Across from them, Mr. Billings, the traveling salesman, snored loudly, his chin resting on his chest. Traveling drummer, she corrected herself. She didn't think she'd ever become accustomed to these funny-sounding Western phrases.

The sobering crinkle of paper from inside her reticule drew her wandering attention and caused

her brows to knit into a frown. Messages from
Richard, left for her at several stops along the te-
dious trip. Atchison . . . Denver . . . Salt Lake
City— all bearing the same distressing news.

Each message held excuses why he hadn't met
her as previously scheduled to travel with her to
meet his family in Deadrange. But Richard would
be at Deadrange, she told herself. There wouldn't
be another message of delay awaiting her. He
would be there.

He damned well better be.

Kate tossed her head. If not, she was likely to
board the next stage back to Boston faster than . . .

The crack of a rifle shot rang out through the
surrounding quiet, and the team of horses lunged
into a wild gallop, throwing Kate onto the floor
of the coach.

"What in tunket?" she muttered, shoving a tangle of curls out of her eyes.

She scarcely had time to scramble up onto the
seat before the coach swerved wildly, and Mr. Billings tumbled face first on the floor, barely missing her feet. The next lurch of the stage threw
Kate against the back of the seat with a hard thud.

"Oh, my," Mrs. Madison screamed and caught
her reticule to her bosom. "We're being robbed."

Two more shots rang out in rapid succession,
and Mrs. Madison promptly collapsed in a faint
against the door. Another shot cracked, followed
by a cry of pain from the driver. As the coach
lurched out of control, Kate grabbed for the edge
of the seat and hung on. The rumble of thunder-
ing hooves echoed.

Now what? She was in a runaway coach with no
driver! How was she supposed to stop the horses

from in here? She reached for the door, but as gunfire sounded, she yanked her hand back.

Gathering up her courage, she reached again and pulled back the leather window covering in time to see two riders gallop past. Shouts filled the air, then the coach jerked and lumbered to a halt.

"Thank goodness." Kate breathed a sigh of relief and settled her dainty bonnet with its plumed feather back into place, then picked up her lace parasol from the floor.

She pulled back the window covering again and peered out. *Right down the barrel of a gun.*

"Well, lookee what we have here." The gunman's wide, toothy grin displayed tobacco-stained teeth. "Come on out here to Joe, sugar." He scratched his stomach, sliding his fingers between two gaping buttons.

Kate resisted the instinctive urge to scoot back onto the seat. Instead, she met the robber's leer with a challenging stare of refusal.

"No, thank you," she answered defiantly.

The next instant the door was jerked open. Joe grabbed her arm, and before Kate could do more than yelp, she was dragged out of the stagecoach. She tumbled into an undignified heap at the robbers' feet.

All about her, horses' hooves shifted, the clop-clop seeming to roar in her ears as the massive animals pranced in a hypnotic two-step around her. Of course, they'd be on horses— the only thing she admitted to being afraid of and avoided at every opportunity. Just her blasted luck. She knew all she needed to know about the beasts; one end kicked and the other end bit.

She jumped to her feet and ducked out of their

way, raising her chin and meeting her fears
straight on. Four men and four horses stared back
at her. The jangle of a bridle alerted her an instant before the men dismounted.

Her actions seemed to amuse them, and Kate's
temper soared with each resounding chuckle.
She'd had enough. She was hot, tired, sore, and
mad. No one, but no one, treated her this way.
She bent down to retrieve her parasol from the
dusty ground.

From the corner of her eye she saw Joe reach
out to grab her arm. She ducked her head and
surged up in a swift move, catching the outlaw
right in the middle of his protruding belly. The
force of the impact knocked Kate's bonnet askew
and Joe flat on his back.

Raucous laughter from the other outlaws warned
her seconds before they converged on her. One
tall skinny man rubbed his fingers over the fine
material of her sleeve. A younger man caught at
her waist and swore when he missed. A strand of
oily blond hair dipped over his eyebrow. She
slapped at him with her parasol.

"Hey, Joe, she sure is feisty, ain't she?" the
young man sneered.

Kate backed away and glanced warily at the outlaws. The one called Joe lay like an overturned
turtle to her right. Taking another cautious step
backwards, she surveyed the area. The stagecoach
driver lay slumped over the seat at a drunken angle, obviously wounded. Or worse.

She swallowed down the sob that rose up into
her throat, fighting down the nausea that followed.
Buck had been nice to her, even suggesting that
she secure a place on the high-backed leather seat

with its back to the driver for a more comfortable ride. The parasol slipped from her fingers.

As the younger outlaw shook back the strand of hair and took a broad step closer, Kate bolted, but there was nowhere to run. And no one to come to her aid. She only got two steps before he closed in on her.

"Maybe she just needs some convincing, Joe." His cruel laugh was far older than his years and made her skin crawl.

Feigning a step to the left, she ducked and lunged away. Her fingers brushed warm metal nestled in a cracked leather holster. His gun. Kate grabbed the gun and jerked away.

When she spun around to face the men, she pointed the pistol straight out away from her. It wavered in her hands, much heavier than she'd expected.

"Bobby, you fool. You let her get your gun." Joe lumbered to his feet.

Kate cocked back the protruding metal part like she'd seen Buck, the driver, do yesterday. As she tightened her grip on the pistol, a deafening roar erupted from the gun, sending her stumbling back against the side of the stagecoach.

"Yeow! Damn blazes to hell!" A scream of pain sounded from one of the men. "She shot me!"

Kate whipped her head to the side where Joe was hopping on one foot. His worn brown boot sported a round hole and a dark stain. Her eyes widened in horror. She hadn't meant to actually shoot anybody, even if he'd deserved it.

She rapidly glanced from Joe to each of the other robbers. They looked as if they would advance on her at any moment. Now what was she supposed to do?

A cloud of dust in the distance caught her attention, raising her hopes. Was it help? Or another robber? The last thing she needed was another of the men's confederates to arrive on the scene. Hadn't she read somewhere that outlaw gangs always posted a lookout near a holdup?

The shot she'd fired must have brought their lookout down on her. She squared her shoulders and tightened her grip on the pistol. From the corner of her eye, she warily watched the rider draw closer.

The reverberation of the approaching horse's hooves drowned out the rider's shout. His black Stetson hid his face, and he was bent low over his horse and coming at breakneck speed. Friend or foe? She doubted the first and suspected the latter. It didn't offer her any reassurance.

As he neared them, she caught the light of recognition in Joe's eyes before he could hide it. That was all Kate needed to make up her mind.

"Oh, ginger!" she muttered under her breath. *Damn,* she added silently.

She braced herself against the side of the stagecoach and waited. Not a sound came from within the coach. She wondered if the skinny salesman had joined Mrs. Madison in a fainting spell of his own.

Almost before she could complete the thought, the lone rider drew his black horse to a halt a scarce few feet from her. In fact, he stopped much too close for her peace of mind.

Dark was her first thought as she quickly noted his black boots and pants molded to muscular thighs. A brown vest skimmed his chest, covering the dust-covered shirt beneath. A black Stetson hat sat rammed back on his head to reveal equally black hair.

Dangerous was her next thought as dark eyes glared at her from beneath slanted brows. A hard man. And, obviously an angry one to boot.

She tried to ignore the way her hands insisted on shaking and the disturbing way her heart set to fluttering every time she met his eyes.

"Hell and damnation!" he swore.

The gun in her hand wavered as she saw him lower one hand to his side.

He was going to draw on her.

The terrifying thought chased through her mind in a scarce instant. She raised her hands the extra inches she needed and aimed her own gun at the center of his wide chest.

"Don't even think of it!" she threatened him with a lot more nerve than she felt at the moment. "And get your hands up," she added.

So much for her heart fluttering at the sight of this handsome man.

She waved the gun at him in what she hoped was a sufficiently threatening gesture. Nothing in her lessons at Mrs. Parker's Finishing School in Boston had prepared her for this.

She watched shock cross his face first, followed in the next breath by anger as he tightened his fingers on the reins. She just bet he was mad. She'd quite obviously foiled his attempt to salvage the outlaws' robbery. But what was she supposed to do now?

Disarm him, a little voice in the back of her head prompted her. *Yes, that was it.*

She searched her mind for how such a thing was said in the forbidden novels she'd sneaked into her room at the finishing school when no one was watching.

"Reach for the sky, mister," she called out, liking the sound of the long-forgotten words. They gave her the bit of added courage she needed to raise her chin a notch in challenge. "And do it real slow, mister," she rushed to add.

He paused for an endless moment, and Kate felt her heart lunge for her toes. Her courage chased right after it.

She could feel the heat of his glare almost scorching her as he turned the full impact of his dark eyes on her. Why, they weren't black at all, she thought, they were the darkest shade of blue she'd ever seen. And the most compelling. She wished he'd quit staring at her so— it caused her heart to race in a funny way she'd never had happen before.

Lucas Brannigan stared down at the red-haired bundle of contrary femininity with a mixture of anger, suppressed amusement, and admiration. Her fancy traveling gown was streaked with dirt, and the tiny hat atop her curls sat at a precarious angle. She was beautiful and single-handedly holding off the gang of robbers. *With a gun aimed right at his own gut,* he thought wryly.

"And if I don't?" he drawled the question out slowly, tauntingly, shifting in the saddle.

She faced him with a rare defiance for a woman, but the quick-silver dart of her tongue across her lips belied her nervousness. He noted how her lips glistened with moistness, and desire suddenly and unexpectedly hit him like a solid punch to the gut.

"I'll shoot you," she stated with bravado. "Now, throw down your weapon, too."

Her response cooled his desire better than a winter snowstorm. Only a fool toyed with a woman who held a pistol pointed at any part of his body.

Gaging his movements, he released the reins to his mount and raised his hands only a few slight inches. His pretended act of agreement seemed to appease her. However, the lady didn't have a hope in hell of getting his six-shooter, he vowed.

The possibility was ridiculous. No way a little bit like her was going to succeed where bigger men than he had failed. And died for it, he added with grim silence.

His rapid-fire glance skimmed her. Damn, just what he didn't need— an interfering city woman. And a right pretty one to boot. If it wasn't such a dangerous situation, he couldn't have restrained his laughter. Fate seemed determined to hound him. His mount shifted in a nervous movement that alerted him.

The chuckle lodged deep in his throat as he saw one outlaw sidle away a step to the left in an attempted flanking move.

Joe Crocker. The recognition hit him with a thud. Crocker wouldn't bat an eye at killing a woman.

"Damn," Brannigan murmured under his breath.

If he didn't do something now, the fancy, interfering Eastern spitfire was as good as dead. And himself right along with her. He eased his hands downward with deceptive slowness.

"Don't even think of it," she hollered at him.

"Lady . . ." Brannigan clenched his teeth until his jaw ached.

"Keep your hands where I can see them, mister," she ordered.

"Lady . . ." His voice was deep, soft, and dangerously menacing. He sent a quick glance

Crocker's way, then lowered his hands another inch.

In the next instant, Brannigan saw her bite her lower lip, then the gun in her hands went off with a deafening roar.

Beneath him, his horse bucked, then reared. Caught off guard with his hands still raised in diffidence to the gun that had only moments before been aimed squarely at his gut, Brannigan lost control of his mount for the first time in his twenty-nine years. As his mount reared a second time, Brannigan tumbled backwards over the horse's rump, landing in a heap on the hard ground.

Joe Crocker howled in laughter and slapped his knee. He took a step towards Kate, and she squeezed the trigger. Nothing happened, and she threw the heavy pistol at him. It hit him full on the shoulder, then bounced harmlessly to the ground.

"Sugar, I'm gonna make you pay real good—"

"Crocker!" Lucas Brannigan's shout halted the outlaw in mid-step.

He spun around to face the gun in Brannigan's hand. "Your day's comin', Brannigan." Joe Crocker glared at him in undisguised hatred. "And I'm gonna enjoy putting the bullet in you myself."

"Care to try it now?" He brushed his thumb across the pistol's hammer.

Crocker acted with the lightning speed of a cornered animal. Grabbing Kate's arm, he shoved her straight at Brannigan.

She slammed into his broad chest, sending him back a step before he steadied her, bracing his booted feet to stop them both from tumbling over backwards. The barrel of his pistol hit her shoulder as he turned his aim in that split second. The gun slipped from his grasp and landed in a cloud of dust.

A short bark of laughter came from Crocker before he yelled, "Mount up, boys. Let's get outta here."

Before Brannigan could sufficiently disentangle himself from the woman, the outlaws were riding out in a cloud of dust. And with *his* horse.

He swore and picked up his gun. He didn't have a hope in hell of catching the men on foot. He slipped the pistol back into his holster, pointedly ignoring the fancy Eastern woman's gasp. Scooping up his hat from where it had fallen, he slapped it against his thigh before setting the Stetson back on his head. He pulled it forward to shield against the glare of the sun.

A low moan drew his attention to the front of the stagecoach. Old Buck waved one hand back and forth at him in an attempt to attract his help. A rush of guilt surged over him; while he'd been concentrating on the woman, his old friend had been hurting. Brannigan spun on his heel and was at the man's side with three long strides. He swung up onto the driver's box.

"How bad is it, Buck?"

"Well, I ain't ready to saddle no cloud and ride to the great beyond yet, if that's what you're asking. I'll make it. If I'd jus' stop dozing off and missing things."

"Let me see for myself."

One quick look showed that Buck had taken a slug high in the shoulder. Thankfully, it didn't look too bad. Brannigan ripped off his kerchief and pressed it against the wound to stop the bleeding.

"Dagnamit, boy, that hurts like blazes. What are you trying to do to me? Finish me off?" Buck complained in a loud gruff tone that matched his mood.

Brannigan smiled at the remarks. Obviously his friend was feeling well enough to complain— a good sign with Buck. While he needed a doctor's attention, he'd make it fine. Brannigan released a sigh of relief under his breath. He wouldn't admit it out loud for the world, but the crusty driver meant a lot to him.

"What happened to Roy?" Brannigan asked in a low tone, referring to the man who usually rode shotgun.

"He took up with a gal in the last town and up and quit on me. Cost us near half a day, too." Buck shook his head and reached for the reins. He winced at the pain the movement brought.

"Stay still," Brannigan ordered. Nothing doing but that he'd have to see the stage and its bundle of trouble to Deadrange himself. Buck wasn't up to driving the team without help. Not with that shoulder.

Ignoring the order, Buck reached for the reins again, then fell back with a yelp of pain.

"Leave him alone!" A woman's cry of alarm startled Brannigan.

He knew instinctively who it was. He swung his gaze in her direction, sparing her merely a glance of disbelief, but he froze when he saw the gun held in her hands once again.

"Hell and damnation, lady— "

"Get down," she ordered.

From the corner of his eye, he could see Buck's

chest shaking with suppressed laughter. He was glad somebody saw the humor in the situation, because he sure didn't. The lady was more trouble than a batch of loco weed. And she was waving the gun back and forth in his direction. He'd better get down before the fool thing went off and hit only heaven knew what or whom.

"Yes, ma'am." Brannigan's sarcasm carried across to Kate as he swung down from the coach. When he got his hands on her pretty neck, he was going to strangle her.

"Why don't you just go join your friends?" Kate motioned him toward the direction where the outlaws had ridden off.

"I don't think so."

She watched him take one determined step towards her. Then a second.

Kate angled the gun toward the ground, shut her eyes, and squeezed the trigger. Nothing happened. She snapped both eyes back open. Looking down at the gun in her hands, she pulled the mechanism again. Nothing.

"Ginger," she muttered.

"Lady, you're in more trouble than you can imagine."

Kate backed up a step. "Are you going to kill me?" she asked in a burst of finality.

"Don't tempt me," he muttered.

"Now, listen . . ."

She backed up another step, and he advanced one. He wore his shirtsleeves rolled up above his elbows, and his thickly corded muscles bunched as he clenched his fists.

"You— " She ran out of words.

"The name's Brannigan."

He took another menacing step forward.

As she continued to stare, momentarily mesmerized, a muscle at the side of his jaw tightened. She watched it in fascination. A faint shadow of stubble covered his jaw and chin. He looked as dark and hard as stone.

He stepped forward again, and the sunlight glinted off a shiny object on his brown leather vest.

"*Marshal* Lucas Brannigan," he added. "And, ma'am, you're under arrest."

He faced her full on, and this time the sunlight highlighted the badge pinned to his vest.

Two

Kate stared at him a full moment before the impact of his words struck her.

Marshal? Under arrest!

She blinked in disbelief.

"What for?"

"Hell and damnation, lady." Brannigan rubbed the back of his neck. "Take your pick."

"You . . . you . . . can't arrest me," she sputtered.

"Watch me."

Kate planted her hands on her hips. "What for, Marshal?"

"Interfering with a properly sworn lawman—"

"But," she cut in, "I thought you were one of them—"

He tapped the badge on his chest and threw her a dark look.

"But—" She curled her fingers around the useless gun in her hand.

"Aiding the outlaws," he continued as if she hadn't spoken.

"But—"

"And costing me my best damned horse," he ended.

She watched him clench one hand into a fist then release his grip. He looked angry . . . no, he looked mad as hell. And he was advancing on her again. One step at a time.

Kate inched back a step, not wanting to give ground, and giving as little as she had to. He towered over her. Before then, she hadn't noticed how tall he was, or the broad width of his shoulders. They shut out the very sun behind him, leaving him silhouetted before her.

Nervous, Kate licked her lips. She could actually feel his eyes watching the movement of her tongue against her lips. Tiny shivers raced down her back.

She swallowed the sudden lump that rose in her throat. She knew it wasn't fear, but he stirred *something* undefinable in her. Something she'd never felt until that moment. His eyes held hers captive, and for an unbelievable instant, she felt as if she'd never be completely free again.

Silly, she scolded herself. They were only another pair of eyes staring at her. True, they happened to be eyes the color of a crystal blue sky, clear and startlingly beautiful and warm— oh, so warm. His gaze had the effect of heating her body all the way down to the soles of her feet. She wiggled her toes in her dainty slippers, trying to shrug off his effect and failing.

Why, the marshal was not much better than an outlaw, she chided herself. Wasn't that what she'd read in the newspaper back home? Yes, the item had said that most lawmen in the West had actually been on the other side of the law at one time or another. What was she doing standing here staring at a man like that? she scolded herself. She was betrothed. Richard was waiting for her in Deadrange. This was utter insanity.

Kate jerked her thoughts up and forced her gaze down to the pair of black boots planted so firmly in front of her, then back up at the marshal. At the first glimpse of his rugged face again, her heart plummeted.

Ginger! she swore silently. *Oh, fiddle.*

"Shouldn't you be riding after them?" she challenged, hoping to put a stop to whatever strange thing seemed to be taking place between her and the marshal.

"Them?" he asked in a low voice.

Kate swung her arm in an arc, gesturing in the direction the outlaws had taken. However, she'd forgotten the pistol still held tightly in her grip. As the barrel brushed across his chest, Brannigan snatched the gun out of her hand in a lightning fast move that took her very breath away.

"Riding on what?" he asked, drawing her attention back and away from the feel of his hand against hers.

She sent him a scorching glance, angry at him as well as herself. It didn't appear to do the slightest bit of good. He persisted in standing tall and straight before her, his very stance challenging her and calling to her at the same time.

"On a horse," she enunciated each word as if she were speaking to a small child.

"Lady, in case you forgot, the *real* bad guys took my horse with them."

"Then what are those?" She pointed to the team still hitched to the stagecoach.

"Those horse are harness broke, ma'am."

"So, unharness them."

Brannigan felt his patience wearing extremely thin. The woman was exasperating. She stared up at him with an expression of impatience, stubbornness, and temptation on her face. It was a right pretty face, he noted, framed in a cloud of copper curls brushing her cheeks. Delicate cheekbones, soft creamy skin, and full luscious lips. For an instant, he couldn't help wondering what she'd do if he caught her close to steal a kiss from those lips. Probably slap him.

But damn, she was a temptation. And irritating. And just about the most beautiful thing he'd ever seen. She brought to mind the excitement in the air just before a big storm. And she'd probably prove to be just as unsettling to his peace of mind.

Brannigan shut his eyes against her tantalizing charms for a moment. The lady was pure trouble. A woman like her was all go with no staying power, he reminded himself. At the first sign of real hardship, she'd light out, right back to the fancy Eastern city she'd come from. He'd seen it happen one too many times; it was branded into his mind. And his heart.

"Lady—"

"The name is Kate Danville," she interrupted in a cool voice, lifting her chin. "From Boston."

She'd stiffened her spine as if a wood plank had been rammed down her back. Definitely a city woman. She'd introduced herself with all the manners of a high-bred lady greeting an unwelcome visitor in her front parlor— an act guaranteed to raise a man's temper.

He couldn't believe her. She raised her chin in a polite rebuff and had the nerve to be looking down her pretty little nose at him. It made him bristle, even while he told himself that it didn't matter a bit. No, not the least little bit. *Like hell.*

"Well, Miss Kate Danville from Boston," he drawled the words out, "you are still under arrest."

Kate faced him, hands on her hips. He watched

her blink her eyes once, then again. They were the greenest eyes he'd ever seen. They brought to mind a spitting mountain lion cub he'd accidentally met up with on the trail one time. The two seemed to possess the same temperament to boot.

Suddenly, the door to the coach swung open with a thump, and Mrs. Madison charged out, her face flushed with exertion and temper. Her serviceable brown bonnet tilted drunkenly to one side of her head, the ribbon bow tangled in her brown hair.

"Don't you touch her," she huffed, clutching her reticule tightly in one hand. She shook the drawstring bag threateningly, then whacked it on Brannigan's forearm. "Now see here, you leave that girl be."

"Ma'am—"

"Marshal, don't you dare go arresting Miss Danville. Why, she likely as not saved our lives."

With this, Mrs. Madison clasped her reticule in both hands and took a step forward as if to put herself between Kate and the marshal. "Just where were you when we needed help from those murdering outlaws? Tell me that."

"I was being detained by Miss Danville." Brannigan felt his temper rising with the ridiculous exchange. Kate Danville was becoming more trouble than any tenderfoot he'd ever met up with yet. Trouble and excitement and challenging— a combination he hadn't felt in a long time.

"Dagnamit, folks," Buck shouted from the driver's box. "Sort it all out later, would you? I'm bleeding."

"Damn," Brannigan swore under his breath. "I'm coming, Buck," he called to his friend.

Turning back to Kate, he noticed that a tiny

smile pulled at the corners of her lips, revealing a small dimple in one cheek. Once again her beauty struck him like a bolt of lightning. Somehow he sensed that the lady was just about as dangerous as that lightning bolt, too.

"Ladies." He offered the women a smile. "If you'd like to get back inside, I'll see you and Buck to town."

Catching Mrs. Madison by the elbow, he helped her clamber back inside the stagecoach. It rocked and swayed with her bulk as she settled herself on the seat opposite Mr. Billings who sat stiffly in the corner as if frozen in place.

Brannigan spared the cowardly drummer only a glance, then extended his arm to Kate. Turning up her nose at him, she picked up her fancy parasol, swept up her skirts, and took a step toward the coach, dismissing his offer.

Not a chance, lady, he thought to himself. He'd been wondering how she'd feel in his arms and now was the perfect chance to find out. He wasn't about to pass up the opportunity she presented to him without good reason, and her snub wasn't near reason enough. Not by a long shot.

He reached out and clasped her by the waist. Kate let out an indignant exclamation in the instant before he drew her body back against his.

Whatever Kate's next words had been going to be, they flittered away from her mind as she felt the heat from Brannigan's chest against her back. It seeped through the fine material of her dress. Her very thoughts scattered as if they'd been caught in a windstorm. She attempted to gather her wits back about her, without much success. Brannigan eased his hands more firmly about her waist, sending the remainder of her senses fleeing.

It was really quite improper, a part of her mind told her. Meanwhile, another part of her thrilled at the feel of his strong hands enveloping her waist. He was . . .

With a smooth movement, he lifted her and shoved her inside the stagecoach. As her feet touched the flooring, she gasped and sat down with a thump. What had come over her? It had been as if every single thought had gone out of her mind, and that certainly had never happened to her before. And she didn't intend for it to happen again. She fully intended to stay as far from the devastating marshal as she possibly could.

Kate swept her skirts aside in a haughty gesture, reached over, and slammed the door closed with a loud thump.

Brannigan released the chuckle tickling the back of his throat. She had fire, he'd say that for her. With a wry smile, he turned his back on temptation and mounted the driver's box beside Buck.

He was insufferable!

Kate fumed to herself and wiggled her backside on the leather high-backed seat of the coach.

He was rude.

She shifted position again.

And . . . and . . . Marshal Lucas Brannigan was just about the most handsome man she'd ever laid eyes on.

Kate tossed her head, attempting to dislodge the image of him from her mind. He was insufferable, she reminded herself. And he was most certainly no gentleman!

Her Richard was a gentleman. He wouldn't take liberties with a lady the way Lucas Brannigan had

dared to do. The way he had slid his hands about
her waist had been positively disgraceful. And
scandalous. And thrilling, a little voice in the back
of her mind taunted.

Kate tossed her head, sending her once perfectly
coiffed hair tumbling about her shoulders in a
flame of curls as her bonnet slid to the floor. She
most certainly shouldn't even be thinking about a
man such as the marshal. She was appalled.

Why, she was an engaged woman, and Richard
would be waiting for her when they reached Deadrange. Somehow, that thought failed to create the
excitement in her that it had only the day before.
Before she'd met Marshal Lucas Brannigan.

"Oh, ginger," Kate muttered under her breath.
"Fiddle."

"What, dear?" Mrs. Madison asked, concern
written on her face. "Are you feeling ill?"

"No, I'm fine," Kate assured her. *Just fine.*

She was tired, she told herself, that's what it was.
However, as if to disclaim this, an unexplained vi-
tality surged through her body. She brushed at a
spot of dirt on the fine material of her lavender
skirt. Her lack of enthusiasm over finally seeing
Richard again had absolutely nothing to do with
the marshal, she told herself firmly. Absolutely
nothing.

Kate was still trying to convince herself of that
fact when the stage pulled into Deadrange. She
drew back the curtain, eager for her first look at
the town. It only took a minute to take in the dirt-
packed street and scattering of one- and two-sto-
ried wood buildings that lined the street. Words
to describe the small western town escaped her. It

was nothing like she'd imagined. Why, the buildings practically sagged in disrepair. And it was dirty!

She let the curtain drop back into place and sat back in her seat. *Richard Hale had better be here.*

It seemed that scarcely had that thought left her mind when the coach pulled to a halt. Almost instantly the door swung open.

Her breath caught as Lucas Brannigan filled the doorway and smiled at her. He extended a hand to help her out, and the instant she'd placed her hand in his she knew she'd made a mistake.

Amusement lit his eyes as if he'd read her thoughts. *Oh, fiddle de damn, that's all she needed.*

He held her hand a moment longer than necessary. A pleasurable warmth began at her fingertips and spread upward. It quickly increased its intensity. When she made to pull her hand away from his, he quickly released her, and before she realized what he intended, he wrapped his hands around her waist and swung her out of the coach.

A small gasp of surprise left Kate's mouth, but any complaint froze on her lips. He held her aloft a long moment, their gazes meeting— hers startled, his full of desire.

Kate stared as if mesmerized, forgetting her surroundings. She hadn't noticed before that his dark hair had lighter strands the color of a rich sable mixed in. She met the blatant desire in his gaze, and once again felt the warmth from his body holding her close. A hundred and one questions surged to her mind.

Instead of merely assisting her down, Brannigan lowered her slowly, holding her close and sliding her along the length of his body. She felt every hard muscle of him against her, and knew she should pull away. It was the proper thing to do, but she couldn't seem to make her body obey.

Brannigan tightened his hold on her, and the air suddenly felt charged, like a thunderstorm moving in too close. A shiver of response raced along Kate's back. Her heart beat faster, and she feared that Brannigan would hear it.

He looked down at her, capturing her gaze with his. How could she have ever thought his eyes were hard, she wondered. The deep blue eyes meeting hers were warm, in fact, heat fairly radiated out from them, practically singeing her with its intensity.

While it seemed that he held her forever, it couldn't have been more than a few moments. Gently, Brannigan lowered Kate until her feet touched the ground.

When he released her, Kate's legs felt too unsteady to hold her up. She clasped one hand against his chest to steady herself. He glanced down at where her hand was wrapped around the edge of his leather vest and smiled. That smile unnerved her more than anything else had.

Kate knew her face had turned red from the way her face heated with the blush. She hurriedly stepped back and turned away from Brannigan's smile and came face to face with her fiancé.

Richard stood not five feet away, his eyebrows raised in censure. He was impeccably dressed in an Eastern suit and looked strangely out of place. His pale blond hair was neatly trimmed, and his face was slightly pink from too much sun.

"Richard!" Kate cried out.

Gathering up her skirt, she ran the short distance to him and threw herself in his arms. He stiffened in disapproval.

"Kate, we're in public," he reprimanded her in a low voice.

She bit back the rest of what she'd been about to say. How could she have forgotten propriety so quickly? Richard had always said that he admired her ladylike qualities, and here she was behaving like an exuberant child. Whatever had come over her?

She stepped back and smoothed a hand over her loosened curls, tidying herself. From under her lashes she observed Richard. He straightened his jacket and tie, then assured himself that his cuffs were still fastened.

Richard looked different here in Deadrange, Kate thought. Somehow he appeared shorter and thinner than he'd seemed in Boston. Or was it just that Brannigan had been so overwhelming, the little voice spoke up again.

"How was your trip, dear?" Richard asked in his well-modulated voice. "Your stage was late and I was beginning to worry." He ran a glance from her tousled hair and missing bonnet down to her dust-covered slippers. "It must have been a difficult trip, you are quite disheveled."

Kate felt a blush of embarrassment creep upward from her neck to her cheeks. She had so wanted to look perfect when Richard saw her.

She brushed at a spot of dust on her sleeve. She imagined that she looked a complete sight. Oh, ginger, she wanted to stomp her foot in anger, but Mrs. Parker's rule about ladies never giving in to displays of anger stopped her just in time.

"Oh, Richard, you wouldn't believe it. The stagecoach was held up."

"What?" His normally even voice rose on the lone word.

Kate nodded her head, and a red curl bobbed in front of her eyes. She brushed it back, tucking it behind her ear.

"Yes, the outlaws—"

"Outlaws?" Richard interrupted, catching her arm. "Were you robbed? Was anything taken? You—" He stopped himself and caught both her hands in his. "My dear, were you hurt?"

"No, I—"

"I'm so glad, dear. But what happened? Did they rob everyone?"

"No," Kate assured him. "Brannigan, I mean, Marshal Brannigan rode up," she paused.

"Then he stopped them from robbing you?"

"Yes," she answered, leaving out the rest of the events. Richard seemed more concerned over the attempted robbery than over her ordeal, she noted with a twinge of irritation.

She was being ridiculous; of course he was occupied with the facts of the robbery. Such things as stagecoach holdups didn't happen in Boston. However, an uneasy feeling plagued her.

"Well, dear, let's get you to your room," Richard insisted. "You should rest."

"But your family?"

"Later."

He placed her hand on his forearm and turned toward the hotel. As Brannigan cleared his throat, Kate resisted the urge to look over her shoulder for one last glimpse of him. Instead she followed Richard's lead.

Brannigan watched the couple walk away. Kate had her fancy parasol resting on her shoulder, and the lace bobbed with each step. Her silly trinket was about as out of place here as a city woman like her.

He saw the man pat Kate's hand in a possessive gesture and felt his gut clench. *It was just as well,* he told himself. He'd been a prize fool thinking of a city woman like her. More than once he'd even caught himself wondering what her lush lips would taste like when he kissed her. He shook his head. Miss Kate Danville of Boston wasn't for him.

The next morning, Kate paused in the hotel lobby and removed her gloves. She couldn't believe how dusty they had become from her sojourn to the telegraph office.

She'd sent a telegram to Papa telling him she was safe in Deadrange and would be marrying Richard tomorrow. She had no doubt that he'd be furious, but he'd get over it once she and Richard were wed. Her father never stayed angry with her for long. Unlike Richard, who still seemed a bit put out. He'd left her at her room yesterday with a kiss on her cheek, orders to rest, and a promise to return for her at noon today.

The door opened behind her, and she turned as Brannigan strode in. He stopped dead at the sight of her. As his gaze held hers, he removed his black Stetson. Kate stiffened in anticipation, but he only gave her a nod, then turned to the man behind the wooden counter.

"Morning, Marshal. How's Buck?"

"Ornery as a mule."

Kate let their conversation wash over her, shamelessly listening to Brannigan's deep voice. The differences between Brannigan and Richard sprang unbidden to her mind. The two men couldn't be more opposite. While she admitted to a slight attraction to the handsome lawman, it was Richard she loved. Didn't she?

Of course, she did. She straightened the ribbon of her sapphire bonnet. She was only experiencing pre-wedding nerves. All brides had them, or so Mrs. Parker always claimed.

A strange sense of unease swept over her as if something were definitely wrong. She brushed her hand nervously down the flounced skirt of her blue gown. Beneath the silken fabric, her petticoats rustled softly as if chastising her thoughts.

She crossed to the stairs. Everything should be wonderful, she chided herself. Tomorrow was her wedding day. By this time tomorrow, she would be Mrs. Richard Hale. The thought brought a smile to her lips. However, as she climbed the stairs, the strange sensation of unease still held her firmly in its grasp.

Turning left down the hallway, she slowly walked the remaining steps to her room. She had one hand on the doorknob when she heard the telltale creak of the wooden floor from the other side of the door. Then the muffled thump of a footfall sounded from within the room. She froze in place, her feet surely rooted to the wood flooring beneath them. She gulped the breath she'd been taking and swallowed.

Drawing in another breath, she cocked her head and listened intently. This time only silence came from the other side of the door. Perhaps she'd been wrong. Maybe her nerves were just what Papa called overwrought— what with the approaching of her wedding on the morrow. That must assuredly be it, she reasoned to herself.

Satisfied with this explanation, she turned the knob to her door. The loud scrape of the room's single, old window being raised halted her in mid-step.

Someone was in her room.

Without stopping to think of the consequences, she flung the door open. As the door banged against the wall, a rush of fresh air hit her in the face. She instantly turned to the open window. It had been closed when she left, she knew it for certain.

Now the slim figure of a man straddling the window ledge caught her full attention. Her scream stopped in her throat as she recognized Richard immediately, and a sigh of relief replaced the fear.

Ah, it was just Richard. Richard! The thought struck her with the force of a blow. What was her fiancé doing in her room? And what was he doing scrambling out her second-floor window like a common thief?

"Richard?" Kate asked in shock.

The sound alerted the man balancing precariously on the window ledge. Richard Hale glanced over his shoulder a moment before turning and scrambling out the opening.

That single look said it all to Kate. Shock . . . amazement . . . guilt. But whatever did Richard have to feel guilty about? she thought to herself. It wasn't as if he'd been caught stealing . . .

The last thought unfroze her feet as surely as if she'd received a shove. Stealing! Her money!

No, she refused to believe her father's warning. Richard loved her, he . . . She still couldn't resist the urge to glance to the bureau where she'd hidden her funds. Surely the money was . . .

She stared at the bureau in horror. The carefully arranged items atop the battered wood surface lay in disarray. Her hair brush teetered on the corner, and her bottle of scent lay drunkenly on its side, while the top drawer hung open at a crooked angle. Most assuredly not the manner she'd left things.

Spinning on her heel, she raced to the bureau. Her worst fears gnawed at her as she yanked open the drawer and tossed things aside, searching for her one special reticule, but she couldn't find even a scrap of black velvet in the drawer. No!

She shoved things out of her way, desperately looking again for the black reticule that hid all her money. She dumped the drawer's contents onto the floor. Kicking aside a white fichu, she dropped to her knees as a piece of dark material caught her eyes. She scooped it up, then recognized the black glove and dropped it back to the floor. Refusing to believe Richard had stolen from her, she sorted through the drawer's contents again, but not a scrap of the reticule was left. It was gone. Gone— along with all her money.

"Dammit, Richard Hale!" Kate screamed her frustration, surging to her feet. "You're not getting away with this."

Grabbing up her skirts she dashed for the hallway. In a blaze of fury, she started down the stairs not caring who might see an improperly displayed curve of ankle. Propriety was the least of her worries.

She spared the man approaching the bottom of the stairs only a glance. She wasn't in the mood to brook any interference in her pursuit and capture of the thieving, no-good Richard.

She turned her head and continued her pell-mell rush after Richard and her money with a single-minded determination. Richard wasn't getting away with this. She'd . . .

She took the last two steps in a single jump and careened right into the broadest, rock-hard chest she'd ever had the misfortune to collide with. The man instinctively tightened her arms around her, steadying her. A tingle of awareness skittered along Kate's body where it pressed against his. She caught his arms to regain her balance, and hopefully her scattered senses.

Beneath her fingers, his arms were firm and strong. And so very warmed by the sun. The unwarranted thought raced across Kate's mind, a mere instant before she regained her misplaced senses.

"Let me go," she ordered, pushing ineffectually at the firm hands now spanning her waist. "He's getting away."

Kate yanked back out of his hold at the same instant that her unwanted rescuer released her. The force of her movement was her undoing. It sent her backwards in a tumble, and she landed on the bottom step with a thud.

Looking up through the two sagging feather plumes of her sapphire blue bonnet, she met the intense gaze of Marshal Lucas Brannigan.

"Oh, ginger," she muttered.

"Hell and damnation," he echoed her sentiments.

Three

"Well, don't just stand there!" Kate shouted.

Brannigan extended a hand to help her to her feet, but Kate slapped it away.

"I don't need your help to stand up. Go and stop him."

Brannigan dropped his hand to his side, withdrawing his gentlemanly offer of assistance. "Stop who?" he asked.

"Richard."

"Who?"

"Oh, never mind." Kate braced her hands firmly on the steps and pushed herself to her feet. "Get out of my way, and I'll do it myself."

She charged forward, smack into Brannigan's shoulder. She reeled back a step from the force of the impact.

"Lady—"

Kate blew out a frustrated breath, causing the two bent ostrich feathers on her bonnet to dance merrily in front of her eyes. She shoved the dainty bonnet to the back of her head, dislodging several carefully pinned curls in the process.

"Oh . . . oh . . ." Anger left her at a temporary loss for words.

"Kate—"

"Oh, damn!" she ended, brushing past the man in her path.

With one hand lifting her skirts out of her way, and the other hand holding her bonnet in place, she dashed across the hotel lobby and out the front door. Once outside, she thoroughly scanned the main street of the town, but found no sign of Richard running down the dirt-packed street or the wood planks in front of the shops that lined the street on both sides.

Kate stomped her foot. Richard Hale was nowhere in sight. Grabbing up her skirts, she ran the length of the street to the west end of the town, but found no sign of him. She spun around and ran until she reached the tiny telegraph office at the other edge of the town, then skidded to a halt, breathing hard.

"Oh, ginger!"

Kate planted her hands on her hips and surveyed the landscape leading away from town. She'd hoped to at least spot a cloud of dust to give away Richard's escape route. Instead, it seemed that dust flew about her in all directions, filling the air and settling around her like a cloak.

She sneezed once, then again. She swore the town of Deadrange had enough dust to bake into cakes and sell. A red curl tumbled down to dangle over her eyes, and she shoved it back up under her bonnet. She held her finger under her nose a minute to ward off another sneeze. Her eyes stung with the effort and suddenly another sneeze broke free.

"Oh." She stomped her foot, sending up a small cloud of dust about her. "Damn you, Richard Hale."

She scanned the main street in both directions,

willing him to appear, but Richard Hale was nowhere to be found. He'd gotten away. And it was
all the fault of that blasted lawman.

Kate spun around and headed back to the hotel.
With each step she took, her temper rose. By the
time she reached the steps of the hotel, she had
worked herself into a fine rage, and that rage focused on the one man she held responsible for
Richard's escape.

"Marshal Brannigan," she shouted, mounting
the steps and entering the establishment.

"Yes, ma'am?" he answered her in a low drawl.

How could he be so casual about what had just
happened? She descended on him in a blaze of
fury.

"He's gone," she announced. "Do you hear me?
Gone. Gone. Gone."

"What are you—"

"And you didn't do one single thing to stop
him!"

"What—"

Kate advanced until she stood toe to toe with
Brannigan's black leather boots. Plopping her
hands on her hips, she tilted her head back and
looked up at him.

"Not one dadblammed thing!" she concluded.

"Hell and damnation, lady," Brannigan fired
back. "Calm down."

"Calm down? Calm?" Kate clenched her teeth,
then sent him a sweetly sarcastic smile.

She leaned forward another few inches and
halted only a breath away from his chest, before
she poked one finger at that broad chest with its
lawman badge pinned to his leather vest.

"I'm supposed to be calm? How do you expect
that to happen? When you just let a criminal es-

cape with all of my money!" She punctuated the
last word with a stab at his chest.

He treated her fury like a pesky mosquito, brushing it aside. Instead he passed a questioning glance
down at where her hand pressed against his chest.
His calm only served to feed her anger.

"Aren't you going to do anything?" she challenged him with a final burst of voice. "What kind
of marshal are you?" She threw up her hands.
"Every time I'm around you're letting criminals
go. Is that because you used to be one?"

She knew she'd pushed him too far. The tiny
muscle that quivered at the edge of his jaw warned
her. His lips straightened, and she saw his blue
eyes darken to practically the same shade of sapphire as the sash at her waist. Oh, oh, she thought
too late to catch back the hasty words.

"Just what the hell are you accusing me of,
lady?"

Brannigan's voice was as cold as the snow in mid-
January back home. Kate bit her lower lip in sudden trepidation. Things like this always happened
when she let her temper get the better of her. Her
tongue had a mind of its own whenever she lost
her temper.

"I—"

"The main word being when *you* are around. If
you recall, *you* were the one holding the gun that
let the outlaws escape. Damnation, you were likely
the one who shot Buck as well."

"I was not," she denied hotly.

"Now, this time, you come flying through the
hotel like a madwoman—"

"Madwoman?" Kate's voice rose.

"Damn near assault a lawman," he continued as
if she hadn't spoken.

"Assault—"

"Then, you dash out of here like a barn afire—"

"A barn?"

Kate couldn't believe her ears. The man had just compared her to a madwoman and a barn!

"Go flying down the street," he proceeded, ignoring her attempts to interrupt. "You take long enough prancing around outside to let any fool get clean away. Then you come back in here with your hackles raised and expect me to fix everything up for you."

Kate's temper increased with each word the marshal said. And she'd had enough.

"Hackles?"

She stomped her foot soundly, forgetting that she stood toe to toe with Brannigan. Her foot came down solidly atop his foot.

He jumped back. "Damnation, lady!"

Kate covered her mouth, appalled at what she'd done.

"I'm sorry," she cried out.

Brannigan stood on one foot and glared down at her. The humor struck her. He looked so funny, standing there on one foot. It spoiled the entire effect of the anger he directed her way.

Although she tried to hold back the laughter that bubbled up, a giggle slipped past her lips before she could stop it. Brannigan's eyes darkened, and he took a step forward.

"Lady, you are a menace."

Kate choked back the remainder of her laughter. It would only serve to aggravate him more, and she certainly didn't need to do it. He looked mad enough to bite a bullet, or whatever a man did out here in the West.

"I'm sorry," she rushed to apologize. "Really, I am. I didn't mean to stomp on your foot."

Without thinking, she laid her hand on his chest. It warmed her palm, his heartbeat strong and sure against her fingers. She looked upward, past the leather vest and open shirt, past the tanned column of his throat, past the square jaw to his lips. There her gaze froze. His lips were firm and full. She wondered for an instant just what those lips would feel like pressed against hers. Would they be as strong and forceful as the man himself? Or would they be soft like Richard's had been the few times he'd kissed her?

Kate jerked her wayward thoughts back. She should be thinking solely of Richard. Sneaking, conniving Richard and her money.

"Well," she prompted, suddenly feeling a little bit desperate. "What are you going to do about that thief?"

"And what would you have me do, ma'am? Go riding hellbent for leather?"

When she nodded, he added, "After who?"

"Why after Richard, of course."

"Richard?" he asked.

"Yes, Richard Hale. From Boston."

"The man who met you when you arrived in town?" he asked in disbelief.

"Yes," she answered. "My fiancé," she added softly.

"Fiancé?" he asked.

"Yes." Kate whispered the single word.

Suddenly, the fight and anger drained out of her, leaving her pale. The muscled chest beneath her fingertips reverberated with the marshal's sigh, and she snatched her hand back as if her fingertips had just been singed. As a matter of fact, she wasn't so certain that they hadn't been.

Brannigan stared down at her. The lady was, without a doubt, the most irritating, noisiest, unreasonable woman he'd ever met. And the prettiest creature this side of heaven to boot.

And why in heaven's name had she been wished on his town? She seemed to attract trouble the way honey drew a bear. And something told him that if she stuck around, this particular little pot of honey was going to attract more trouble than a person could count.

The anger that had surged up in response to her accusation drained away. It seemed that Kate Danville brought out a side of himself that he had almost forgotten existed.

"Why don't you start by telling me what happened?" he asked in a low voice.

"I returned from the telegraph office and found Richard sneaking out my window. With all of my money!"

"All your money? How much would that be?"

Kate raised her chin and stiffened her spine without thinking of it. Mrs. Parker's rule of finances sprang to mind, and she recited it automatically in answer to his question.

"A lady never discusses money with a gentleman."

Brannigan burst out laughing. "Lady, you're telling me that you were just robbed and that you shouldn't discuss *money* with me?"

Put that way it did sound ridiculous. Kate's cheeks heated in a blush. This was all Richard's fault.

"Well, of course this is an exception. But shouldn't you be trying to catch him or something?"

"He's probably long gone, but— "

His words sparked a memory and a twinge of hope. "Richard wouldn't have left town," she murmured. "His family's here."

"What?"

Kate gave him a tentative smile. Maybe this was all a misunderstanding. Richard wouldn't do something like steal from her; he'd told her he loved her. Besides, his parents lived here.

"I was supposed to meet his parents this afternoon. Mr. and Mrs. Roger Hale. They live in Deadrange."

A shadow crossed Brannigan's face. "There aren't any Hales living around here."

"No, you're mistaken. Richard— "

"Lied to you. There are no Hales in Deadrange, or anywhere else close," he said with finality.

Pain shot through Kate at this statement. It crushed the last of her belief in Richard. Papa had been right. He'd only used her.

Brannigan flexed his fingers around the brim of his Stetson. Dusting off the hat out of habit, he sat it firmly on his head and turned back to Kate.

"Like I said, he's probably long gone, but I'll ride out and see if I can pick up his trail."

With this, he strode out of the hotel and down the steps before she could even think of a response.

Sighing, Kate turned away and slowly climbed the stairs to her room. Her door stood ajar from her hurried chase after Richard. She was most assuredly lucky that everything else hadn't been taken while she was downstairs answering Brannigan's questions.

She entered her small room and shut the door

behind her. She turned the key in the lock immediately, then chided herself. It was a little late. She doubted that she had anything of value left to steal; Richard had seen to that.

A horrible thought struck her. She no longer had the money needed to pay her fare back home. Kate dropped onto the edge of the bed, tossing down her blue beaded reticule that she'd chosen so carefully to match her gown such a short time ago.

She'd been so excited to get back to the hotel and finish the last minute preparations for her wedding tomorrow. Hah! Well, there most certainly wasn't any need to complete the tasks now. There wasn't going to be any wedding.

How could she have been such a fool as to believe Richard loved her? It had been like Papa had insisted. Richard Hale had only been pretending to love her so he could get her money.

Oh, how the truth hurt. Kate bit her lip to force back the tears that sprang up unwanted to burn her eyes. She wouldn't cry. She wouldn't. Crossing to the bureau, she picked up the discarded items heaped on the floor, placed the contents in the drawer, and shoved it closed.

"Oh, ginger!"

Kate whirled and paced the length of the room. Turning at the door, she crossed back to the open window and looked out. If anything the town looked more rundown than it had from the street. From her vantage point she could see from one end of the town to the other. The shops' false fronts hid the rundown, tiny single-story eyesores, concealing their true identity in much the same way that Richard's fine manners had hidden the thieving heart within.

She admitted to herself that the chances of finding Richard were very slim. If only Marshal Brannigan had gotten after him sooner. If only she hadn't left the money in her bureau. If only . . .

She stopped herself. She could go on like that all day, and it would accomplish nothing. *If onlys* were useless.

She leaned out the window for a better look. The same ledge Richard had sneaked out, she suddenly recalled. She stepped back and slammed the window shut, then whirled away from the reminder.

"I wish you'd broken your neck, Richard Hale."

She strode across the room to the washstand with its pitcher and bowl. Grabbing up the pitcher, she poured a splash of water into the bowl. A black bug scurried over the sloped side in an attempt to escape the water.

Kate screamed and dropped the pitcher. It shattered on the wood flooring. Water splashed up, soaking the skirt of her gown. It was the final insult.

"Ginger!"

She bent down to pick up the pieces of broken pottery and nicked the tip of her finger on a sharp edge. Sucking on the injury, she dropped the other pieces on the washstand. The black bug skittered across the rim of the painted bowl and she snatched her hand away.

The bowl teetered, and she reached out to catch it, but missed. It landed on the wood floor with a loud smash, shattering into small pieces.

"Fiddle de damn," she swore.

The owner would likely as not add the cost of the broken items to the cost of her room. Her unpaid room, she added.

"Damn you, Richard Hale."

Turning around, she grabbed up her beaded reticule and hurled it across the room. It landed against the wall with a soft, harmless thud.

Unsatisfied, she kicked off her slippers, then sent first one and then the other sailing across the floor. They hit the wooden door with satisfying thumps.

The sound brought a smile to her face. However, the loud pounding of a fist on the other side of the door quickly drove her smile away.

Swallowing down her trepidation, she walked to the door and opened it a crack. Marshal Lucas Brannigan filled the doorway.

"What are you doing here?" she accused.

"Answering a complaint of disturbance of the peace, ma'am." He tipped his hat to her.

Kate knew her mouth dropped open, but she couldn't seem to stop herself. She released her hold on the door, and it swung inward with a rusty creak.

She watched Brannigan survey the broken pottery, puddle of water, and miscellaneous items scattered across the floor of the room.

"Had an accident, ma'am?" he asked with a smile.

"A bug ran out of the bowl, and I . . ." She let the remainder of her explanation trail off.

The smile on Brannigan's face widened, and her anger began to grow once again. This wasn't a laughing matter.

"Did you catch him?" she fired out the question.

Brannigan had the grace to look sheepish. "No, ma'am, he— "

"He got away," she finished. "I should have known. Just my luck. In fact, I should have listened to my father." She threw up her hands. "He warned me, but would I listen? Oh, no. I knew better. I knew Richard loved me. Hah!"

"Kate—"

"Do you know what he loved? Papa's money. Well, that's the last time I'll ever become involved with any man who isn't every bit as rich as Papa. And of my social class," she added for good measure.

Well, that left him out, Brannigan assured himself. He should thank his lucky stars for his escape from her attentions. A fancy lady like Kate Danville of Boston was the last thing he should be interested in, or needed.

He watched the play of emotions cross her lovely face and tapped down the desire that insisted on plaguing him. *All go and no stay,* he reminded himself. She'd hightail it out of Deadrange as fast as she could now. Just wait and see.

Meanwhile, he was smart enough to know that he should keep as far away from her as he possibly could. He'd dealt with enough dangerous men in his career to be able to smell trouble far off. And this woman was trouble all the way to her dainty toes. He took a step backward.

"You're leaving?" Kate asked.

"Well, it seems the disturbance is over."

"But what are you going to do about Richard?" she challenged.

"I've telegraphed the nearest towns. If he passes through, they'll arrest him."

"That's it? If he passes through?"

Brannigan sighed in irritation. "I'm riding out again at first light."

"And what am I supposed to do?"

"I suggest that you try and stay out of trouble."

Brannigan rammed his hat on his head and strode away.

Kate bit back the sharp reply that sprang up. This predicament wasn't his fault. Well, not all of it, she amended. She slammed the door on his retreating back.

Now what was she going to do?

Her mind refused the obvious answer. She would not telegraph Papa for money. She wouldn't!

Kate resumed her pacing, carefully avoiding the damp spot on the floor. She ran her options over in her mind. They came down to telegraph Papa or starve.

There was nothing to do but grovel and admit that he was right about Richard and ask him to wire money immediately for her to return home. How she hated to do it! Crossing to the door, she scooped up her blue beaded reticule, stepped into her slippers and strode out the door. If she telegraphed him now, she should have an answer by morning.

Kate reread the telegram from her father for the third time. All the wishing in the world didn't change the words. They remained as unyielding as when she'd first read them only minutes ago in open-mouthed disbelief. She curled her fingers over the edge of the paper, her anger mounting.

Kate, my darling girl. I'm sorry for your predicament. Stop. My answer must be no. Stop. I cannot keep fixing all your mistakes. Stop. You made your bed, now you'll have to lie in it or find your own way out. Stop.

Kate stomped her foot. Fiddle de damn. Now whatever was she going to do? She didn't have enough money to get home to Boston without her papa's help. Suddenly the realization of her situation struck her full force.

She was alone in Deadrange. A memory of Buck's gravelly voice telling her that the stage ran regular as could be once a month suddenly sprang to her mind.

The stage only ran once a month. Every thirty days. It wouldn't be back for another twenty-nine days.

The facts piled up on her one by one, and she reeled with the realization. There would not be another stagecoach for twenty-nine more days, and she didn't have money to hire other transportation back home.

She was stranded in the broken-down town of Deadrange.

Four

William Danville unfolded and refolded the sheaf of papers. A lot of good the Pinkerton man's report on Richard Hale had done him. He'd never been able to show it to his beloved Kate. Now it was too late.

She had learned the truth the hard way. The fortune-hunting scoundrel had stolen her money and abandoned her— just as he had known the no-account would do.

He'd been proved right, but the hollow victory left a bitter taste in his mouth. The only good thing to come of this was that the marriage hadn't taken place. At least Hale had the decency to abscond with her funds *before* the wedding, instead of afterwards.

Now the only thing left to do was to clean up after his wayward daughter. Again. He withdrew his kerchief and mopped his brow. *The girl was going to be the death of him yet.*

He admitted that due to his overindulgence Kate was stubborn, spoiled, pampered, and far too used to getting her own way every time. That combined with her too-soft heart was sure to get her hurt again and again.

He drew his kerchief back over his brow. She couldn't see that he only had her best interests at heart, that he was merely watching out for her. Oh, no, she always had to go her own way.

The blame for Kate's willfulness was his alone. After his wife had died of a fever when Kate was only three years old, it had been the natural thing to do to spoil her. She'd needed extra love, but perhaps he'd gone too far in giving her almost anything she wanted. Now look where it had gotten her.

According to her telegram she was staying at the local hotel in Deadrange, Nevada. *Deadrange*. What in the name of heaven had prompted Kate to stop over at a town named Deadrange? Surely even the name had boded no good, but Kate never looked for things like that.

He tossed the sheaf of papers down onto the table and picked up the painted miniature of his daughter he'd commissioned for her last birthday. Whatever was he to do with her?

Had he done the right thing in refusing Kate's request for money? Surely if he kept bailing her out of every situation her impetuosity catapulted her into, no good would come of it. No, there had been no other choice, he assured himself. He had done the right thing.

Kate had to learn this lesson, then perhaps she'd listen to him when the next handsome fortune hunter came along. He had no doubt more would follow. They always did. The potent combination of his daughter's beauty and his wealth presented too strong a temptation for any greedy young man to resist.

Worry ate at him, but he forced it aside. It was time she learned to take responsibility for her actions. He'd been right in refusing her request for money. As the worry rose again, he assuaged it.

He'd ensured that someone kept an eye on her for him.

He'd telegraphed the local lawman in Deadrange, offering him a handsome amount to watch over Kate. He had no doubt a mere lawman would be pleased to have the money. In William Danville's world, no one refused money.

Lucas Brannigan reined his horse in and scanned the early morning countryside. Nothing but green-gray sagebrush and cactus met his gaze. Obviously Hale had ridden hard and long, and put a good distance between himself and Deadrange.

Brannigan questioned how any man could abandon Kate Danville. A memory of her pretty, downcast face had haunted him, sending him riding out shortly after dawn in hopes of finding her thief for her. But no luck. It looked like her "fiancé" had made a clean break of it. Hale must have been planning this for some time and had his escape all set up in advance of stealing Kate's money.

He shook his head. He couldn't imagine any man leaving a spirited and beautiful woman like Kate Danville willingly. Why, if she were his—

He brought himself up quickly. Whatever had taken possession of his mind to conjure up a thought like that? The lady in question might be a beauty, but she was also more trouble than he needed in his life. No, he was better off keeping as much distance between himself and her particular temptation as he possibly could.

He resettled his Stetson on his head and frowned. Keeping his distance presented a problem. That is, if he was to do as her father asked.

Sighing deeply, he withdrew the telegram from his pocket. He'd been wakened at dawn when his deputy delivered the missive. Kate's father had taken it for granted that he'd be willing to "keep an eye on his daughter for a fee, of course." At least that's how the telegram read.

"Hell and damnation," he muttered.

He did feel an obligation to Kate for not catching her thief, as much as he hated to admit it. Well, it looked like there was nothing else to do but try to take care of her. Until she left town on the next stage. However, he could never accept her father's money for doing his job.

He'd see to it that she stayed safe. Pain of a never long-forgotten memory clouded his thoughts and the serene view for a moment until he shoved it back into the far part of his mind. He would not let anything happen to Kate. Not like what had happened to . . .

Cutting off the thought, he turned and shoved the telegram in his saddlebags. A high-pitch whirl alerted him a split second before a bullet whizzed past his ear, barely missing him. He bent low over his mount and kicked him into a gallop, riding hard to get out of the range of the bushwhacker. The wide, open space separating them offered no cover.

A quick glance over his shoulder revealed a man with a raised rifle standing behind a cluster of rocks off on a low ridge to his right. Brannigan recognized the paunchy build of Joe Crocker without difficulty. His band of outlaws wasn't far away, one could be certain of that.

Another shot echoed. The fact remained that the outlaws had cover and he didn't. That's what he got for letting his thoughts wander instead of keeping his eyes and attention where they belonged. Disgusted, Brannigan spurred his horse on back towards town.

There'd be a next time for meeting up with Crocker, he knew that for certain.

Joe Crocker slammed his rifle against his thigh. He couldn't believe he'd missed Brannigan. The man sure had a long streak of luck playing on his side.

"Damn lawman has more lives than a tom cat," Crocker swore out loud.

"Joe?" his brother Bobby asked, leaning his hip against the rock beside Crocker. "That lawman's getting away. You gonna let him ride off like that?"

"Oh, shut up before I shut you up. What d'ya want I should do? Follow him right into that town and a jail cell?"

"No, I reckon not." Bobby stared down at a lizard scurrying across the ground. With a cruel smile, he caught the lizard's underbelly with his boot tip and flung it against a rock.

"Well, shut your yap and let me think," Joe snapped. He propped one elbow on the flat rock. Slipping his hand between the bulging buttons of his shirt, he scratched his exposed belly.

Yup, he'd get that lawman yet. All he had to do was make up a real good plan, then ride into Deadrange and kill him.

"Joe?" His brother walked up beside him and nudged him hard in the ribs. "Ya been thinking on us robbing that bank again?"

"Maybe." Joe spit a stream of dark tobacco juice into the dust by his brother's feet.

His brother had given him a right good idea. A vision of stacks of money spread out before him, and a greedy grin split his face. Money! Enough money to get him to St. Louis and pay for a big room in one a them fancy hotels he'd heard tell about. And even a *separate* room for Bobby. They'd never had separate rooms before, rarely could they afford one.

"Joe? Hey, Joe?"

At Bobby's voice the vision faded away. "Dammit, what are you yapping about?"

"Are we gonna rob that bank?" Bobby's eyes gleamed with excitement.

"Yup." Joe scratched his stomach again, and a wide smile split his face.

"When?"

"Soon enough."

"Hey Joe?"

"Will you shut up and let me be to think on a plan?"

"It'll work this time, won't it?" Bobby asked earnestly.

Joe winced at the question. Trust Bobby to recollect on that. The last time he and his boys had ridden into that lawman's town of Deadrange, they'd met up with Brannigan firsthand. Because of his meddling, their hold up of the bank had failed. Their day's work had gotten them nothing, and the lawman had killed one of Crocker's best men, too.

He figured he still owned him for that. The next time he and his boys rode into town, they'd clean out that bank, and he'd finish Brannigan off once and for all.

Kate looked at the pile of clothing on her bed in the dingy hotel room and brushed her hands

on a lace-edged handkerchief. She'd done quite
well. Everything lay in readiness, stacked in neat
little rows across the lumpy bed. The clothes she'd
convinced herself to part with should bring more
than the necessary funds to see her back to Boston.
Wouldn't Papa be surprised?

She smoothed down the skirt of her emerald silk
gown. The extra money it had cost to travel with
so many clothes would prove worthwhile. Stepping
back, she surveyed the total of two day dresses, one
ball gown, a plain wool cloak, and three bonnets
piled in orderly stacks across the bed. Yes, they
would most assuredly sell quickly, and she'd be on
her way back home in no time. Quite a nice two
hours' work, she thought proudly of her accom-
plishment.

It had actually been fun doing for herself, instead of relying on a maid to make her decisions
for her. Papa hardly ever allowed her to make a
decision on her own. She rather liked the idea of
thinking for herself.

She smiled. Everything was in readiness. The
bonnets alone, with their ostrich feather plumes,
would likely bring quite a tidy sum. After all, the
ladies in a town like Deadrange hardly had ready
access to the latest European fashions. Or any fashions for that matter.

The only place she'd seen so far that could possibly have clothing of any kind for sale would be
Peabody's General Store. She would start there.
She picked up her green bonnet, placed it atop
her curls and tied the satin ribbon. As she stepped
back, she caught a glimpse of herself in the room's
one lone mirror. The matching green ostrich
plume of her bonnet dipped at a jaunty angle.

She turned cautiously to one side and then the

other, then leaned closer to peer at her reflection. Would anyone be able to tell that she wasn't wearing a corset? She cringed inwardly at the thought.

There was nothing that could be done to help matters. She'd spent the better part of half an hour twisting and turning and reaching every which way, but still failed to fasten her corset. Finally, she'd tossed the offending garment across the room. No matter what decorum might order, there was no way she was wearing a half-laced corset anywhere.

She questioned how any woman managed the feat of lacing herself without a maid. However, that was a luxury she couldn't afford now. Yesterday had been her last day of being a pampered lady. Richard Hale had seen to that.

Satisfied with her appearance, she turned back to the bed. Yes, what items she felt she could reasonably spare should bring her more than enough funds to see her home to Boston. Wouldn't her papa be surprised when she arrived at their home all on her very own? She'd show him that she could take care of herself with or without the likes of Richard Hale.

Sniffing disdainfully, she gathered up the items into her arms, careful not to wrinkle them more than absolutely necessary. *A lady wouldn't be seen in public in a creased gown.* Mrs. Parker's admonition rang in her ears. Most assuredly then, a lady wouldn't care to purchase creased gowns either.

Careful to hold the garments and hat boxes high in her arms, Kate stepped out the into the hallway and eased the door to her room closed with her foot. She shouldn't have to spend more than one more night in this dreadful place.

With a smile, Kate traversed the distance to Pea-

body's General Store. As she stepped up onto the
wooden boardwalk in front of the store, the ping
of tobacco juice resounded, and a stream of disgusting brown liquid hit the dented spittoon. She
quickly stepped around the two men lounging in
the doorway of the store, careful to hold her precious bundle out of their way, and entered the
store.

The sudden change from bright sunlight to in-
doors startled her and she blinked several times.
Once her eyes adjusted to the change, she glanced
around the store, taking everything in with amazement.

The single room was crowded with a wide as-
sortment of items—things she would never expect
to see displayed in a store back home. Hams, ba-
con, luggage, and men's hats hung from the ceiling. She tilted her head back for a better look.
There was even a large black Stetson hat like the
one Brannigan wore. She blushed at her recollection.

Embarrassed, she quickly turned to study the
store more carefully. It was wise to check to see
what gowns Mr. Peabody might carry for sale, although she was certain that her own were of much
better quality.

Hardware lined one wall. She dismissed it and
continued her survey of the store, skipping over
the barrels and the pot-bellied stove in the center
of the room. Along a second wall, groceries of all
sorts were displayed.

However, the third wall held what she was looking for—the dry goods. She walked over for a
closer look, carefully dodging the barrel of pickles
with its pungent smell. She scanned the small as-

sortment of blouses and skirts and noted that several bolts of yard goods were also stocked.

Soundly gathering up her courage in both hands, Kate turned and strode across to the counter with a lot more confidence than she felt and carefully laid her garments out atop a bolt of calico fabric on the counter. With loving care, she smoothed the sash of an apricot gown. She really hated to part with that dress. It was one of her favorites, however, she sucked in a deep breath and thought, desperate times call for desperate measures.

At least that's what her papa always said whenever he found himself in what he termed a financial dilemma. However, his little dilemmas usually consisted of deciding how much money to put into a new venture. Hardly the situation she found herself in at the moment.

A fortyish gentleman, wearing a pair of spectacles perched on his nose, approached her with a distrusting look that almost sent her courage skittering away right out the door she'd just come through. Almost but not quite.

Instead she rushed into her planned sales pitch. She'd rehearsed it over and over in her hotel room until it sounded pretty good to her own ears.

"I'm here to see Mr. Peabody." She raised her chin.

"You're looking at him, ma'am." He smoothed his hand over his bald head with its rim of coal black fringe.

"Ah," she swallowed down the nervousness that rose up. Sucking in a breath for courage, she plunged ahead. "Mr. Peabody." She extended her hand. "I'm Kate Danville, and I'm here from Boston on a little trip—"

"Right sorry to hear about your recent misfortune, ma'am."

Kate gulped.

Her recent misfortune.

"Mis . . . misfortune?" she repeated. Her voice came out sounding a lot less determined than it had only moments earlier.

"Why, yes, ma'am. Any fella would have to be a downright scoundrel to up and run out on a filly as pretty as you."

Did everyone in the entire town know about Richard abandoning her? Kate shuddered at the possibility.

She'd thought of a lot stronger words than *scoundrel* to call Richard Hale since he'd sneaked out of town with her money, but she didn't see any need to share this fact with the proprietor.

Kate tossed her head in disgust, and the green ostrich plume of her bonnet bobbed. Plastering on her best and she hoped her prettiest smile, she stiffened her back the way Mrs. Parker had taught her.

"Well, Mr. Peabody, I thank you for your concern. And I appreciate your kind compliment." Kate struggled not to stumble over the words that threatened to stick in her throat.

She hated to pander to anybody. But, right now, as Papa was fond of saying *desperate times call for desperate measures.*

"Well, sir, it seems that I have found myself with a few extra garments that I would be willing to part with for a price. They're quite fine materials, as you can see. I assure you they are the best that Boston has to offer."

Her papa always insisted on buying only the

best. Right now she found herself thankful for that.

"As a matter of fact," she paused to pick up the apricot gown from the top of the stack. Smoothing out a wrinkle with her hand, she smiled over at the balding store owner. "This gown came from one of Europe's finest courtiers— "

"A what, ma'am?"

"A . . . ," she paused. "A famous dressmaker," she rushed the explanation out.

"Why didn't you just say so?"

"I just did," she snapped, then smiled again and gentled her voice. "This gown came from a famous dressmaker— "

"I got all the dress goods I need, ma'am. People don't buy too many dresses this time of the year around about here."

"Oh." Disappointment colored her voice.

"Your things are mighty pretty, but they're not worth much out here. They're not the sort of things most women hereabouts wear," he continued his explanation.

"Oh," Kate repeated, at a loss for more words.

What was she going to do now? Her beautiful, expensive clothing had no value here. Shock stole her voice for a moment; she'd been so sure that the money from selling her gowns and bonnets would finance her trip back home.

Mr. Peabody pushed up his spectacles in a nervous gesture. He appeared to be searching for words himself.

"But, come to think of it, if you're needing to sell these goods, maybe Belle would be interested. She has a liking for pretty things. And she always looks mighty nice, too. She— "

"Belle?" Kate interrupted the store owner, not

interested in how nice the woman looked only in
the identity of the person who might be the solution to her dilemma.

"Yes, ma'am. Belle Wilson. She runs the local . . . ah . . . she . . ."

Embarrassment brought a flush to the man's
lean face. He pushed up his spectacles again and
let the explanation trail off to an uncomfortable
silence.

"Howard Peabody! What are you telling this
young thing about me?"

At the other woman's husky laughter, Kate
turned toward the source. A pretty woman, several
years younger than Mr. Peabody, leaned toward the
counter and tapped him playfully on the arm. She
was dressed in a bright blue gown, quite low cut
for so early in the day, and her dark black hair was
piled in curls atop her head. She looked more like
she was on her way to a party, than to the general
store.

"They're lies, all lies." She laughed again and
turned to face Kate. "Don't you believe a single
word he said about me."

Kate returned the woman's friendly smile. "He
was quite complimentary—"

"Oh, was he?" The woman turned back to Mr.
Peabody with a coy smile. "Imagine that?"

"Morning, Belle, you're out awfully early, aren't
you?" He smoothed the rim of fringe on his head
and smiled at the woman.

Belle flashed him a wink in return, and he
glanced away as if nervous or flattered. Kate wasn't
certain which one.

"Ma'am, this here is Belle Wilson," Mr. Peabody
rushed to introduce Kate. "Belle, this here is Miss

Danville. I was telling her that you might be interested in buying some of her things."

Belle raised her brows at him, and Kate could swear that she saw the store owner's lean face redden. His smile faltered.

Suddenly, Belle turned away from him and fingered one of the gowns. Kate watched her peek up at the owner again, then look away.

"Ah, Miss Wilson— "

"Call me Belle. Nobody calls me anything else. Well," she paused and laughed good naturedly. "Leastwise not to my face."

Puzzlement clouded Kate's face.

"Honey, I'm not exactly the best woman for you to be seen talking to," she offered Kate the piece of advice. "And I don't know how the ladies of this town would take to you selling me your things— "

"Why would they care about that if they don't want to buy them?"

Belle chuckled. "Oh, they'd care all right. Me and my place aren't too popular with the women folk."

"Your place?"

"My business establishment," Belle explained with a chuckle. "You might say it's a place where a man can find a little comfort and companionship. For a price."

As full comprehension dawned on Kate, her face reddened. The woman ran a . . .

She gulped back the word. But Belle Wilson was so nice and so friendly. And so likeable.

Belle picked up the apricot gown and held it up in front of her, then chuckled. The top was several inches shy of covering her generous bosom.

"I don't think we could let it out enough, do

you?" She stuck her chest out and turned this way and that, with a coy smile for Howard Peabody.

He gave a choked cough as she leaned forward to lay the gown back on the counter.

"Sorry, honey. If you ever need a job, stop in and see me." Belle winked at Kate, then turned and waltzed out the door with her curls bouncing. Her laughter followed in her wake.

Kate stared after her, openmouthed.

"Ma'am," Mr. Peabody lowered his voice to a conspiratorial whisper. "If it's a job you want, I hear that Miss Sally is needing some help over at the restaurant. She's a bit outspoken and all, but she's right nice once you get to know her. If you'd like to go talk to her, it's the third building on the right."

Kate knew that she turned several shades of red, ranging from pink to flaming red. *A lady never discussed financial matters.* Mrs. Parker's words resounded in her ears so loud that she was certain Mr. Peabody could hear them, too. The finishing school instructor would be absolutely horrified if she were here now. The woman would view her student as a total failure.

Work in a restaurant? Mrs. Parker would deny ever knowing her. Kate stiffened her back again the way she'd been taught. Right now, she needed money, and she needed it badly enough to do almost anything.

She swallowed down her affronted pride and offered the store owner a sincere smile. How hard could it be to work in a restaurant?

"Thank you, sir." Her voice came out as stiff as her back. "I'll go speak with Miss Sally. Besides, I do believe that I'm quite hungry. Could I leave these things here for a short while—?"

"Of course."

Mr. Peabody scooped up the stack of clothes and laid them over a barrel behind the counter. Kate tried not to cringe at the casual treatment of her clothing. Well, wrinkles be damned, she was hungry and she needed to check on that job. She'd worry about her gowns later.

Nodding goodbye, Kate turned away. She nibbled on her lower lip. What exactly did a job in a restaurant entail? And how was she going to convince the owner to hire her? She didn't have any experience . . . or know anything about running a restaurant . . . or . . .

Kate raised her chin in defiance. She wasn't about to act defeated without even giving it a try. She needed this job. And she intended to get it.

She'd eaten in several fine dining establishments in Boston, and she'd acted as hostess for her papa many times in the past. That was a start. If need be, she'd exaggerate her meager qualifications until the owner couldn't resist hiring her.

Deep in thought, she walked to the door. She should be able to pull off the pretense quite well, if she tried hard enough. Yes, she was certain to get this job.

Kate stepped through the door into the bright sunlight and stopped suddenly. A tall, broad man sidestepped in anticipation of her oncoming path, then halted in mid-step.

Startled, Kate looked up and met the deep blue gaze of Lucas Brannigan. Her heart raced for the vicinity of her toes, and she hadn't the slightest idea why it would do a thing like that. It wasn't as if the good-looking marshal was a threat to her.

Oh, but he could be, a little voice whispered.

Kate felt the strong tug of some unknown sensation. This was nothing like what she'd felt for Richard. Her feelings toward Richard had never left her breathless, anticipating what she didn't even know.

Kate's mouth dried, and her lips felt as dry as dust. Nervously she moistened her lips with her tongue. Brannigan's eyes followed the movement of her tongue, making her even more nervous. Her heart skittered in her chest, and suddenly began to beat quite loudly. In fact, it beat so loud in her ears that she feared he would hear it.

Kate cleared her throat and forced her eyes away from his. Her gaze lowered to the strong, tanned column of his throat and seemed to lock there. She watched him swallow, unexplainably fascinated with the movement. His skin was richly tanned by the sun. Warm too, she imagined.

For an instant, she practically ached with the need to reach out and see if his throat was as warm to her touch as her imagination claimed it would be. She thought that the skin would likely singe her fingers if she touched him.

Wherever had that scandalous thought come from? She drew herself up with a sharp reprimand. What was happening to her since she'd arrived in this town?

It wasn't the town—it was the devastating marshal. She knew that as sure as she knew the sun shined brightly today.

"Morning, Kate."

His voice flowed like thick honey. Warm and rich to her ears. Lucas Brannigan tipped his dark hat to her, and Kate's thoughts scattered like a cloud of dust in a strong breeze.

"Ah . . . ," Kate stopped, completely at a loss for words.

Disgusted with herself, she attempted to regain control of her wandering mind. She was behaving worse than the young ladies at Mrs. Parker's Finishing School on their first day of training.

"Oh, ginger," Kate muttered under her breath.

"One of these days I'm going to have to find out what that means," Brannigan whispered to her, resettling his hat on his head with a broad smile.

"Food," Kate stammered in a burst of inspired explanation. "I do believe that I skipped breakfast, and it means that I am hungry."

Embarrassment threatened to turn her cheeks red. She could feel them heating as he continued to stare down at her. Damn, the man was tall. And broad. And . . .

Kate forced her mind away from Brannigan and back to the task at hand. Raising her chin a notch, she swept up her skirts the proper way she'd been taught.

"If you'll excuse me, Marshal— "

"Brannigan," he interrupted in a low velvety voice.

That voice stroked her, bringing all her nerve endings to full life, making her body tingle all over. It was a very pleasant feeling. And a very improper one.

Kate tightened her grip on her emerald reticule. Forcing a smile to her lips, she lowered her gaze. She'd never leave this spot if she continued to look at the man.

"I was saying that I must be going. I was on my way to the restaurant and— "

"Good luck on getting that job, ma'am," Mr. Peabody called out helpfully from his recently acquired spot by the doorway.

She was sure that he hadn't missed a minute of the interchange between herself and Brannigan.

"Damn busybody," Kate muttered to herself.

Now the marshal knew that she was going to the restaurant to look for work, not to merely eat a leisurely late breakfast as she'd hoped he would think.

"Good day," she said the last with a crispness designed to hide her humiliation.

Sweeping her skirt to the side, she strode down the boardwalk to the restaurant. It practically killed her not to look back over her shoulder, but she forced herself to keep her chin up and continue walking.

"What was that about?" Brannigan asked in puzzlement.

"I told her Miss Sally is looking for some help at the restaurant. Reckon she's going to go and inquire about a job. Hope she gets it. Things could get real interesting with that little filly around." Mr. Peabody winked at the marshal.

The corners of Brannigan's lips pulled into a smile. He might just stop in the restaurant for a late breakfast himself as soon as he finished his business at the general store.

As a matter of fact, the more he thought about it the hungrier he got.

Five

The nerve of the man.

Kate resisted the impulse to glance back at Brannigan and continued her steps on the wooden planks in front of the shops. Why, he had practically accosted her. And right there in broad daylight on a public street. Well, she supposed that the main thoroughfare of Deadrange, which was only wide enough for a wagon to turn around in, was as close to a public street as it could manage to get.

That didn't matter. What mattered was the scandalous way Marshal Lucas Brannigan made her feel!

How could she be feeling anything for another man so soon after Richard had abandoned her? Much less the way Brannigan made her feel. It couldn't be possible to fall out of love that fast, could it?

Maybe she hadn't really been in love? The question appalled her. Of course, she'd loved Richard. The very thought that she hadn't was ridiculous. She'd defied her father and ran away to elope with Richard, hadn't she? She *had* loved him, hadn't she? The question pricked at her conscience.

Richard had never made her feel the funny things she felt when she was around Lucas Bran-

nigan. Why, the marshal made her feel positively
unladylike!

Kate tossed her head, sending her copper curls
bouncing. How could she so quickly forget the vow
she'd made not to ever become involved with any
man who wasn't every bit as rich as her father?
The pain of Richard's betrayal still haunted her.
She never wanted to hurt that badly again. Never.

Remembering that heartfelt vow, she staunchly
resisted the strange fascination that Brannigan
seemed to hold for her. A marshal in a town like
Deadrange would most assuredly not be wealthy,
and wasn't likely to ever be wealthy. She wanted to
be loved for herself— not for her father's money.

In spite of the attraction Brannigan held for her,
instinct warned her that getting involved with him
would be like getting involved with a diamondback
rattler— deadly, at least to her heart.

Kate put her hand over her chest, shielding her
heart in a subconscious gesture of protection. At
the movement, her stomach rumbled loudly, reminding her she was hungry. It quickly brought
her attention back to the restaurant only steps away
and her mission.

She paused at the door and read the wooden sign
hanging overhead. Black painted letters hailed it as
"Miss Sally's Restaurant." She mentally crossed her
fingers for good luck. This had to work. It had to.

Kate stepped through the doorway and stopped
in bewilderment. All thoughts of Marshal Lucas
Brannigan fled from her mind. The small restaurant looked *nothing* like the restaurants she was accustomed to frequenting in Boston. Tables with
checkered tablecloths were scattered in a haphazard
arrangement across the room, and half a dozen
people sat around the tables.

Whatever tasks would she be expected to perform in a place like this? No one stood ready to welcome the patrons; in fact, she doubted if the position even existed here in this establishment.

Even this early in the day, heat rolled out of the back room housing the kitchen to envelop the dining area. The heat brought with it tantalizing aromas.

Kate sniffed at the delicious smells wafting through the restaurant. Her stomach growled in response to the enticing aroma of fresh biscuits mingling with ham and eggs, making her realize that she hadn't eaten last night. Well, it certainly seemed as if her appetite, which had fled with Richard, had returned full force and with a vengeance. However, it had chosen a poor time to do so. She was penniless.

"Don't just stand there," a woman's gruff voice called out from the kitchen. "Hell's fire, sit down! I'll get to you as soon as I can."

Howard Peabody's warning about Miss Sally's "outspokenness" came to mind. The woman yelling at her certainly fit his description.

"Miss Sally? I'm here to speak with you about—," Kate stopped, realizing that the woman couldn't possibly hear her clearly from the other room unless she raised her voice to a shout. She wasn't about to yell out her business for all to hear.

Kate waited where she was, tapping her foot impatiently and ignoring the people staring at her. How much longer was Miss Sally going to be?

As she waited, the smells from the kitchen enticed her, pulling at her, commanding her to sit down and order a plateful of the sure-to-be-delicious food. She placed a hand over her stomach and resisted the persistent urging. It was imperative that she

inquire about the job. Food had to wait. As if to
argue, her stomach emitted another distressing
growl.

As three men seated at a nearby table turned to
stare at her, Kate made up her mind, boldly striding to the back of the room; she'd search out this
Miss Sally herself and convince her to hire her.
She paused at the kitchen doorway, closed her eyes,
and took several deep calming breaths just the way
Mrs. Parker taught her students to do before facing a trying situation. If there'd ever been a "trying" situation, Kate thought disparagingly, this was
most assuredly it.

She opened her eyes, paused a moment for her
courage to catch up with her, and shoved the door
open. It was now or never.

"Yeah?" A rotund woman wearing a large apron
turned at the sound of her entry. She eyed Kate
from the fancy bonnet sitting on the crown of her
head to the matching green slippers on her feet.

Kate flashed her best smile, and reminded herself to stand tall like Mrs. Parker had taught her.
"Miss Sally, I'm Kate Danville—"

"What do you want?" The other woman wiped
her hands on her apron and crossed her arms over
her chest.

Kate refused to be intimidated. "Howard Peabody," she carefully used the proprietor's first
name to imply a friendship with him, "suggested
to me that I might be able to assist you."

"Is that so?" Miss Sally tucked a stray strand of
mouse-brown hair back into the stern knot she
wore at the nape of her neck and nodded for Kate
to continue.

"Howard recommended that my expertise might
be useful to your establishment."

The first lie pricked at her conscience. Mr. Peabody hadn't actually recommended her, or the sudden expertise she'd developed since walking through the doorway. Resolute, she ignored her plaguing conscience and pushed onward.

"Back at my home in Boston, I acted as hostess for my father's dinner parties." Kate smiled with the second lie.

She hadn't actually been the hostess, but she had helped him with the guests' cloaks. Surely that counted for something?

"I've helped prepare the party menus, as well."

As the third lie stabbed her conscience, she was certain that she'd killed it. However, her remark hadn't been a complete lie, she soothed her conscience. She had suggested the turtle soup that one time.

"Howard Peabody sent you?" Miss Sally bellowed the question in obvious disbelief.

"Yes, he did," Kate answered with honesty. "I came straight here from his store."

Miss Sally looked her over again, and Kate had the distinct feeling of being thoroughly inspected as if the restaurant owner was considering rather or not to buy a particularly questionable horse. She didn't like the feeling one little bit.

"You ever wait tables?"

The sudden question cornered her, and Kate paused a minute before answering. She had helped to clear the table that time that the maid had taken ill. Did that count? She decided it did.

"Yes, I have."

Miss Sally looked her up and down. "Well, I do need help real bad. Etta up and left sudden like to go take care of her sister. Likely as not she won't be back for a week at least."

Kate crossed her fingers in the folds of her skirt. *Oh, please,* she begged, *let me get this position.*

Miss Sally's unexpected wide smile told her that her prayer had been answered, even before she spoke.

"I guess you can stay on till then. Grab an apron and set to work, gal. Those clothes of yours are a mite fancy for working in."

She'd got the job. Kate could scarcely believe it had been so easy.

"Ah, Miss Sally, what will my duties be?" Kate asked, pushing aside the uneasiness the realization of her new job brought. She hoped she sounded a lot more confident than she felt.

"Why, the usual. You'll be waiting tables and washing dishes." She waved her arms in a all-encompassing gesture. "And whatever else needs to be done."

"Yes, ma'am," Kate answered with a full smile, ignoring the "whatever else" Miss Sally meant. She'd worry about those things when she came to them.

After all, how difficult could waiting tables be? Or washing dishes for that matter? She pointedly ignored the fact that she'd never done either.

Less than a quarter of an hour later, Kate had learned how difficult the tasks could be for her. Washing dishes had sounded so simple, even easy when Miss Sally told her to do the dishes while she took care of the customers. However, she had neglected to inform Kate that soap suds made the pottery very hard to hold onto. By the time she'd learned this sufficiently, she'd broken a half a dozen plates and two cups.

Within the next half hour, she learned that swearing came as natural as breathing to the robust Miss Sally. Kate never dreamed that a woman could even know the words her employer used so freely. And so often.

The dishes finished, Kate escaped the kitchen into the now empty restaurant, happy to be away from Miss Sally's outspokenness, as Mr. Peabody had referred to it.

The woman was certainly that. And then some. Kate swore the woman had an opinion on everything, and didn't fail to voice it without even being asked.

Kate glanced around to make sure the room was empty, then slipped one of Miss Sally's biscuits out of her pocket and bit into it. She sighed in pure delight. The biscuit practically melted in her mouth. No matter what else the other woman was, she could cook— a feat that Kate herself had never attempted. She absently chewed and swallowed the remainder of the biscuit, then dusted off her hands.

Glancing around, she noticed that a table had a generous heap of dishes remaining on it and crossed over to the table. There were so many of them— goodness, she'd have to make two trips to the kitchen. Miss Sally would likely scold her for taking too much time as well.

Sizing up the number of dishes, Kate began to stack them in the crook of her one arm. She had almost succeeded in getting them all into her arms when one cup tilted. She grabbed for it, and that's when disaster struck. The cup slipped, then another slid after it, then a plate. The entire lot crashed onto the floor one right after the other.

Kate was left with one undamaged plate clutched in her arm. She closed her eyes at the damage scattered around her. Perhaps if she scooped it up quickly enough, Miss Sally wouldn't . . .

"What the hell!"

The door to the kitchen slammed against the wall with a bang. Miss Sally came bustling out into the room, her cast iron skillet held overhead with both hands.

"What's the trouble out here?" She faced Kate.

"No, there's no trouble," Kate rushed to assure her employer. "I . . . I just dropped something. And it broke."

"It looks like a lot of somethings to me." She lowered the skillet with a heavy sigh. "I'll add them to your list of damages owed."

Kate had no doubt whatsoever that Miss Sally would do exactly as she said. She could imagine that list growing and growing with each mistake she made.

Miss Sally turned away and walked back to the kitchen, muttering the whole time. Kate didn't particularly wish to hear the words she was using this time.

Kate had scarcely finished clearing away the broken pottery when she heard someone enter the restaurant. A man cleared his throat, and a tiny fissure of excitement skittered up her spine as she straightened up and turned around.

Lucas Brannigan stood just inside the door. In some unexplainable way she had known it would be him. She didn't bother to question the fact.

He smiled at her and walked through the room, straight towards her. He stopped at the table beside where she stood.

"Good morning." His deep, low voice stroked her.

It made her feel as if he'd slowly run a finger

down her arm from shoulder to wrist. She shook off the feeling. It was really quite unladylike. And she was a working woman now.

"Good morning, Marshal Brannigan," she greeted him in her best Boston hostess voice.

"Brannigan."

He lowered himself into the chair beside her.

Kate swallowed. "Would you like breakfast?" The words tumbled out as nervousness suddenly overtook her cool composure.

Whatever was happening to her?

Smiling as if he were aware of her unspoken question, he gave his breakfast order. His smile and the knowing look in his eyes unnerved her. As soon as he finished speaking, Kate slipped away, weaving around the other tables to the relative safety of the kitchen, but she could feel his heated gaze following her.

Brannigan watched the provocative sway of her hips as she crossed to the kitchen with his order. A smile tipped his lips. *This was going to be one enjoyable breakfast.*

He pushed back his chair, stretched out his legs and waited for her return. Minutes later, she walked back through the doorway, a steaming plate clenched in her hands. He watched her approach.

Kate smiled, almost shyly at him. Continuing to grip the plate in an overly tight hold, she stopped beside his table and gave his long legs a challenging look. When he didn't move, she leaned over, then stopped inches short of the table.

"Ah, I'll need you to move your legs," she finally asked.

Brannigan straightened in his chair, and that's when he noticed the steaming food level with his nose. The eggs looked as if they'd congealed, and several pieces of white egg shell stood up across the expanse of the eggs. He gulped.

In his three years as marshal of Deadrange, Miss Sally had never sent out a breakfast order with the shells along. Why was today different? He knew without asking that the answer stood directly in front of him in a flour-stained dress and tousled hair.

Surely Kate hadn't been doing the actual cooking! The very thought brought a knot to his stomach. He knew without a doubt that the fine Eastern lady from Boston couldn't cook. He doubted if Kate Danville could boil water without scorching it.

"What did you do to my eggs?" he asked in a strained voice.

"Your eggs?" Kate asked in attempted innocence.

Brannigan forced his gaze away from her and back to the plate in her hands. He pointed to the food.

"Yes, my eggs. You didn't cook them, did you?" he asked, praying she'd say no.

"Of course not." Kate drew herself up, insulted at his tone.

"Thank God," he muttered under his breath.

"What's wrong with them?" Kate leaned closer to look at the generous helping of eggs piled on the plate. "They look fine to me."

"There's egg shells in them," Brannigan informed her.

"Oh."

"Oh?"

"Well, I guess that must have happened when I broke a few."

"A few?"

"All right," Kate snapped, "a dozen." She lowered her voice, "or so."

Brannigan continued to stare at her.

"I tried to salvage them for Miss Sally, and I guess I didn't get all the shells out."

Brannigan looked from Kate to the food. She followed his gaze, shifting her hold on the plate. Then, to her horror, the plate tilted. She tried to balance it, but too late.

The entire steaming meal of scrambled eggs, thick slab of ham, biscuits and gravy slid right off the plate and onto Brannigan's lap.

He yelled and surged to his feet. Kate screamed, and Miss Sally ran into the room, frying pan in hand.

"Kate," Brannigan sighed, brushed at the steaming food clinging to his pants, and clenched his jaw.

"Kate!" Miss Sally roared from behind her.

Squeezing her eyes closed a moment, Kate opened them to meet Brannigan's accusing gaze. She quickly turned away and came face to face with her employer's wrath. The woman looked furious. In fact, her face was mottled a displeasing shade of red. Her formerly neatly pinned bun hung down below her neck in limp strands. Why, the woman looked positively frazzled, she thought.

"Yes, Miss Sally?" Kate smiled her best, most pleasant finishing school smile, assured to soothe.

The other woman merely shook her head. "Hell's fire, gal. I can't afford you."

"What?"

Kate hoped she'd heard her incorrectly. Surely Miss Sally couldn't be intending to dismiss her so soon. Why, she hadn't even been working here a day yet. Actually, she'd been employed at the restaurant for less than a full morning.

The look on the older woman's face warned Kate that her worst fears were about to come true.

"You've broke a half a dozen plates and two cups," Miss Sally started out by listing Kate's first fiasco.

Kate cringed. How was she to have guessed how slippery soap made the dishes? She'd never washed dishes before in her life.

"And so far today," Miss Sally continued, "you've cost me a dozen eggs, not counting those that the marshal is wearing."

"But, it was an accident," Kate injected her innocence. It wasn't as if she'd dumped the plate of food on Brannigan's lap on purpose.

"And you've likely damaged him for life. Or at the least made him mighty uncomfortable. That's not the way I treat my paying customers."

Miss Sally shook her head in disbelief.

"How a little thing like you can cause so much trouble in such a short time is beyond me. You can cause more damage than a tenderfoot set loose at a branding."

"But— "

"Listen here, I'll even feed you for free if you'll just promise never to touch another thing in here. Do you promise?"

"Yes," Kate agreed.

She grabbed up a napkin and began to brush the food off Brannigan's thighs. She noted that he got the most peculiar look on his face.

"Kate," Brannigan said in a choked voice.

"Kate!" Miss Sally shouted. "Don't. Don't touch *anything.*"

Kate froze in her action and looked from Miss

Sally to Brannigan. The woman appeared heartily
disapproving, and Brannigan's eyes could almost
melt her where she stood. Her stomach did a fast
flip-flop, her eyes held fast by the heat in his gaze.
Desire, so strong it reached out and stroked her
nerve endings, emanated from him.

The napkin slipped from her fingers to drift to
the floor. Kate didn't even notice its descent.

Miss Sally quickly stepped between the two people, separating them. She shoved a flour sack towel
into Brannigan's hands.

"I'm mighty sorry for this, Marshal. I'll fix you
another breakfast right away."

"That's all right, Miss Sally," he spoke in a low,
soft voice. "I'm not very hungry anymore."

The woman spun around on Kate, frowning at
her. "You," she pointed to the door, "go back to
your hotel before you cause anymore damage. And
don't come back in here until supper time is almost over."

"But—"

"I'll see Miss Danville back to the hotel," Brannigan volunteered. However, the tone of his voice
didn't encourage any arguing from either woman.

Kate sniffed and raised her chin in defiance.
"No, thank you. I can see myself back to the hotel
quite fine on my own."

She quickly snatched off her apron and handed
it to Miss Sally. "Thank you, Miss Sally," she forced
the words out. "I appreciated the job."

With this she turned and strode to the door. She
felt like a good cry, and no one ever saw her cry.

Before she'd taken a step outside, Brannigan was
at her side. He clamped his hand on her arm,
drawing her to a stop. Kate could feel the sting of

tears behind her eyes. Oh, ginger, she swore to herself, she would not cry here. She wouldn't.

Crying would only make matters worse— as if that could be possible, she thought. She'd just lost her first and only job. At the price of fine china, she estimated that she now owed Miss Sally more money for the damages she'd caused than she could earn in a week. And she was still stranded in Deadrange.

The burning tears worsened, and she knew that if she didn't get away from Brannigan soon she was going to completely embarrass herself.

Jerking her arm from his hold, she whirled about and strode down the boardwalk at as fast a pace as decorum allowed.

"Kate!"

She ignored Brannigan's voice calling her name. Catching up her flour-stained skirts, she broke into a run. Intent on reaching the privacy of her hotel room, she dashed out into the main street and didn't notice the horse-drawn wagon rumbling down the street. Straight for her.

"Kate!" Brannigan yelled.

The authority in his voice slowed her, and she glanced up— right at the oncoming wagon and horses. A scream lodged in her throat.

Brannigan jerked her back into his arms and out of the path of the wagon in the last second before the team galloped past. The rumble of the horses hooves shook the ground beneath her feet, and Kate clung to Brannigan. She tightened her hands around the edges of his leather vest, savoring the warmth of his chest against her now suddenly icy hands.

"You little fool. You could have been killed," he shouted at her.

Kate bit her lip and held to him tighter. She could still hear the clang of the horses' harnesses and the echo of the rumbling wagon wheels. At the reminder of how close the wagon had come, a shiver of fear ran up her spine, and she shook in reaction.

"Oh, damn," Brannigan muttered.

He drew her away from the street and down an alley. For once in her life, she followed meekly.

He stopped a few steps into the alleyway. Kate stood there trembling slightly. Sighing, he ran his hands up and down her arms, trying to rub some warmth back into her. She shivered under his ministration.

"I'm sorry for yelling at you," he apologized.

Kate nodded, fighting back tears of reaction to the near accident.

"Are you all right?" he asked.

Kate only nodded. Keeping her face averted, she stared down at the ground.

Several loose tendrils of copper hair trailed down to brush her shoulders, tempting him to loosen the rest and let the cloud flow free about her face and shoulders. A man could lose himself in her so very easy.

Brannigan stepped away from the temptation. "Kate, are you hurt?"

She didn't answer, only shook her head and continued to fix her gaze on the ground.

"Hell and damnation, Kate. Why won't you talk to me?"

"Because I'm trying not to cry!" she shouted back at him, then cupped her hand over her mouth.

Brannigan burst into laughter, the unwelcome

sound firing her temper, and Kate kicked him soundly in the shin.

"Hell and damnation, what was that for?" He jumped back from her.

"For laughing at me crying."

"I thought you were trying not to cry."

"I was!" she sniffed and raised her chin with pride. "I don't cry in public," she answered haughtily.

Unable to help himself, Brannigan laughed again. Catching her shoulders in his hands, he stepped back out of the reach of her feet this time. He looked down at her upturned face, and suddenly his breath left in a rush.

What he'd heard said about a woman being beautiful when she's angry must be true, he thought in an instant. Kate's green eyes sparkled with the promise of fire beneath the prim Eastern facade. Color graced her cheeks, making them look as touchable as soft pink velvet. Her lips were full and parted, as if waiting for her next outburst or his kiss. Desire hit him with the power of a lightning bolt.

The laughter left him. He tightened his hold on her shoulders and drew her closer. Kate's gaze met his, and for the first time in his life, he was held spellbound by a woman.

He wondered how her luscious lips would feel beneath his, and if she would be as soft and inviting as she looked right now. He longed to pull her into his arms and find out.

He knew he should let her go. He knew he shouldn't kiss her. He knew he couldn't stop himself.

"Brannigan?" Kate asked in a whisper.

Her soft voice held confusion, and wonder, and

invitation. He took the invitation, and damn the consequences.

He pulled her fully into his embrace, lowering his head and capturing her lips with his. Her breath rushed out in a tiny whimper of sound, and he caught that, too.

She fit perfectly in his arms, her curves conforming against the hard planes of his body as if she'd been made for him. He slanted his mouth more fully over hers and deepened the kiss.

Kate gave herself up to the wondrous feel of his kiss. She was rocked to her toes with the force of his desire.

Richard had never kissed her like this.

Six

The next instant all thoughts of her former fiancé fled Kate's mind. Only Brannigan filled her thoughts.

His kiss was strong and forceful, like him. He kissed her with a demand that left her breathless, and somehow she'd known it would be like this when he kissed her.

Kate burrowed her hands into the thick hair at the nape of his neck. As she curled her fingers, she wondered for a second how her hands had gotten there, when last she'd known they'd been holding onto her skirt.

She brushed all conscious thought aside and gave herself up to the pleasurable feel of his lips against hers. His lips were warm and firm. His kiss demanded, desired, and possessed. And she revelled in it.

Kate leaned closer, wanting to be nearer to him if possible. She felt as if she were being absorbed into him.

"Marshal? Marshal?" a voice repeated over and over in the distance.

Finally it penetrated Kate's thoughts, forcing her eyes open. Her confused gaze met Brannigan's heated blue one. Whoever said that blue was an icy color had been wrong, she thought to herself.

Brannigan's deep blue eyes practically blazed, and Kate felt as if she'd be consumed by the fire within.

"Marshal?" a man's voice called out again.

Marshal. Suddenly reality returned to her, and Kate realized where she was and what she was doing— standing in a common alley kissing the town marshal. In broad daylight. And thoroughly enjoying it.

The realization of her impropriety acted like a splash of cold water to Kate's heated skin and passion-numbed senses. She pushed Brannigan away, her face turning red with embarrassment. Why, she had behaved no better than a . . . good heavens!

"Hell and damnation," Brannigan muttered.

Kate studied the dusty toes of his boots, unwilling to meet his eyes and the censure she'd surely see reflected there. When would she learn to control her unladylike tendencies? If she'd behaved like this with Richard, he would have pushed her away in disgust. What must Brannigan think of her?

"Kate?" he murmured against her ear.

His breath stirred the fine tendril of hair dipping over her ear, and she weakened a moment, leaning towards him again.

Gently, Brannigan pushed her from him slightly, then stepped back. She was horrified at her actions. What was happening to her?

"I . . . I have to go, Kate."

She stiffened at his words, drawing on her finishing school training to endure the humiliation. "Then go."

"Kate— "

"Go," she ordered.

She pushed him away forcibly, angry with herself. How could she have allowed such a thing to take place? Mrs. Parker would be appalled. Richard would be . . .

"Marshal?" Deputy Tom Avery rounded the corner. "There's a ruckus going on over at The Silver Slipper."

"This early?" Brannigan sighed and looked from his deputy to Kate.

Kate stared up at him, unable to resist the insistent pull of his gaze on her. There might be a "ruckus" going on at the saloon, but there was an all out war going on in her mind. And her heart.

She was appalled at herself, and what she'd allowed to happen. Allowed? She'd not only allowed Brannigan to kiss her, she'd kissed him back. And in public, too.

"Well, go and do your duty," she snapped at Brannigan. "I am quite capable of seeing myself to my hotel."

She sniffed and straightened herself to her full height of five feet and one inch. It didn't do any good. She still felt dwarfed by him and the intensity that emanated from him.

"We're not finished," he told her in a low voice, heavy with meaning.

"Oh, yes we are, too," she fired back.

She wasn't about to allow herself to be found in this situation again. She intended to steer as far away from the sinfully tempting Marshal Lucas Brannigan as she could manage.

Kate swept up her skirts and turning her back on him strode away. Brannigan's low chuckle of laughter followed her, and a smile tugged at her lips in spite of her resistance.

* * *

"Have a seat, boy." Buck waved Brannigan to a nearby chair. "You got the looks of a man with trouble on his mind. The Silver Slipper—"

"Just a disagreement between some Granger and Rustin men." Brannigan brushed the incident aside. Buck didn't miss anything that went on in town, not even from his sickbed in the rooming house. "They settled down pretty quick."

"So, what's troubling you?"

Brannigan sank into the straight-backed chair. Sweeping off his hat, he rubbed his hand through his hair, his irritation plainly showing. Kate had almost made him forget his daily visit to the wounded driver.

"Trouble is that woman's first name."

Buck slapped his leg and chortled. "I take it that the she-critter in question is Kate Danville?"

"Yes."

As if it could be anyone else, Brannigan thought. No other woman had even caught his passing attention since Kate Danville of Boston rode into his life. The woman had turned his life completely upside down in almost no time, and he didn't have the slightest idea how to right it again. Or if he truly wanted to do so.

His only hope was that his world would return to normal when she returned to Boston, but he was beginning to doubt if that would be the case.

"Hear tell she got herself stranded here in town."

"Her fiancé ran off with all her money. She can't leave Deadrange quick enough for my peace of mind," Brannigan added.

Buck chortled at his remark. "It ain't your peace of mind she's got in an uproar, boy."

Brannigan rubbed the back of his neck, trying to knead out the ache that had settled there ever since he'd first laid eyes on Kate, then sent his friend a disgusted look meant to silence him. Neither worked.

"Dagnamit, boy, I ain't ever seen you this tied in knots over a woman before." Buck laughed again.

"I'm glad somebody sees the humor in this," Brannigan answered in a sharp voice.

He surged to his feet and strode to the window. Looking out, he jammed his hands down onto the sill.

"She's got you tied up tighter than a calf at branding time. Yup, all that's left for her to do is put her brand on you."

Brannigan turned around to face his friend. "The lady isn't interested."

A sudden recollection of Kate in his arms brought the touch of a smile to his face. There was interested and maybe there was "interested." She certainly hadn't been completely immune to him.

The slight smile didn't go unnoticed by Buck. "Do tell," he drew the words out.

Brannigan turned back to stare out the window glass without really seeing what lay outside.

"She reminds me of Elizabeth," he said in a soft voice that did little to hide the pain underneath.

"Dagnamit, the two ain't nothing alike, you hear me, boy. Open your eyes and see past Kate's pretty face. That gal's got more guts than a lot of men I've met up with in my time."

Brannigan met this with silence.

"That gal's just plumb full of sand and fighting tallow."

"And that could get her killed," Brannigan added with finality.

"Humph. That little gal's too ornery to up and die easy like Elizabeth."

Brannigan sucked in his breath at the mention of the name. He spun around to face Buck, but the torment in his eyes did little to discourage the older man's meddling.

"It's past time you let her rest in peace, boy. It's been three years since she hightailed it out of here— "

"And died because of me."

"Weren't your fault. Only a fool would keep taking the blame for something that wasn't his doing."

"But it was my— "

"Like hell. It was her who did the deciding to go. And she sneaked off in the middle of the night. That was plumb asking for trouble."

Brannigan leaned back against the wooden sill, turning his head away from the man propped up in the bed. "I don't want to discuss it."

"Fine with me, but someday you're going to have to face it and put it behind you."

"Buck— "

"All right, I'll quit exercising my jaw." The old man held up his hands in surrender, then a smile slowly widened his face, turning into a broad grin. He cleared his throat and glanced to the ceiling. "Heard tell that you didn't care much for Miss Sally's breakfast."

"Sounds as if your jaw has been exercised plenty so far today. Has the entire town been in to see you?"

Buck slapped his knee and laughed. "Pretty near

to it. And you can guess who everybody's jawing about."

"Kate," Brannigan said in resignation. He straightened away from the window.

"Dagnamit! Will you sit!" Buck hollered from his bed. "I swear you're worse than a pup trying to find a spot to lie down."

Chuckling, Brannigan strode away from the wall and crossed over to the straight-backed chair.

"Well, what are you going to do about her?" Buck asked, the curiosity evident in his gravelly voice.

"Nothing," Brannigan answered.

Buck raised his eyebrows in an exaggerated gesture of disbelief.

"The last thing I need is a fancy Eastern lady who draws trouble like honey draws a bear," Brannigan added. His head might be listening to that, but his heart was having no part of it.

"She'd make a right good blanket companion."

"Buck—"

"Now, don't tell me your mind hasn't gone down that road?"

"Buck—," he tried again.

"She sure is a sight for sore eyes, and a little trouble keeps life interesting."

"Kate is more than a *little* trouble."

Buck grinned. "Given some time, that little gal will fit right into this town like it were made for her."

"Not even when hell freezes over."

"We'll see." Buck chuckled. "We'll see."

Kate plopped down on the lumpy mattress and stared at the flour stain on her skirt. What was she going to do now?

She'd lost her first and only job, and was worse off than when she'd started, for now she owed money to Miss Sally for the damages she'd caused at the restaurant.

"Oh, ginger."

Her stomach rumbled as if in response. Miss Sally's offer of free food tempted her, offering some small way out of her financial dilemma, but she refused the temptation. She wouldn't feel right eating at Miss Sally's restaurant for free. Kate Danville wasn't a charity case.

And she wasn't about to become one. Not if she had anything to do with it, and she did. She'd show Papa and the town of Deadrange a thing or two. Not to mention a certain lawman.

Kate jumped up from the bed and strode across to the armoire. Jerking open the door, she sorted through her clothing, looking for just the right gown.

She pulled out a demure gown of soft blue with a band of darker blue velvet trim about the neckline and the two flounces. Before she could lose her burst of courage, she stripped off her flour-stained dress, changed into the fresh gown, and repinned her hair. Securing a dainty bonnet atop her curls, she surveyed the results in the only mirror the room had to offer.

Kate eyed herself critically, turning first one way and then the other. After straightening her bonnet and retrieving her parasol, she pronounced herself ready. She thought that she looked like the perfect candidate to be employed at a general store. All she had to do was to convince Mr. Peabody of that fact.

* * *

When Kate entered Peabody's General Store, it appeared unusually busy to her. It seemed that half the town was either browsing or standing about the cold pot-bellied stove—talking. The room suddenly fell silent as she walked further into the store, then conversation started up again, more intense than before.

She ignored the customers in the store, searching for Mr. Peabody, and found him on a ladder pulling down a Stetson hat. She debated with herself, then decided not to interrupt him when he was attempting to make a sale. Kate recalled that always irritated Mademoiselle Piermont at her millinery shop back home in Boston. It was best not to start out by upsetting the owner.

Kate strolled over to the area where the dry goods were displayed. Bolts of fabric leaned haphazardly, and a length of bright yellow ribbon dangled down across a calico print on the floor. The display could most assuredly use some straightening; it was the perfect way to show the owner how helpful she could be to him. Scooping up the bolt of calico, she sat it atop the stack with the other fabrics. Next, she rewound the spool of yellow ribbon and hung it on a nail in the wall where other colorful rolls of blue, pink, and green ribbon streamed down.

Cocking her head, she surveyed her efforts. Very nice indeed. She gathered up a spool of lilac ribbon from atop a barrel and replaced it on a hook, then straightened the roll next to it.

"Ma'am, I'd like some of that pretty lilac ribbon you just sat out."

A feminine voice behind her startled Kate, and she spun around. A tall woman faced her with a wide smile on her thin face.

"Oh, but I . . ."

"And while you're at it, young lady," another cheery voice piped up from Kate's other side, "would you cut me off some of that calico?"

Kate opened her mouth to inform the women that she wasn't employed at the general store, and then just as quickly shut her mouth. What better way to show Mr. Peabody how much he needed her services and how capable she was than to attend to the customers already milling about the store?

"I'd be happy to assist you," Kate answered both women without hesitation.

She scooped up the bolt of fabric and retrieved the spool of ribbon from the wall. Wouldn't Mr. Peabody be surprised when she made her first sale?

"Would you like some of the yellow ribbon to go with your fabric?" she tentatively asked the one woman, crossing her fingers in hopes of an additional sale.

"Why, yes."

Kate eagerly grabbed up the spool and led the women to the counter. Once there, she sat the material and ribbons down onto the scarred wooden counter, then stopped suddenly at a loss of what to do next.

She frantically searched her mind to recall what Mademoiselle Piermont did after she'd secured the ribbons from her display case in her shop back home. Kate remembered that the Frenchwoman had cut the ribbons. That left the question of how much to cut off for these women? Did they expect her to know?

"The measure is over there," the first lady pointed out helpfully.

Kate flashed her a smile. The woman had won her undying gratitude.

"You're that Boston lady, aren't you? I didn't know you were working for Howard," the second woman put in.

Kate merely smiled in answer. She couldn't see any reason to correct the woman's assumption. At least not yet. If everything followed her plan, she would be working for him.

Over the next twenty minutes, Kate retrieved a length of red ribbon, a sack of flour, and a ham at patrons' requests. Feeling quite proud of herself, she jumped when Mr. Peabody clamped a hand on her shoulder.

"What are you doing, ma'am?"

Kate swallowed down a yelp and turned to face him, raising her chin in defiance. "I'm showing you how much you need an assistant." She smiled her prettiest smile and added, "Me."

"Now, ma'am— ," he began, but Kate cut him off.

"Don't you 'now ma'am' me. So far, I've sold fabric and ribbon to one patron, two lengths of ribbon to another, a whole sack of flour." She ticked the items off on her fingers in front of his nose. "And a ham," she ended in triumph.

"Well— "

"Well?" Kate repeated. "Am I hired?" She planted her fists on her hips. "Or do I go find those patrons and have them return the items?"

"No, there's no need for that." He faced her in defeat. "You're hired."

Kate could have hugged him, but settled for shaking his hand. With a smile of triumph, she untied her bonnet and placed it on a shelf under the counter. She was staying.

Over the next hour, Kate worked harder than she'd ever worked in her life. She swore every single resident of Deadrange came into the store for one item or another. She suspected the increased business was in part due to the whispers that flew around the store like flies at a picnic. Apparently seeing the stranger from Boston held quite a fascination for the townsfolk. She shrugged off the uncomfortable thought; at least the increased business ensured her position. Howard Peabody truly needed her help, she thought with pride.

A loud "humph" jolted her out of her reverie, and Kate whirled around to face Miss Sally's scowl.

"Broken anything here yet?"

"No, ma'am," Kate answered proudly.

She was beginning to heartily dislike Miss Sally. The woman's next words didn't do anything to further endear her to Kate.

"Hell's fire, old Peabody must be richer than I am to be able to afford you."

"How may I assist you, Miss Sally?" Kate's voice was tight with anger, but she forced herself to hold her tongue.

She wouldn't give the nasty-tempered woman the pleasure of seeing her dismissed for being rude to one of Mr. Peabody's customers. She plastered on her hardest learned finishing school smile, the one with which Mrs. Parker told her ladies would withstand anything. Kate was certain that the finishing school instructor had never met someone like Miss Sally.

"I'm checking to see if my special order is in yet," Miss Sally spoke in a low voice.

"Your special order?"

"Yeah."

Kate waited a moment for the woman to elaborate.

"Well, what are you waiting on? Is it here or not?" Miss Sally snapped.

Kate bit back the sharp retort that sprang to the tip of her tongue. How on earth did the woman expect her to know if an order was in when she hadn't informed her what that order might be?

She forced herself to widen her smile and inquire, "What was your order?"

Miss Sally mumbled something Kate couldn't discern.

"What?" she asked.

Miss Sally grumbled out a response that Kate still couldn't understand.

"I'm sorry but I didn't hear what you said. Could you speak up?"

"Hell's fire, it's my underwear," Miss Sally whispered in a voice that carried several feet away.

Two women turned at the words, their eyes wide. Kate knew that her lips twitched, but she couldn't help herself.

"Don't you dare laugh, girl."

Kate bit the corner of her mouth to stop the laughter that was bubbling up. She blinked several times and cleared her throat. Finally, she thought that she could safely speak without releasing a giggle or two.

"I'll check on your order."

With this, Kate scurried off to find Mr. Peabody, who had retreated to the back room minutes earlier. She covered her mouth with her hand, trying to hold back her laughter. Poor Miss Sally, she thought in sympathy.

Kate found Mr. Peabody working on his books.

He was sitting on a stool, bent over the papers and didn't hear her approach.

"Mr. Peabody," she called out.

He jerked up and almost fell off the wooden stool he'd been perched on.

"Miss Sally is outside, asking about her special order of underwear?" Kate asked with a smile that persisted in slipping out despite her attempt to hold it back.

"Oh, she means her long johns—"

"Long johns?"

"Long woolen underwear," he explained with a grin. "They're in a brown package on that shelf up over the hardware."

Kate nodded and turned away.

"Kate, you'll need a ladder to reach them. I can get them for you."

He started to stand, but Kate stopped him.

"Oh, no. You just keep working on your papers. I can get it just fine," she announced with a thread of pride in her voice.

She strode out of the back room in search of a ladder and Miss Sally's package. On her way by, she gave the pickle barrel a wide berth. Every time she'd passed the barrel that afternoon she'd held her breath. In spite of that, the pungent smell practically overwhelmed her, causing her to wrinkle her nose in distaste. She hurried past in search of the ladder.

Thankfully, she found it leaning against the back wall. Half-lifting and half-dragging the ladder, she pulled it over to the wall where the hardware was displayed. She leaned the top rungs against the wall and stood back and searched out the parcel.

Once she'd scooted the ladder beside the brown-wrapped package, Kate began to gingerly climb the rungs. Unfortunately, the ladder was propped a scarce foot from the distasteful pickle barrel. Wrinkling her nose, she carefully held her skirt out of the way of her toes and climbed one step at a time.

"Are you going to take all day on that?" Miss Sally complained. "Slow as molasses."

"Would you rather I missed a step and landed on you?" Kate snapped back before she thought.

"Humph!" sounded loudly from below.

Gritting her teeth to hold back any further comments, Kate climbed to the top shelf. She reached out and caught up the package. However, her fingertip tore a hole in the brown wrapping, and one sleeve of bright red material fell through, now in plain view.

"Hell's fire, don't wave it for everyone to see," Miss Sally ordered in a sharp voice, glancing in the direction of the two women nearby.

Kate glanced down at the woman. Flashing her an appeasing smile, she tried to tuck the bright red wool back out of sight in the wrapping.

"Red wool is good for rheumatism," Miss Sally rushed to explain. "But you don't need to show it off to everyone who's looking," she reprimanded.

Kate attempted to cover up the bright red material that persisted in easing out the hole in the package, and hang onto the ladder at the same time. The ladder tilted, and Kate frantically attempted to regain her balance, waving one arm. She temporarily forgot all about the bright red long johns and their plain brown wrapping.

As the ladder tilted to one side, Kate leaned to the opposite side. The ladder quivered, then straightened. Kate released a premature sigh of relief. A second later, the ladder tilted the other way.

Kate grabbed hold of the wood with both hands,

completely forgetting about Miss Sally's long johns. In her haste to secure a solid hold on the ladder, she let go of the package.

The brown wrapping fell away, and the bright red woolen underwear tumbled down. Right into the pickle barrel!

Miss Sally shrieked, then let out a bellow of rage.

Kate cringed and shut her eyes. A second later, she opened them and dared to look down. Miss Sally's long johns floated on the top of the pickle brine.

"Oh no!"

Kate scrambled back down the ladder as fast as she could.

Cuss words tumbled from Miss Sally's mouth, and her face turned an unbecoming shade of beet red. "Hell's fire! Look what you've done."

Kate ran over to the barrel, and wrinkling her nose in distaste, she pulled the soggy wool from the pickle barrel. A stream of sticky pickle juice ran down her hands.

"I'll . . . I'll clean these right up for you," she offered.

"You— " Miss Sally took a step towards her.

Kate backed away, the dripping material held in her outstretched arms.

"I'll just take these outside— "

"Don't you dare— !" Miss Sally shrieked.

"They'll be fine," Kate tried to reassure the almost hysterical woman. "I saw a horse trough outside. I'll just go rinse this pickle brine out of them— "

"No!"

The other woman lunged for the underwear. Kate spun on her heel and dashed outside.

"Don't you dare go waving my things around for everyone to see!" Miss Sally shrieked after her.

By the time Kate reached the water trough and dropped the smelly material inside, Miss Sally came huffing and puffing up behind her.

Mr. Peabody ran out of the store with each and every patron behind him. Almost instantly a small crowd began to gather, encircling the water trough.

"What's going on?" Mr. Peabody asked Kate.

"It's all taken care of, I— "

"She dumped them in the pickles," Miss Sally accused in a loud voice. "And now, she's parading them for the whole town to see."

A ripple of laughter started through the crowd, then turned into guffaws. Kate winced at the unwelcome sound. It would not improve Miss Sally's temperament to be laughed at.

"Kate— "

Mr. Peabody cut off what he'd been about to say as Miss Sally lunged for Kate. He caught the angry woman and held her back with effort.

"Kate, maybe you'd better get on out of here," he suggested.

"This will rinse right out. I'm sure. See?" Kate held up the underwear to show Mr. Peabody that it was going to be fine. Water streamed down her arms.

The sight of the red material enraged Miss Sally as if it had been waved in front of a bull. She bellowed in rage and reached for Kate again. The crowd erupted in whistles and laughter.

"Howard, you better keep her out of Sally's reach," Belle Wilson shouted. A hoot of laughter followed.

Kate squeezed her eyes shut. She'd done it again.

The cluster of people in front of Peabody's store drew Lucas Brannigan's attention the instant he left the rooming house. A chill ran down his spine. The burst of laughter from the crowd did little to reassure him.

As he strode over to investigate, he heard Kate's voice. "Now, Miss Sally—"

"I should have known," he muttered.

Trouble and Kate Danville just naturally went together.

"Marshal?" Howard Peabody called out over the din of laughter and hoots.

Brannigan turned to him.

"Marshal, will you get this tenderfoot out of here before Miss Sally up and has her lynched?"

Seven

One quick glance at the look of fury on Miss Sally's face convinced Brannigan that getting Kate away from there was exactly what he'd best do. And it couldn't be soon enough.

"Folks!" he called out to the handful of people in front of him. "Let me through."

The crowd parted, making a clear path between Brannigan and Kate. That's when he caught his first good look at her. He barely resisted shaking his head at the sight. Her fancy Eastern gown was streaked with dirt and droplets of water. A smudge of dirt graced her chin, while her usually pert little hat was missing. He was coming to expect seeing her copper curls tumbling about her shoulders in sensual disarray. She didn't disappoint him.

He didn't know whether to give into the temptation that urged him to sweep her up into his arms or give into the laughter that tickled the back of his throat. He staunchly resisted both.

She was concentrating so hard on something in the horse trough that at first she didn't notice him. He shifted to get a better look at what held such interest for her. At that moment, she pulled a dripping clump of red from the trough.

As Kate shook the object, two red sleeves dangled down and he recognized what she held. Biting the inside of his cheek, he bit back his laughter. Someone's underwear was receiving a thorough dunking from Kate. From the sound of Miss Sally's bellowing voice, the clothing in question belonged to her. Laughter tugged at his lips, but he stilled it.

He had a job to do. He was the law in Deadrange and assigned with keeping the peace, and if he didn't get Kate out of there soon, there wouldn't be any peace left. With three long strides he reached the water trough.

"It's best if you leave, Kate," he spoke in a low, but firm voice.

"But I can fix these, I know I can." She dunked the red wool back into the water and swished it around. "If you'll— "

"Marshal, I don't know how much longer I can hold her," Howard yelled.

Miss Sally jerked her arm out of his grip. Brannigan stepped between the irate woman and Kate, earning a solid whack in the ribs from Miss Sally. He cut off the word he'd been about to say.

"Now, Sally, best you calm down some." Howard caught her arm again and pulled her back. "Marshal?"

"I'm fine," Brannigan gritted out the words.

Ignoring him and the ruckus around her, Kate pulled the red wool back up out of the water. Brannigan knew the action would have an effect like waving it in front of an enraged bull if Miss Sally saw it.

"Kate, let it be," he ordered.

"But— "

"I said leave them."

He caught her arm, and she dropped the sodden material. The long johns splashed back into the trough, sloshing water over the side. Dismissing her struggles, he pulled her along behind him through the crowd.

One quick glimpse of Miss Sally's beet red face convinced Kate of the wisdom of keeping up with his long strides. Laughter and Miss Sally's sworn threats followed them.

"How did you get into this mess?" Brannigan asked, exasperation tingeing his words.

"I work for Mr. Peabody," Kate rushed to explain. With her free hand, she swiped at the mixture of water and pickle juice that ran down her arms.

Brannigan drew to a halt in front of the hotel, releasing his hold on her. "I wouldn't take any bets on that now." A faint hint of laughter edged his voice.

"Oh, ginger."

Kate spun on her heel and strode into the hotel. Brannigan pushed back his Stetson and followed her. This was one story he had to hear. Kate muttered all the way up the stairs to her room, and he stayed only a pace behind her.

Once upstairs, she unlocked her door, stepped inside, and slammed the door shut behind her. It landed with a dull thud against Brannigan's palm.

Shoving the door open, he strode into the room and whipped his hat off.

"What happened this time?" he asked. "How did you ever get Howard to hire you?"

Kate shrugged. "I got the job all on my own. And without telling a single lie," she announced.

At his quick look, she amended it to, "I mean stretching the truth."

"I wondered how you got Miss Sally to hire you.

You'd never worked in a restaurant before, had you?"

"I, ah, I stretched the truth a bit about my qualifications."

"A bit?"

"Yes, a bit," she answered back, chin held at a haughty angle.

A smile pulled at his mouth, but he forced it back. He recalled that Kate hated to be laughed at, and he had the bruise on his shin to prove it.

"And this time?" he prompted.

"Howard Peabody needed my help, and I was doing a good job— "

"What went wrong?"

Brannigan knew beyond a shadow of a doubt that this was one explanation he had to hear. Kate stared down at her hands, entwining her fingers.

"Well?" he prompted.

"Everything was going so good. Then I was retrieving Miss Sally's special order— "

"Special order?"

"Don't keep interrupting." She shot him a stern glance. "Mrs. Parker says it isn't polite."

Before he could ask who Mrs. Parker was, Kate plunged on.

"As I was saying, I was retrieving Miss Sally's special order *of long johns,*" she added the last with emphasis.

"The ones in the horse trough?"

"They weren't in the trough then."

"I figured that."

"Do you want to hear this or not?"

Brannigan choked back his laughter. He wouldn't miss this for anything. "By all means proceed." He waved her on.

Kate took a deep breath and launched into her

explanation. "I wanted to convince Howard I could work on my own without needing his help. I got the ladder all by myself. Then, I was retrieving Miss Sally's order from the top shelf when she yelled at me, and I lost my balance, and the ladder started tilting, and the package tore worse . . ."

Brannigan tried to follow the chain of events as the words tumbled from Kate's luscious lips, but instead he found himself watching the way Kate's lips tipped up at the corners. The memory of how her lips had felt beneath his plagued him. They had been so soft and yielding.

"And Miss Sally started yelling, and the ladder swayed, and," Kate paused, cocking her head to study the man across from her. "Are you listening to me?"

"Yup."

His one word answer had the effect of silencing whatever she'd been about to say next. That one word had been spoken in a low drawl that seemed to feather over her and stroke her softly.

"Ah," Kate forced her gaze away from Brannigan. Somehow she couldn't seem to look into his deep blue gaze and find the words to carry on a conversation at the same time.

She forced herself to concentrate hard on the events that had transpired in the store. She almost blocked out the picture of Brannigan standing across from her, his arms crossed over his broad chest. Almost, but not quite.

"Yes?" he asked in a low voice.

Kate felt the word skim along her skin, from her neck all the way to her toes. She forced herself to stare at a spot on the wall over his shoulder and continued her explanation. It was the only way she could manage to get a single word past her dry lips with him, looking at her the way he insisted on doing right now. It made her feel all shivery inside like she'd been riding in a carriage that had just driven over a big dip in the road and left her stomach behind.

"The . . . the ladder tipped," she forced the words out. "And Miss Sally started yelling at me, and the ladder kept moving." The words came faster as she tried to avoid the feel of Brannigan in the room. "I tried to hang onto the ladder and her package both, but I guess I let it go." She met Brannigan's questioning look, then rushed on to the awful end of her story. "The long johns fell in the pickle barrel."

Kate scrunched her eyes tightly closed, waiting for the explosion that was sure to follow her words. None came. She peeked up at him and could have sworn she saw his lips twitch.

"The pickle barrel?" he asked in a strained voice.

This time she was certain she saw his lips twitch. She nodded in agreement. "The pickle barrel."

Brannigan's laughter rolled over her, sweeping her up with it. She gripped her hands tightly together as her stomach performed that strangely pleasant flip-flop again.

When Brannigan's laughter came to a sudden stop, her heart did, too. His gaze was locked on a spot just below her neck. Unable not to, she followed his gaze down to the top of her gown and her breasts, which were clearly outlined by the damp material. It was evident she wasn't wearing a corset, and the dark shadow of her nipples showed through the damp, now nearly transparent fabric of her gown.

"Kate . . ." His hat slipped from his fingers to glide unnoticed to the floor.

She straightened her clenched fingers.

"Ah . . ." She swallowed down her words, separating her sticky fingers. She wrinkled her nose as the smell of pickles wafted up to her. "I need to take a bath."

Brannigan's eyes darkened at her statement. A mental picture of their bodies, slickened with water, close together in the metal tub arose before her, taking her breath away.

"I could stay and help." His voice lowered to a pitch above a whisper.

The soft drawl stroked her. It tempted her. She couldn't have spoken if her life depended on it.

"Rinse the soap off your back for you," he continued his offer, still in that velvety-soft voice that held her practically mesmerized.

She knew that if she closed her eyes she'd be able to feel his calloused palms against her soapy bare skin, so real was the mental pictures his words evoked.

It was so very tempting, and the very thought shocked her. And offered a most tantalizing enticement.

"Kate, come here," he ordered, still in that voice full of temptation. This time it also held a command that would not be denied.

She could no more resist its lure than she could willingly stop her own breath. She took a step forward. Then another.

Brannigan met her halfway, drawing her into his arms in one smooth movement. He cupped her chin in his palm and lowered his face to a mere breath from hers, so close that their very breathing

mingled together until she didn't know where she
stopped and he began.

He trailed his other hand down her neck, flicking
back a wayward curl with his finger. Running the
pad of his thumb over her lower lip, he gazed down
at her as if he would devour her. The thought excited and shocked her.

His thumb tasted salty against her lips, and she
resisted the sudden unknown impulse to draw it
into her mouth and suckle it. Wherever had that
thought come from!

He trailed his thumb across her lip and down
her chin, sending an enjoyable shiver across her
shoulders and downward. As if he'd felt it too, he
slipped his hand down her neck to her shoulders.

His palm rubbed against her skin, dragging
against the sticky residue from the brine, but the
friction only served to heighten the pleasure his
touch brought with it. It was roughened and tender at the same time. It amazed her. And delighted
her.

No sooner had that realization slipped into her
thoughts, then Brannigan slid his fingertips beneath the damp bodice of her gown, stroking the
tops of her breasts. As his fingers brushed lower
against her nipples, a gasp rushed past her lips.
He answered with a deep groan and crushed her
against his length; the force of his desire sent her
heart skittering down to the bottom of her stomach, where it met up with the flurry of butterflies
that had taken up residence there. It was a most
unusual sensation. Slightly dangerous, exciting,
and oh so pleasant.

All the strength fled her legs, leaving her knees
strangely weak. She caught his shoulders to steady
herself. They were firm and finely muscled be-

neath her fingertips. Resisting the unexplained
and unladylike urge to rub her fingers back and
forth across those muscles, she stared up at him.
What she saw reflected in his eyes held her spellbound. Heat, fire, and blatant desire so intense it
practically engulfed her. Then he kissed her.

He took his time with his kiss, letting his lips
caress hers, tasting, sucking. Kate stretched up on
tiptoe, striving to get closer. He wrapped his arms
around her, molding her to his length. His body
was hard and hot against hers.

He continued the kiss, slanting his mouth more
firmly over hers. He gave the impression that he
had all day in which to kiss her. There was none
of the hurried, distracted way that Richard kissed.
None at all. Brannigan concentrated his full attentions on that kiss. Why in comparison to Richard . . .

Kate's mind snapped to full attention and her
senses came crashing to a halt. She'd been prepared to marry Richard only days ago. Hadn't she
learned anything? One by one, each of her senses
cooled. Whatever was she doing? She wasn't about
to marry the town marshal. This had to stop. Now.

She was horrified at her behavior. How could
she be letting him kiss her, much less in this improper manner? And all alone in her hotel room?
And kissing him back. Mortification swamped her.
What had happened to her since coming to this
town?

She straightened her fingers from their hold on
Brannigan's shoulders and pushed against his
wide chest. It was like trying to move a wall. She
pushed harder, trying to put a respectable distance
between their melded bodies. Shame flooded her
cheeks. Anger followed right on its heels. What

gave the marshal the idea that he could treat her this way?

She planted both hands firmly against his chest and shoved. The action broke off the kiss, and Brannigan blinked his eyes open to stare down at Kate.

Dear, dear Kate. The words whispered within his mind.

She stiffened against him, pushing again with both hands. It took a moment for the fact to penetrate past his arousal. The lady had turned colder than a winter storm, and just about as quick. The passionate woman of moments ago had disappeared. Now she was every inch the prim and proper Kate from Boston, he thought to himself.

From Boston. The recollection hit him hard, and he felt his blood slow and cool in his veins. *She was all go and no stay.* Just like . . .

He cut the painful memory off and released Kate at the same instant. He drew in a ragged breath, ordering his body to return to normalcy. There was no future in this foolishness.

Remember, Kate Danville would be hightailing it out of Deadrange as soon as she could gather up enough money to do so. Their time together would be no more to her than the dust she'd brush off her fine fancy Eastern gowns. But dammit, in spite of knowing this, he still wanted her.

Brannigan called himself every kind of a fool. He stepped back and set Kate from him with a forced effort of sheer will. Drawing in another shuddering breath, he looked down at her.

"Let me go," Kate ordered, stepping back another step.

Her hair lay in tousled disarray about her face, the copper strands shimmering with a vibrancy that was pure Kate. Her green eyes slanted, half closed with intensity, recalling to mind that mountain lion he'd met up with that one time. She had about as much fight and spit to her as well.

He had hated to push away from her almost as much as he'd hated having to do anything in his entire life, but he knew that he didn't have a choice. A woman like her wasn't for him. He wanted a woman who would stand by his side. He needed a woman he could count on not to run off. And right now, Kate was running.

A shuttered look came over his face, locking away the thoughts and painful memories. He stepped back a difficult step, then another, knowing he needed to put distance between himself and Kate's potent brand of temptation. She made a man lose all sane thought when he held her in his arms. That was something Brannigan couldn't risk.

"You'd best be taking that bath now," he spoke in a cool voice that gave away nothing of what he'd been thinking about, or the battle he'd just fought. And lost.

With this, he scooped up his hat from where it had fallen to the floor and settled it on his head and turned toward the door.

Kate watched him leave in bewilderment. He wasn't going to argue or even question her. It was as if he couldn't get away fast enough. Whatever in tunket had brought that sudden change in him? Richard had never reacted so oddly after a kiss. He'd never left as if he'd been scalded the way Brannigan had left.

The door shut with a soft click behind him, and it was as if the sound unfroze her. Kate took a step toward the door intending to call him back, then stopped herself.

If he wanted to go, then let him go!

"Oh, ginger!"

She stomped her foot. No man had ever simply turned his back and walked out on her like that, much less rushed away. But, she'd never met a man like Marshal Lucas Brannigan before either.

She hoped his self-righteousness up and hit him. It wouldn't be anymore than what he deserved.

What was it about her that sent men scurrying away? It seemed they couldn't flee from her fast enough. Look how Richard had left her. A sharp stab of pain caught her. Had Brannigan recalled that she was penniless? Her father's remark that men only wanted her for his money returned to haunt her.

She would not believe it would always be this way. She wouldn't. Someday there would be a man who would love her for herself, and not her father's money.

Her anger at Brannigan's departure resurfaced, driving out the harsh reminder of her father's attitude. The marshal was the most irritating and confusing man she'd ever met up with.

One instant he kissed her as if his life depended on it, and until she became convinced that her next breath depended on his next kiss as well. Then, he stepped away, sat that danged black hat on his head, and calmly walked out the door.

"One of these days, Brannigan," she muttered, "one of these days." The marshal needed to be taught a lesson.

The campfire crackled in the night air. Joe Crocker stared hard into the meager flames and swirled his coffee around in the cheap tin cup. The

sound of laughter drew him out of his dark
thoughts.

"Bobby, get over here!" Joe took a long swallow
of the cooling coffee. "I got me a plan all thought
out."

"What's that, Joe?" Bobby rushed to join him
at the campfire, leaving his two cohorts to their
own devices and their bottle of whiskey.

A wide grin split Joe's face as he stood, stretching
out the silence until it about snapped. He took another slow swallow of coffee, making his younger
brother wait in anticipation for his answer.

"Joe?"

His grin tightened as he took enjoyment from
watching his younger brother wait on his words.
Leisurely, he reached his fingers between the buttons of his dirty, faded shirt and scratched his
belly. His brother shifted from one foot to the
other.

Finally, Joe spoke, "We're gonna ride into that
little old town of Deadrange and rob us a bank."

"But, the last time we tried that, Drago got killed
by that town's marshal."

"This'll be different." Joe's grin widened, showing dark, tobacco-stained teeth. "That's why I plan
to kill the marshal while we're there this time."

Bobby sucked in his breath, then chortled. "Yeah,
Joe, that'd even the score real good. But, what about
Pete and Jensen? Ya think they'll go along with your
plan?" Bobby thumbed to where the other two men
stood several feet from the campfire, drinking from
a bottle.

"They'll do what I tell them to do." Joe spat
out a mouthful of coffee grounds. "I'm still the
head of this outfit."

"Yeah, Joe. Nobody'd be fool enough to say you weren't."

"Keep that fixed in your mind, too."

"Sure, Joe."

"And Brannigan's mine. Don't nobody better shoot him afore I gets my chance." Joe lowered his hand to rub the cracked leather of his gun belt.

The two brothers grinned at each other, then erupted into coarse laughter.

"When are we gonna do it?" Bobby asked, when they'd stopped laughing. "When, Joe?"

"I'll let you know when it's time. Don't you worry, I'll let you know."

Joe Crocker's eyes glazed into a grimace of pure hatred, and he threw his tin cup to the ground. "But Brannigan's mine."

Kate clenched her hands into fists and threw an angry glance at the mirror over the saloon bar. She didn't know when she'd been so frustrated as she was at this moment. She'd spent the last ten minutes trying to convince the aging saloon owner to hire her. But to no avail.

First, Frank Jones had politely inquired about her health, then proceeded to comment on the weather— in great detail. Anything but agree to her request for a job.

Then to add to the insult, he'd refused to face her straight on. Instead, he kept focusing his gaze on a spot above her head, or on the glass in his hands that he kept polishing so studiously.

"Mr. Jones— "

"Ma'am, I got to say no to you." He straightened his bent back, reminding her of a gnome.

"But, why?"

"Ah . . ."

He was most definitely searching for an excuse, but she was having none of it. He might look like a kindly old shopkeeper, but he was as wily as a wild animal. She'd ascertained that by now.

"I happen to know for a fact that you need the help," Kate challenged his refusal.

Although she wondered why he needed assistance. The saloon was practically empty, one lone patron sat at the tables, his head leaned back, snoring loudly. It was the only sound in the big room.

"And that you have been looking to hire someone," she added.

Tommy Tyler, who clerked at the hotel, had told her that very thing when she'd descended the stairs after scrubbing herself free of the pickle brine and all memory of Lucas Brannigan. He had also complimented her on her "sunny yellow dress" as he'd called it, then cleared his throat to force his young voice to a deeper tone. She had rewarded him with a wide smile.

She wasn't smiling any longer though. "Well?" she queried the saloon owner. "You are looking for someone. Tommy told me."

Frank Jones took his time polishing the glass until it shone. Finally, as the silence stretched out, Kate could stand it no longer. Light from the overhead lighting reflected off his bald head, reminding her of the set of billiards back in Papa's study. He was paying her about as much attention as one of those billiard balls, too.

"Mr. Jones?" she demanded, hands thrust on her hips.

With an effort of will, she refrained from stomping her foot to get his full attention. Although the action was becoming more and more tempting. He was obviously stalling as he raised the glass to his lips and blew out a long breath, then began to repolish an imaginary spot on the rim. Probably hoping she'd give up and leave.

"I'm waiting for an answer." She raised her chin up and faced the owner head on. "And I'm not leaving here until I get that answer." She crossed her arms over her chest. "I intend to wait right here."

Frank set the glass down and stared hard at her a moment, then sighed in defeat.

"Ah, hell." He ducked his head. "Beggin' your pardon, for the swearing, ma'am."

Kate tapped her slippered foot in a statement of impatience and continued to stare at him. He flushed under her steady perusal. The temptation to stomp her foot became stronger.

As the seconds stretched into minutes, he shifted from one foot to the other. "Why can't you just be like any other female when a man says no, and turn around and leave, ma'am?"

"Because I'm not leaving until I have my answer, and I'm not like the women in town."

Brannigan stepped through the saloon door, and stopped in his tracks at Kate's statement. She was certainly right on that fact. Kate Danville wasn't like any other woman in town, or anywhere else, that he'd ever met up with before.

Or ever will again, a little voice prodded in the back of his mind. He silenced it and listened to the interchange between Kate and the saloon owner.

"Ah, well, ma'am. You asked for it." Frank threw the towel down on to the top of the polished wood bar. "You got yourself a reputation for bringing trouble with you wherever you go."

"What?"

"Ma'am, it just seems that trouble follows you around like a newborn calf following its mama." Frank scratched his bald head. "I swear I've never seen anything like it in all my days."

He stopped and smoothed one hand across the top of his head, obviously at a loss for words.

"I promise that I won't cause any trouble here, Mr. Jones," Kate said earnestly.

He shook his head vehemently. "No, ma'am." He softened his voice, "I'm sure you start out meaning well, but I can't do it. I got too much whiskey stock here. It's too costly. I can't let you work here."

"But— "

"I know you don't mean to cause trouble, but it's like you just can't help yourself. It's as if you go borrowing trouble."

The saloon owner echoed her father's sentiments so exactly that Kate fell silent for a minute. She didn't *try* and cause trouble. It just seemed to happen. No matter what she did.

"I'm right sorry, ma'am, but I can't afford your brand of trouble in here." The owner shook his head in resignation.

As Kate opened her mouth to protest; he held up his hand. "Now, I already know that you don't have the money to pay for any damages done in here. You already owe money to Miss Sally for her place, and to Howard Peabody for . . . ," he trailed off and coughed back a snicker of laughter. "For Miss Sally's order."

In spite of his efforts to the contrary, a grin split Frank Jones's face.

"I— ," Kate tried again, but was silenced.

"No," Frank answered with a decisive note of finality.

Brannigan listened to the interchange with in-

creasing interest. He couldn't blame old Frank for
refusing her, but he questioned how he managed
to do it. Kate was so insistent. She faced the owner
squarely with what Buck would call "sand and
fighting tallow." He had to admire her for that.

It was then that Brannigan saw her bottom lip
quiver. Hell and damnation. It was nearly his undoing.

He would *not* intervene. He wasn't about to step
in and help her out. All it would take was one
word from him, and Frank would give in. But he
wasn't going to do it. No, he . . .

Hell and damnation.

One more look at Kate's downcast expression
cinched it. He'd do it, and somehow he knew he'd
regret it. He stepped forward, drawing their attention.

"I'll stand good for her, Frank."

"Marshal? Did I hear you right?" He scratched
his ear, tugging at his earlobe.

Brannigan made the mistake of glancing Kate's
way again. The flash of hope and the smile that
could light up a dark night sealed his fate as surely
as if she'd laid an official stamp to it herself.

"Yes." His answer was curt.

At his single word, the smile on Kate's lips softened for him alone, and his heart told him it was
worth any amount of hard-earned money to bring
that look to her face.

However, his head told him that he'd come to
regret it.

his eye, and he mumbled something she couldn't
understand.

"I sorried and said, 'like "Shore got her spooked
"..........to the saloon talk.

Eight

Brannigan called himself seven kinds of a fool.
What had he up and done? Why had he given into
the sweet look of entreaty in Kate's eyes?

He'd been a fool to let her affect him that way.
The only reason he'd volunteered to stand good
for Kate was because he'd felt sorry for her, at
least that's what he told himself over and over.

He wasn't doing this for any other reason— certainly not because he was developing feelings for
her. He felt absolutely nothing for Kate, he assured himself. Absolutely nothing.

He was a liar.

Truth was he didn't want her to leave Deadrange. It seemed that willing or not, he was fast
becoming Kate's keeper.

Angry at himself for his weakness for her, he
spun away from Kate and the saloon owner and
slammed back through the doors, leaving them
swinging after him.

Kate stared after Brannigan. Now what had she
done? She turned back to Frank Jones and caught
his puzzled frown.

"Marshal's turned off grumpier than a peeled
rattler," Frank pronounced.

Rubbing his smooth head again, he looked Kate
up and down in speculation. An odd expression lit

his eyes, and he mumbled something she couldn't understand.

It sounded oddly like, "She's got him cinched to the last hole."

Whatever did that mean, Kate wondered with a frown at the saloon owner.

"Begging your pardon, ma'am."

"What did you say, Mr. Jones?"

"Oh, nothing, ma'am. Just thinking out loud." He swung away from her as if he were embarrassed.

"Oh. When should I start?" she asked him.

"From the looks of the marshal, you're already just about done. Yessiree," he chuckled below his breath.

Kate had to strain to hear him. "What?" Her voice tightened.

"Oh, sorry, ma'am. Thinking out loud again. Why don't you come back tomorrow night, you can start helping out then. Unless you'd rather wait till Monday night to start?" he asked hopefully.

Glancing her way, he muttered something that sounded suspiciously like, "That ought to give me time to remove most of the breakables."

Kate's temper rose, and she squelched it back down. She forced herself to smile her sweetest, most innocent smile at him.

"Why, tomorrow would be fine," she answered.

He gulped, and she watched his throat bob with the effort it cost him.

Frank Jones was most certainly a peculiar person, she thought, but wisely kept that opinion to herself. She had no intention of giving him any excuse to fire her before she'd even started working for him.

She'd be a success at this job. She'd make it work this time. Wait and see. She'd show Lucas Brannigan a thing or two.

"Hear that Kate's in trouble with Miss Sally again?" Buck motioned Brannigan into the room, greeting him with the question.

"That's an understatement if I ever heard one." Brannigan swept off his Stetson and slapped it against his thigh to shake off the dust out of force of habit.

"Well, you know you could add to it a mite," the old man prompted without trying to disguise his eagerness to hear whatever his friend had to say.

Brannigan grinned. Buck liked nothing better than listening to the latest news. "How do you survive driving that stagecoach and being away from the town gossip? It sure is a wonder to me."

"You think I don't get an earful out there?" Buck thumbed toward the window and the land stretching away outside.

Brannigan shook his head. "Come to think of it, I don't doubt that you do."

"Well?" Buck urged. "Get on with it." He shifted impatiently in the bed.

Brannigan sent his friend a searching look, attempting to gauge the man's health and recovery. He didn't appear to be in pain, and his eyes were bright and alert. However, concern forced him to ask, "How are you—"

Buck anticipated the question, cutting him off. "Told you before, I'm fine. Now sit." He jerked a thumb in the direction of the straight-backed chair.

Brannigan ignored his order and started toward his preferred spot by the window where he could keep one eye on whatever happened outside, but Buck's bellow stopped him in mid-step.

"Dagnamit. Will you sit!"

Biting back a chuckle, he changed direction and sank down into the chair, stretching out his long legs. He didn't want to upset the old man. He appeared plenty excited already.

"Well?" Buck prompted, leaning forward in the bed and giving the pillow behind his back a good punch.

"Well, what?" Brannigan teased.

"Heard tell that Miss Sally's red woollies got a good washing in that horse trough. In front of half the town, too."

Brannigan grinned back at his friend. "News travels fast."

"I got the folks around here trained 'bout as well as a good team of horses."

Brannigan chuckled out loud.

"But what nobody could tell me was what happened once you got that little gal safely out of Miss Sally's reach? And out of sight, humm?"

"Buck— " He stopped for he had no intention of letting the old busybody know what had happened upstairs in Kate's room. At the memory of the feel of her in his arms, his body hardened. He shifted uncomfortably in the straight-backed chair.

"Yup, seems I was sure right." Buck snapped his mouth shut with a smug grin.

"About what?" Brannigan asked, knowing that he likely didn't want to hear the answer.

"Told folks if that gal stuck around, things would get mighty interesting, didn't I? Yup, sure did."

Brannigan felt a red flush steal up his neck.

"Yup. Kate's sure livened things up around here. Ain't had this much excitement in town since the Crocker gang rode into town a-trying to rob the bank six months ago."

Buck slapped his knee and chortled, then coughed. Shifting in the bed, he punched his pillow again.

"Are you all right?" Brannigan asked in concern.

"Dagnamit, I said I was fine, didn't I?" He turned his head and gave the pillow a look of disgust. "I'm tired of being stuck in this here bed."

"Doc says it'll only be a couple of more days."

"Humph."

Brannigan jumped at the chance to change the subject away from Kate and what had gone on between the two of them in her hotel room. "Settle down and listen to the Doc. He knows— "

"Now, don't go changing the subject on me. We was talking about Kate."

"Can't fault a man for trying." Brannigan smiled across at his friend.

"Humph. Well, what's that little gal going to do now that that fool Peabody fired her? That little gal's got herself such a reputation for causing trouble, I don't know who'll take her on now."

Brannigan cleared his throat that had suddenly gone dry as dust. He had the unpleasant sensation that his collar was too tight. He could feel Buck's keen gaze watching his every move.

"Ah, she's going to be helping out at The Silver Slipper."

"Now, I wonder why Frank Jones would up and hire her?" Buck scratched his chin and sent a deliberately speculative look at the marshal. "Don't suppose you got any ideas on that, do you?"

"Maybe he felt sorry for her."

"Frank Jones? That miserly fool ain't ever felt sorry for a soul in his life."

The silence lengthened between the two men for several seconds as Buck waited for him to elaborate, then stretched into minutes.

"You're gonna have to do better than that," Buck chuckled.

Brannigan shifted in the chair. He might as well admit it, the old man wasn't going to let it rest until he had the truth.

"All right. He might have hired her because I agreed to stand good for her damages."

After a startled grunt, Buck's mouth dropped open. "You did what? Well, I'll be danged."

Setting his Stetson back on his head, Brannigan stood to his feet. "I think it's time I got back to the jail."

"Now, you— "

"Not another word," he ordered.

"Well, I'll be danged," Buck repeated. "You agreeing to stand good for— "

"Somehow I know I'm going to regret that." Brannigan slammed the door closed behind him.

Buck's snort of laughter followed him out of the room anyway.

The next evening when Kate walked into The Silver Slipper Saloon, it was filled with noise and people, mostly all men. A far different sight met her than that of the previous afternoon. The noise level attested to the fact that the saloon had shifted into full swing. Why, at night the place was completely unlike its daytime pretense of a quiet, struggling business.

Someone plunked out a tune of sorts with one finger from the piano that stood against one wall. Meanwhile, the din of voices struggled to be heard over the tinny discord. Kate stared about her in disbelief.

She belatedly realized it was her first trip inside a drinking establishment of any kind, discounting her visit the day before. Yesterday she hadn't really bothered to inspect the near-empty saloon; she'd been too intent on getting the job. However, she stopped with the swinging half-doors at her back and took stock now.

While the name, The Silver Slipper, may have deigned to give the place a sense of class, it in no way fit the saloon. Why, the place didn't even have tablecloths on the wooden tables. The tops of the scarred tables stared back at her nakedly. Bottles of golden-brown liquid and shot glasses littered those same tabletops. She wrinkled her nose and identified the smell of whiskey.

A fog of blue-gray tobacco smoke hung over the room, and Kate wrinkled her nose again in distaste as the smoke burned her nostrils. She stifled a cough. Was it always like this? The air was absolutely foul in here.

Why, she suspected that she wasn't going to like this job one little bit. Raising her chin a notch in stubborn determination, she walked the seemingly endless distance to the bar where Frank Jones was leaning over the bar's wooden surface talking with two men.

Kate stood politely waiting for them to finish their conversation. She didn't want to start out with upsetting the owner by interrupting what might be an important business conversation.

She smoothed a wrinkle out of the wide skirt of

her apricot gown and straightened the matching sash of darker ribbon along her waist. Since she couldn't manage to sell the dress, she'd decided she might as well wear one of her favorite gowns for courage. She wanted to look her very best on her first night of work.

Brushing a stray curl back over her shoulder, she checked to make sure that the hair ribbon was still in place. Without the assistance of a maid, she hadn't been able to arrange her hair in her preferred style of curls atop her head. Instead, she'd been forced to try to brush some order into her curls, and then be satisfied with using a ribbon to hold the curls away from her face. She shoved another tendril back.

The conversation appeared to be taking an inordinately amount of time to her. She was certain that she'd been waiting for at least five minutes. After giving the men what she judged to be another minute or so, she cleared her throat firmly, but still in what Mrs. Parker would consider in a polite gesture.

The sound had the effect of bringing the conversation to a sudden halt. Kate swallowed nervously.

The man nearest to her swung around, almost dropping the drink in his hand at the sight of her. The man beside him followed his movement and froze stock-still as well.

Kate could almost swear that the entire room was holding its breath in anticipation. Of what she wasn't sure.

"Good evening, Mr. Jones," she addressed her new employer.

After a quick, nervous greeting and what Kate was certain was disappointment at her showing up in his eyes, Frank Jones assigned a pleasant brunette named Abbie to "help Kate settle in" as he called it.

Kate held a strong suspicion that in truth Abbie was "keeping an eye on her" at the saloon owner's orders. She'd had enough experience with that to recognize it, since Papa had been quite inclined to hire people to do so repeatedly. Did everyone think she needed a keeper?

Holding her temper in check, Kate did as she was told and followed Abbie back to the storeroom. Under the other woman's tutelage, Kate learned where things were stored, how to fold the bar towels just the way Frank Jones liked them, and even how to balance a small tray of drinks without letting the glasses slip off the edge.

Kate and Abbie also shared several minutes of pleasant conversation, with Kate learning an alarming amount of the other woman's past. Something about her forlorn expression when she spoke of her home in Missouri prompted Kate to suggest she return there for a visit.

Her remark was met with sudden, uncomfortable silence. Then after a moment's hesitation, Abbie began to chatter once again, telling Kate about practically every person in the bar.

With Abbie's help and advice, it took Kate a remarkably short amount of time to learn how to dodge any unwelcome advances and to put the few men who dared try to touch her soundly in their place.

By the time she'd been serving drinks scarcely an hour, one of the Rustin ranch hands was favoring his right foot for daring to address Kate improperly. In the space of another fifteen minutes, the Rustin's foreman, Clancey Newman, was sporting what would turn out to be quite a shiner on his left eye. After that, the ranch hands gave Kate a wide berth.

Three hours later, Brannigan pushed open the doors to The Silver Slipper with a sense of expectancy and dread combined together. He knew Kate Danville was the reason for the disturbing mixture of feelings.

Uneasiness tugged at him, reminding him that he was to ride out within the hour. And leave Kate on her own for the better part of a week. His unease increased. Only heaven knew what kind of trouble she could get into in that amount of time.

He shot a glance around the saloon, half expecting to be greeted with Kate's particular brand of trouble. However, the saloon looked like it did every night, perhaps a little more crowded, but no disaster stood waiting to meet him.

"Well, Marshal, what brings you in tonight?" Janie sidled up to his left side. A knowing smile tipped her lips.

"I have to ride out, and I wanted to check on things before I left town."

"Things?"

As he narrowed his eyes at her, Janie giggled.

Brannigan resisted the urge to shake his head in disbelief. The entire town had gone loco since Kate arrived. He'd lost the respect he'd worked so hard to earn; now when he walked down the street he received knowing glances from the townspeople.

Word of his agreement to stand good for Kate's damages had spread through the town like a wildfire backed by a strong wind. The woman could cause an uproar without doing a thing.

"Those things wouldn't happen to include Kate?" Janie leaned closer to ask.

Brannigan fired a seeking glance around the saloon, but Kate was nowhere in sight. His gaze strayed to the stairs and the private rooms above where Frank's "upstairs girls," as he called them, entertained. His gut clenched. Surely Kate wasn't . . .

He took a determined step forward, but Janie caught his arm.

"She's not up there." Janie pointed to the back with her thumb.

"Where— ?"

"Frank sent her to fetch something from the storeroom." She lowered her voice. "If you ask me, he jus' came up with an excuse to get her out of here for a bit."

Janie looked pointedly around the crowded room.

"Business looks good tonight," he observed.

"And Frank wants to keep it that way. He claims that something about Kate puts the men off his liquor. But there's been a steady crowd anyway."

"Been quiet so far?" he asked, sending an assessing glance around the room.

"Most of the boys are here waiting to see what Kate does next."

Brannigan groaned. "What's she done now?"

"Clancey Newman is sporting a black eye. And Abbie left." Janie tapped her lower lip with her fingertip. "It was the strangest thing I ever saw. In no time at all, after just a few hours of working with Kate, Abbie up and decides to pack her belongings, quit, and go back home to Missouri."

Brannigan raised his brows in disbelief. Abbie had been working upstairs for Frank the better part of a year. He didn't know that anyone knew exactly where she'd come from.

"Frank was plenty upset, but he got over it. Seems that business has increased enough since Kate started working here to make him happy enough to forgive her for Abbie leaving."

Sighing in relief, Brannigan glanced around the room. His pay was safe for now. At least Frank wasn't holding Kate responsible for the loss of money from the other woman's departure.

"Anything else?" he asked, then stiffened in preparation for the answer.

"Nothing," Janie rushed to answer. "Matter of fact, the folks are kinda getting used to her managing to stir things up."

Kate could definitely do that, Brannigan thought to himself. Just the thought of her stirred his blood, making him want to see for himself that she was all right. He admitted that he also wanted almost desperately to hold her in his arms.

"Mind if I go find her?"

"Go on, you know the way." Janie nodded to the storeroom.

That's where Brannigan found her. Kate was stretched up on her tiptoes, trying to reach a package on the shelf above her head with one hand. In her other hand, she clasped two shot glasses.

A smile tipped Brannigan's lips as he watched her bottom sway seductively with each stretching movement. He stood silently and took in the sight with appreciation.

The apricot-colored gown rippled and shimmered with each move she made. Her hair trailed across her shoulder and down her back in a riot of curls that begged for a man's touch. Temptation pulled at him with a force and intensity that caught him off guard.

Kate stretched one arm higher, and he noticed how her gown hugged her breasts and her waist, and he found himself wishing it were his hands hugging those curves. The temptation crept up again to taunt him, and this time he gave in to it.

Slipping his hands around her slender waist, he bent down and whispered in her ear, "Need any help?"

Kate shrieked and spun around, dropping the two glasses in the process. She landed right in his arms. Right where he most wanted her.

The silk of her gown flowed like liquid beneath his fingers, and he couldn't resist caressing her back. He'd bet it was as smooth as the silk material covering her skin, and he longed to find out for himself.

"Brannigan!" His name was a shocked whisper on Kate's lips.

He drew her closer, preventing her instinctive withdrawal. He ran his hands upward from the small of her back to caress her shoulder blades, then back to the sensitive spot at the base of her spine.

"Brannigan." Kate's soft whisper invited, tempted, begged.

He complied. It was beyond him to refuse, especially when refusing was the last thing on his mind.

Her lips drew him with the same intensity that a flame draws the moth. He couldn't have stopped himself from taking her lips with his, not even if his life had depended on it. He took her lips hungrily, savoring the taste and feel of her mouth beneath his. But it wasn't enough.

She smelled of wildflowers, and sweetness, and pure woman. He drank in deeply of her scent, committing it to memory. In return, it claimed him.

He teased her lips apart with his tongue, then slid it into her velvet depths, tasting her fully. As he dragged his hands up to her cheeks, Kate curled her fingers around the edge of his leather vest. Her fingernails skimmed his chest, and he sucked in his breath.

No other woman had ever made him feel like this with only her kiss. But with Kate it was far more than a kiss; it was a melding of two spirits, closer and closer together until they raged to become one.

Kate slid her hands along the edge of his vest, the leather buttery soft beneath her fingers. Beneath it his flesh was warm and tensely bunched into iron-hard muscles. She ran her hands up his chest to sink her fingers into the thick hair at the nape of his neck.

Standing up on tiptoe, she ached to get closer to him. His vest skimmed back and forth across her arms, teasing, mimicking the action of his tongue against hers. Sighing, she leaned into him, her own tongue darting in a quickly learned lesson as she followed his movements.

Brannigan slanted his mouth, sliding kisses along the edge of her mouth and down to her chin. He suckled on the dainty point of her chin, and Kate moaned, her voice a mere mew of sound against his roughened cheek.

As he drew his mouth downward along the slim column of her throat, he pressed closer into her, his leg sliding intimately between hers. His action brought a startled gasp from Kate.

He wanted her. Oh, how he wanted her. The

thought penetrated his mind along with a sharp prick of his conscience. He was ready to take her here in the storeroom of The Silver Slipper.

The realization struck him with the force of a bucket spray of cold, dirty water. It had the same affect on his desire. He forced himself to regain control back of each of his senses and muscles, achingly one by one.

This wasn't one of Frank's upstairs girls. This was Kate. He had no doubt that she was the kind of woman who wanted a wedding ring and a home and kids— in Boston. Not here in Deadrange.

All go and no stay. The phrase rose up to condemn him.

No matter how hard he tried, he couldn't see himself wearing one of those tight collars, sitting in a fancy Eastern drawing room, and drinking tea. That wasn't for him.

And neither was Kate Danville.

He stiffened and stepped away from her, putting a distance between them that spoke louder than words to Kate.

"I'm sorry."

His apology acted like a slap to Kate. She winced from its impact.

"I stopped by to, ah, to tell you that I'm leaving." He bent down to scoop his hat up from the floor, wondering how it had gotten there. He hadn't even remembered having the Stetson in his hands once he'd entered the storeroom and seen Kate.

Leaving?

The single word chased away the feelings of rejection his action had brought. However, the pain of his rebuff fled much slower, easing away bit by bit before realization of his words struck her like a sharp slap, jolting her into speech.

"You're leaving?"

Her heart stopped for the space of a second.

"I'll be back," Brannigan rushed to reassure her.

Her face creased into a puzzled frown.

"Kate, I received word today from Carl Green over in Redmondton that Crocker and his men have been sighted in that area."

"Oh." It was the only sound she could manage to get past her lips.

"Joe Crocker was head of the gang that held up your stage," Brannigan began to explain, without having the slightest idea why he was doing it. He had never explained himself to anyone before.

"I recall," Kate stopped him.

She remembered the outlaw well. She didn't think she'd ever forget his crude invitation to "come on out here to Joe, sugar." No one had ever called her sugar in her entire life.

"I have to ride out tonight. Now. And I'll be gone a few days at the least."

She wanted to ask him what he'd do if he caught the men . . . she wanted to ask if he'd be in danger . . . she wanted to ask him to stay. But couldn't.

Fighting the sinking feeling that insisted on settling in the pit of her stomach, she told herself she wasn't concerned. She wasn't going to miss him. No, not one little bit.

She was lying.

Pride made her stiffen her spine in the manner that would have made Mrs. Parker proud. She couldn't let him know she cared. She couldn't. What of her vow? she reminded herself. Hadn't she learned anything from Richard's betrayal?

"Kate?"

Her resolve wavered at the sound of her name on his lips. It threatened to break down all her defenses.

"Well, hadn't you better get going?" She hated herself for saying the words the instant they were out. "Ah, I mean, if you have to go," she stopped, uncertain what to say next. "Be careful," she finally whispered.

A grin pulled at his lips an instant before he bent down and kissed her soundly. Just as quickly, he turned away and strode out the storeroom door.

Kate resisted the impulse to call him back. She watched him walk out through the saloon, and held back the unexplained sense of disappointment that swamped over her. She had work to do, she told herself, and if she didn't get back to doing just that, Frank Jones was likely going to fire her. Then Brannigan would owe him for the two glasses she'd broken.

The next days passed with agonizing slowness for Kate, finally stretching into a full week. She refused to accept that Brannigan's absence had anything to do with the slow passage of time. Instead, she blamed it on being busy, honestly busy, for the first time in her life.

At the thought of her work, a feeling of pride arose. She'd been doing a good job. Why, Frank had even complimented her last night on her work. It seemed that without Brannigan around to make her nervous, she didn't have so many mishaps.

She was beginning to honestly believe that she could succeed at this job. Kate raised her chin in satisfaction and pride.

That's the exact moment that five men from the Granger ranch spread chose to enter The Silver Slipper Saloon. The atmosphere in the place changed almost instantly. The laughter became subdued, voices were lowered, and several men shifted uncomfortably in their chairs.

"Who are they?" Kate whispered to Janie, who was never too far from her side since Abbie left. It seemed that Janie had been assigned to take the other woman's place and keep an eye on her now.

"Oh, damn." Janie swiveled to stare at the group of men who'd stopped inside the doorway.

"What?"

"Trouble. They're Milt Granger's men. And Marshal Brannigan is out of town."

Kate knew the latter information quite well. She'd lost count over the past week how many times her gaze had strayed to the doorway, seeking his tall frame.

"Shouldn't somebody send for the deputy?" Kate asked, still speaking in a whisper.

"They haven't done anything. Yet."

Janie tore her gaze from the men in the doorway and glanced over her shoulder at the table of Rustin ranch hands behind her. Then she looked back to Milt Granger's men. One young man with bright red hair stepped out in the lead.

"Oh, no. Not Hank Granger, too," Janie groaned.

"Who's Hank Granger?" Kate asked, peering around the other woman's shoulder.

It brought the attention of the man in the lead straight her way. He pursed his lips in a soundless whistle and stepped away from the door with a broad smile on his lean face. That smile plainly said he didn't know the meaning of the word no.

Janie slipped in front of Kate, trying to block her from the man's view.

Too late.

A tenuous peace, at best, had existed between the Rustins and the Grangers the past few months, but everyone knew it would take only the tiniest spark to send it into a pile of burnt cinders.

One look at Kate in her fancy gown and copper hair had the effect of lighting a match to overly dry kindling.

"Oh, no, Hank's seen you." Janie groaned and closed her eyes.

"So?" Kate asked, turning to look back at the slim, redheaded man. He gave her a wide grin.

"I wish Marshal Brannigan were here," Janie mumbled under her breath.

So did Kate, but for entirely different reasons. She brushed the fingers of her right hand across her lips, remembering the feel of his kiss.

It had been a week since he'd left her after the kiss that had rocked the foundations of her too-unsecure world. Without realizing it, she took a step back, closer to the table and the group of Rustin men seated around it.

Her lips tingled with the memory of Brannigan's kisses. Her thoughts on him, she let her attention wander from the tray in her left hand.

The tray gradually tilted sideways. More and more. A lone glass of whiskey followed, sliding off the edge of the tray. The glass landed right onto Clancey Newman's upturned face, spilling the amber liquid across the foreman's cheeks as the glass bounced off his hawklike nose to land on the floor with a crash.

Nine

"Oh, no!" Kate yelped, attempting to steady the tray too late.

Clancey Newman leaped to his feet with a bellow of rage. Swiping his hand across his wet face, he turned on Kate, but before he could do more than glare at her, Hank Granger strode across the room.

"Let the lady be." Hank's voice held a note of challenge.

He flashed her a practiced smile, one she was sure he'd tried on numerous ladies before. It had big-man-with-the-ladies written all over it.

Kate had the distinct feeling that defending her was only an excuse for starting trouble with the angry Rustin foreman. Everyone in town, including her, knew about the on-again, off-again feud between the two neighboring ranches. It seemed the men involved went out of their way to find reasons to start a fight.

"Shut up, pup," Clancey Newman sneered. "This isn't your fight."

"It is now," Hank returned with a grin that didn't reach his eyes.

Almost before she knew what happened, Hank shoved Clancey, and the fight was on. Clancey threw a punch that caught Hank under the chin, sending him reeling back. Kate started forward to intervene, but Janie grabbed her by the arm, pulling her back.

"Oh, no, you don't."

"But they can't keep fighting, I—," Kate began.

"Oh, yes they can. And we're staying out of it," Janie ordered.

Hank lunged forward, catching the older man squarely in the gut. The two men collided with the next table, overturning it. It slammed to the floor with a crash, sending glasses and men in all directions. Hank and Clancey continued their fight as if nothing had happened.

Kate held out her hands as if to try and stop the fight. She hadn't meant to splash the whiskey in Clancey Newman's face. Or for Hank Granger to step in. Much less for a fight to start.

All she'd done was let her mind drift to thoughts of Brannigan, and see what happened!

Had just the thought of Marshal Lucas Brannigan caused this? she questioned. All week she'd tried to keep her mind off of the too-disturbing marshal and concentrate on doing her job for Frank Jones. And she'd been doing just fine— no accidents or catastrophes. At least until tonight.

Janie grabbed her arm again and pulled her out of the way of the two men as they brushed past, grappling with each other. Beside them a table crashed to the floor as more men joined in the foray.

Another man staggered past Kate and Janie, blood streaming down his chin from his nose. Two more men bumped into him, knocking over chairs in the process.

Janie dodged, dragging Kate along in her wake. Nearby a bottle crashed to the floor. The scuffle of boot heels against the wood floor grated, crunching the glass underfoot.

"Now we can call the deputy," Janie said in resignation, sending Kate a speculative look.

A whiskey bottle sailed across the room to smash against a wall. Janie dragged Kate down to crouch behind the safety of an overturned table.

Kate peeked up over the edge of the tabletop and looked around the room in disbelief. Everywhere there were men fighting. Whatever had happened to turn her little mishap with Clancey Newman into this?

How could two men fighting become an entire roomful of fights in the blink of an eye? She, Kate Danville, who had never even witnessed a fight before, was smack in the middle of a brawl.

"Come on!" Janie yelled into her ear. "Make a run for the stairs." She leaped up and dashed across the room, leaving Kate behind.

Within seconds Kate lost sight of her in the crowd of flailing fists and flying bottles. Beside her, a chair toppled over, narrowly missing her. She jumped up out of the way.

Around her, the shouts, grunts of pain, and yells blurred together to be joined by the discordant clang of piano keys. The din turned into a roar of noise. She distinguished the thud of a fist against flesh barely in time to sidestep as two more men fought their way past the spot where she stood.

As one of the men swung his arm back to throw a punch, Kate jumped back out of their way and right into Frank Jones. The box of liquor he'd been carrying to the bar slipped from his arms and fell to the wooden floor with a resounding crash.

"Kate!" he yelled.

She spun around, caught one glimpse of his reddened face, and scurried away in the opposite direction. It would be best to allow him time to cool off before she apologized, she thought with a grimace.

Pushing her way through the fighting mass of bodies, she headed as far away from her employer as she could get for now. If possible, the noise around her got louder, but she could still hear Frank Jones shouting her name over the din. It might take him quite a while to cool his temper from the sounds of it.

She sidestepped one man and quickened her pace as much as feasible in the crowd. Another bottle crashed to the floor beside her, splattering the hem of her gown, but she kept going.

As she whipped past, Clancey Newman reached out to grab her arm. She slapped his hand away. Once. Twice. He reached for her again, and this time succeeded in catching her arm. Kate abandoned her last vestige of ladylike demeanor for the sake of survival, and she bit his hand. Clancey yelped, releasing her instantly.

Kate ducked to the side, then whirled away from him. She glanced back over her shoulder in time to see two other men throw a third man out through the saloon's batwing doors. A cloud of dust signalled his landing on the boardwalk outside.

Brannigan heard the commotion from the other side of the street. Instinctively, he knew that as sure as he breathed, Kate Danville would be involved.

It sounded like an all-out brawl— at The Silver Slipper. It was his job to break up the brawl, no matter who'd started it. But, without even asking, he knew the answer would be Kate Danville.

He turned and strode across the street, making his way to The Silver Slipper. In his mind he could see his pay vanishing, dollar by dollar. Whatever had possessed him to agree to stand good for the woman's damages? He stepped over the man crumpled in front of the boardwalk and shoved open the batwing doors to the saloon, then stopped dead still.

The scene before him was total chaos. There wasn't a single person in the room who wasn't involved in the fight. Fight, hell, it was a brawl!

Where was Kate? He knew she'd be in the middle of this. Somehow, he knew it for a fact.

He was right.

He spotted her across the room, one hand on her hip and one arm raised over her head. In her delicate, little, upraised hand, she held a whiskey bottle. As he watched in disbelief, she swung it.

Increasing his pace, he shoved his way past a Granger ranchhand and a Rustin man locked in battle. For an instant he lost sight of Kate, and his chest tightened. Then he saw her duck behind an overturned table. She was safe. For now. Until he got his hands on her.

As Brannigan waded through the mass of swinging fists and flying bottles, he couldn't help wondering that if Kate had managed to cause this much trouble within ten minutes of his riding into town, what had the last week been like? He didn't want to even know the answer. As it was, he was surprised to find the town still standing.

He drew even with the table where he'd last spotted Kate, but when he shoved it aside, she wasn't there. A loud crash followed by a grunt of pain from behind him sent him spinning around, one hand on his gun.

He came face to face with Kate, holding the neck of a broken whiskey bottle. Crumpled at her feet lay Hank Granger.

"Hell and damnation," Brannigan muttered under his breath. There'd be hell to pay for this.

He reached out and yanked Kate to him. Her yelp of surprised insult didn't even give him pause. He scooped her up, slung her over his shoulder to free his fists in case he needed them, and started shoving his way past the heart of the brawl.

"Put me down!" Kate pounded one fist against his back, hanging on with her other hand.

He ignored her attempts to free herself.

"Brannigan!" she shouted in his ear.

He still ignored her.

Kate's screams of indignation echoed in his ears as he made his way towards the door. Damn, but the woman had a healthy set of lungs on her.

Reaching the edge of the room, he shoved his shoulder through the batwing doors, propping them open. With his free hand he drew his gun and fired one shot into the air outside.

The shot had the effect of freezing the action inside the saloon for the space of a heartbeat. Then, one by one, the men turned toward the sound.

"The next one of you to throw a punch ends up in my jail!" Brannigan charged.

Silence blanketed the room.

Suddenly, Deputy Tom Avery appeared beside him, shotgun in hand.

"And I'm here to back up his words," he announced in a voice full of authority.

Brannigan turned to him, swinging Kate along with his action. "Tom—"

Kate's yelp stopped what he'd been about to say to his deputy. He shifted his hold on her, planting one hand firmly on her behind.

"Put me down!" she yelled.

"If you don't want me to put you down in my jail, you'll stay quiet."

Brannigan's voice was a deep rumble beneath her ear. She opened her mouth to answer, then thought better of it and snapped her mouth closed again.

"I'll take care of things here, if you want to handle your problem," Tom Avery offered in a strained voice.

Brannigan noted the twinkle of laughter in his deputy's eyes and how his cheek muscles twitched with the effort to hold back his chuckles.

"Thanks," Brannigan answered curtly.

"Looks like you got your hands full," Deputy Avery choked and a snicker slipped out.

He did at that, Brannigan thought to himself. His deputy didn't know the half of it. He pulled his hand away from Kate's backside as if he'd been burned.

"Tom, shut up."

Choosing to ignore the hearty chuckles that followed, Brannigan spun on his heel and stepped down off the boardwalk. A billow of dust rose up around his boots as he hit the dirt.

"Where are you taking me?" Kate asked, her voice now an embarrassed whisper in his ear.

As he tried to ignore the warm breath against his neck, she shifted, trying to turn around. All she accomplished was to almost dislodge herself from his shoulder.

"To your—," Brannigan stopped.

He swung up an arm around Kate's waist to

steady her and keep her from toppling to the hard-packed dirt beneath his feet. His fingers rested on the gentle curve of her hip, and his breath caught in his throat. He'd been about to say to her hotel room.

Right now he didn't think that might be such a good idea. She felt too good in his arms. Beneath his fingers he could feel the warmth of her flesh through the fine material of her gown.

He jerked himself up, forcing his wandering attention away from the feel of her pressed against his shoulder, and tried to resurrect his earlier anger. For heaven's sake, the woman had started a brawl. She could have gotten herself hurt. He noticed that her thigh was firm where it brushed against his chin. Frustrated, he realized the more she wiggled her cute little rear against his shoulder, the less his anger mattered and the further it got from his mind.

No, her hotel room was the last place he should be taking her.

He changed course and headed straight for the jail. Once inside, he strode to the center of the room, bent forward, and sat her down on her slipper-clad feet.

She faced him defiantly, her tousled hair hanging free in sensual abandonment. Her right sleeve was torn at the shoulder and hung drunkenly halfway down her arm, giving a tantalizing glimpse of silken skin. She looked more tempting than she had a right to look. She also looked like she'd most definitely been at the heart of a brawl.

His gaze traveled in quick observance of her damaged gown, littered with streaks of dirt and damp splotches of liquor. Even her satin slippers hadn't escaped the wreckage. He quickly stepped back out of the range of those feet just in case she decided to kick him like he recalled the one time before.

Kate noticed his backwards movement and watchful glance at her feet. She resisted the urge to do exactly what he was expecting. Instead, she curled her toes with the effort it took not to give into the raging impulse to kick him soundly. Why, he'd carried her out of The Silver Slipper with no more regard than a sack of flour!

Biting back the words that begged to be let loose, she kept her gaze glued to her toes. For the first time in her life she was too downright mad to speak. Anger simmered to a boil, churning in her. How could he have *dared* carry her out of the saloon *that* way!

Concentrate on something else, Mrs. Parker would say. Kate glanced around in an attempt to follow her instructor's orders. The jail was nothing like what she'd expected or what she'd read in those forbidden novels. It was clean, if a bit worn. She concentrated on examining the room and forgetting her fury and the way his hand had felt on her hips and . . .

Brannigan found himself shifting uncomfortably at Kate's appraisal. The way the office looked had never mattered to him before; the room was serviceable and worked fine for him. Now for the first time, he saw his office through someone else's eyes.

He noted how old the wooden desk looked, its top scarred with boot heel marks and spur scratches, some of them his. Formerly he'd been proud of his initials among those carved in the wood, one set by each marshal who had spent time behind that desk. Now he noticed how the floor below was worn from too many boot heels and too many years.

"Kate," his voice came out harsh and demanding to cover his unease.

It grated on Kate's raw nerves, and she narrowed her eyes on the small jail surrounding them. A jail! He'd brought her to a jail. And after the way he'd carried her out of the saloon. Why, he'd . . .

Her anger grew anew with each recurring memory of the humiliation he'd heaped upon her. It threatened to engulf her until she couldn't stand still another moment.

Planting her hands on her hips, she faced him squarely. Several curls tumbled forward and dangled over her eyes. She shoved them back, glaring at Brannigan. Her torn sleeve slid down her arm, and she tugged it back up. Her beautiful gown was ruined, she smelled of liquor, and *he* had brought her to jail for something that wasn't even her fault! And he hadn't even allowed her to explain, he'd just thrown her over his shoulder like a bag of Mr. Peabody's flour.

"You . . . ," she sputtered, taking a step forward. "You lowdown excuse for a—"

"Kate," Brannigan warned in a tight voice.

She snapped her mouth closed on the rest of her words. Remember Mrs. Parker's rule, she ordered herself, silently beginning to count to ten or however high it took to calm her.

"Kate."

She pointedly ignored him, tapping one dainty whiskey-stained slipper on the wood flooring and counting to twenty. The silence stretched between the four walls, threatening to break into pieces.

"Hell and damnation," he finally shouted at her. "Will you look at me?"

Kate tilted her head back. "I'm looking."

Her tone clearly said she didn't much like what she was looking at, and Brannigan regretted his sharp outburst, but it was too late to take it back now. Besides, he knew if he dared show any sign of softening to her, she would walk all over him with those dark-stained, satin-clad feet of hers. He knew that for a fact.

"What did you do to start a brawl?" he asked in frustration.

If she'd actually started it by hitting someone, would Frank Jones insist he lock her up in the jail? It was a definite possibility.

Kate ignored his question, one hand still firmly planted on her hip. She tapped her fingers in a nervous gesture that only served to focus his attention on the curves that lay beneath those fingers.

Brannigan ran his hand back and forth across his neck, rubbing at the knot of tension that had formed there. It was the only way to keep his hands from straying where they longed to be— on Kate's sweetly curved body.

"What makes you think I had anything to do with that fight?" Kate asked, her voice the epitome of innocence.

"Fight?" he said in disbelief at her show of pretended innocence. "Honey, that was a brawl."

"All right, brawl. Why do you think I— "

"Honey, I don't think. I know. It had to be you," he said with resignation.

"Why me?"

"Because *somehow* I know that you're at the bottom of this mess."

"Me?"

"Yes, you," he fired back. "Who did you hit?"

"Me? I didn't hit anybody," she denied.

"You sure?" he asked, trying to hide the relief he felt. "At least I won't have to arrest you."

Kate snapped her mouth closed. She wasn't about to offer him any explanation now. She stepped back a step, striving to put more distance between herself and his imposing body. She bumped into the edge of the desk, and he took a step forward.

"I didn't hit anyone," she repeated.

"What about the bottle you broke over Hank Granger's head?"

"That was different."

"How?" Brannigan shook his head in exasperation. "I can't believe you broke a bottle over Hank's head. I know he can be a bit—"

"He was going to hit you," Kate interrupted, defending her actions.

Suddenly realizing what she'd admitted, she clamped her hand over her mouth, but it was too late to call back the words. He'd already heard them.

Brannigan paused and blinked several times at her admission. Clearing his throat, he asked, "Kate, exactly how did it start?"

"I, ah, I dumped a drink in Mr. Newman's face."

"Clancey Newman?"

"Yes."

"Whatever possessed you to do that, woman?" his voice raised in spite of his efforts to keep it calm. "Newman can be mean as an angry rattler when he's been riled."

"It was an accident."

"That's one hell of an accident."

"I was thinking about you," she snapped, an-

swering once again, before she thought of what
she was revealing.

The anger rushed out of him, her admission
pricking it as surely as if she'd stabbed holes in it.

She was thinking about him.

How was he supposed to answer that? Frustration and desire rose up in him, each battling for
the upper hand. As Kate turned her head and
looked up at him, the desire won a decisive victory.

Brannigan took a broad step forward, putting
him only a breath away from her. Kate scooted
back closer against the desk, then stopped. She
continued to look up at him, meeting the possessiveness in his gaze with sudden, wide-eyed wonder. He could have resisted almost anything but
that.

"Ah, damn," he muttered, hauling her up
against his body with one arm.

She felt so good. So damn good.

He drew her closer against his chest. Kate's
mouth opened ever so slightly in a soundless protest, or welcome, he didn't know which. He was
past caring.

She tipped her head back to meet his gaze, and
a copper curl brushed her cheek. Raising his free
hand, he started to tuck the tendril back, but almost of their own will, his fingers slid into the
mass of curls at her temple. The curls coiled and
rippled around his fingers, enslaving him as surely
as if they had been bindings of steel.

He stared at her upturned face. Her hair spread
out about her in tumbled disarray. Sensual, tempting, demanding his touch.

The curls glowed and shimmered almost with a
life all their own in the light of the lamp that had
been left burning in the room. The soft light

turned her copper curls to deep golden red. He ached with the sudden desire to bury his face in those tempestuous curls framing her face.

He brushed his thumb across her cheek. Her skin was silken smooth beneath his calloused thumb. Kate licked her lips with a quick flick of her tongue. Giving into the temptation, he traced her lower lip with the tip of his thumb. It was petal smooth beneath his touch, and more of a temptation than any sane man could be expected to resist.

He slid his hand into the curls surrounding her cheeks, burying it in her tousled hair. Applying pressure to the back of her head, he drew her closer. Ever closer. Until his lips brushed hers. Once. Twice. Thrice. With a ragged sigh, he took her lips in a breath-denying kiss that left them both shaken.

Kate leaned into his embrace, sliding her hands along the hard planes of his chest. Her palms skimmed his firm muscles, roved over his shoulders, and came to rest around his neck. She tightened her hold on him.

He swung her up, lifting her feet off the hard wooden flooring. A long moment later, he eased her downward, setting her atop the corner of the desk. His arms never let go of her. Nudging her legs open, he stepped between her thighs.

Kate knew she should say no, but the word never made it past her lips. Her behavior was shockingly unladylike, but as Brannigan kissed her again, she was beyond caring. He slanted his mouth across hers, tasting, tempting, calling her with unspoken words.

She'd never felt such sensations as those coursing through her body at that moment. The very blood within her veins raced. Her heart beat so fast and loud that she was certain he could hear it. Waves of delicious heat rolled over her, and everywhere he touched, her skin came alive beneath his hands.

As Brannigan's lips left hers she wanted to cry out and call him back, but before she could, he lowered his lips to trail kisses against her chin. Slowly, he rained more kisses down the column of her throat. Kate moaned her pleasure, unable to utter a word as she buried her hands in the springy dark curls at his nape.

Obeying the entreaty in her soft whimper, he returned his lips to hers. Kate clung to him, giving him back kiss for kiss, then opening her mouth to him. His tongue plundered her velvet moistness, and she wiggled on the hard desktop in an attempt to get closer. Closer to what she wasn't sure, except that *something* separated them.

Sliding his hands down her back, he answered her entreaty and clasped her buttocks, lifting her up off the desk and drawing her tighter against his growing hardness. His breath came out in a ragged rush of need, feathering her lips.

"Kate." He whispered her name softly against her lips. Then trailed his tongue slowly down along her jaw to the hollow of her throat.

She tilted her head back to give him better access, gazing into his face. Brannigan's eyes had softened, the deep blue color reminding her of a gentle summer day. She bit her lower lip without realizing it.

"I'm sorry for starting the fight," she admitted to him.

"It only cost me more than a month's pay," he muttered against the fair skin of her throat. Pulling back, he smiled down into her face and added, "And worth every bit of it."

He leaned forward again and lowered his head to take her lips with his.

The words eased their way through Kate's mind, past her senses, then slowly took hold. All sense of pleasure left her.

Cost . . . a month's pay . . .

Kate jerked herself up with a start.

Pay.

There it was. Money again. Pain cut through her with the sharp thrust of a knife, and her lips went numb beneath his. Was he telling her that he expected her to repay him with her body? Was that what this was all about?

The questions chilled her, and she stiffened in his arms. The kisses they were sharing meant little or nothing to him while they shook the very foundation of her life. She was nothing more to him than a means to collect for the money he'd lost.

Well, for all she cared, he could just count that money as lost for good. At least until she could return home to Boston and send him the funds. She shoved the hurt deep inside and locked it tight. Anger sprang upward, and she allowed it free rein. If he thought she was going to repay him in *that* way, he was in for a rude surprise.

Raising her hands, she braced them against his broad chest. She pushed away, breaking both the kiss and his embrace. Before he could reach for her, she jumped down off the desk and took two steps sideways, putting as much distance between them as she could.

"It seems you've made a mistake." Her voice dripped icicles. "You will have to lock me up, Marshal."

The coldly spoken words had the effect of cooling Brannigan's heated passion. He stiffened his own body and stepped back from her.

"What the hell— ?"

"I'd say about the time it freezes over. That's when you can expect me to repay you in *that* way."

"Kate— "

"Don't 'Kate' me."

She stepped back with two more quick steps, then took another step for good measure closer to the door. She wanted to be certain she stayed out of his reach; she didn't think she could stand it if he touched her right now. For she'd either slap him or give into the heart-rending temptation to wrap her arms around him and beg him to kiss her, and she didn't know which one.

"I pay my debts with money." She tossed her head back, glaring up at him. "Or with hard work. And not the kind you have in mind."

Before he could stop her, she rushed to the door and flung it open.

"Kate— "

Brannigan took a long stride after her, but her next words froze him in place.

"If I wanted to do that kind of work, Belle offered me a job."

The second toss of her head unfroze him.

"Dammit, Kate."

"Don't you swear at me."

"I'll do what I damn well please," he shouted back at her. "And you stay away from Belle Wilson's place."

"Is that an order, Marshal?" she asked in a voice tight with suppressed fury. Her eyes narrowed so much they hurt.

"Yes, it is," he bit out the words.

"I'll do as I please," she echoed his words back at him.

With a swish of her liquor-stained skirts, Kate stepped outside and slammed the door behind her.

Let him chew on that!

Ten

The next morning when the bright sunlight streamed through her window Kate awoke with a pounding headache and a disturbing sense of loss. She placed the blame for both soundly on Marshal Lucas Brannigan.

How could he have ever thought that she'd agree to repay him *that* way!

After all, the brawl hadn't even been her fault. In fact, she'd been doing fine at her job until Brannigan returned to town.

She decided that if she never laid eyes on him again, it would be too soon. In the next instant, she decided it would be too long.

"Oh, ginger," she swore, plummeting her pillow in frustration.

What was wrong with her? She wouldn't miss Brannigan. No, not one little bit, she fiercely denied. *Why should she miss him?* she chided herself. All he could think about was how much money she'd cost him and how she was going to repay him.

A jab of pain hit her. She'd hoped he was different, but she'd learned that he was as caught up by the all-consuming desire for money as every other man she'd ever encountered.

Resolute, she renewed her vow to never allow

herself to become involved with any man unless he was at least as rich as her father. That most definitely crossed one marshal off her list of prospects. She blinked back the hint of moisture in her eyes.

Dwelling on money reminded her that she now owed even more money than she did the day before. She owed Miss Sally for the breakage . . . owed Howard Peabody for the special order . . . and worst of all she owed Brannigan for the damages from the brawl!

"Oh, ginger."

She groaned aloud and pulled the pillow over her head. She wasn't doing a very good job of showing the people of Deadrange a thing or two.

She wanted to crawl back under the covers and never come out. Couldn't she do anything right? Was she a failure at everything, is that why no one could love her for herself instead of for her father's money? It all came back to money.

Kate clenched her hands into fists and flung the pillow away. She wasn't about to simply lie here abed and let life walk all over her. Nothing got better unless you did something about it. Well, she was about to do that very thing.

That evening found Kate dressed in one of her best gowns of a rich emerald green hue and firmly established in Belle Wilson's front parlor. She shuddered to even think of what Mrs. Parker would have to say about her new circumstances.

Say? Why, her finishing school instructor would faint dead away if she saw her working here now.

Things couldn't be helped, she consoled herself. She'd had little choice in the matter. Over the course of the morning, she'd visited four business establishments in Deadrange. Not one of the proprietors would even consider retaining her services!

About the only place she hadn't sought employment had been the town's stable. Somehow, not even her dire financial predicament could induce her to work for a horse. Not that it mattered, she had no doubt that the owner wouldn't have hired her.

Once word of last night's brawl at The Silver Slipper had spread through town, Belle Wilson had been the only person willing to give her a job.

At a knock on the front door, Kate crossed the lavishly appointed room with its polished wood floor, glittering chandelier, and inviting plush sofas. She opened the door, swinging it inward with the slight flourish that Belle had taught her earlier that day. The open door revealed Howard Peabody.

Kate scarcely stopped the gasp from leaving her lips. She wished she could find a hole to crawl into, or that Belle's gleaming wood floor would open right up and swallow her.

However, since neither seemed likely to happen anytime soon, she raised her chin with all the dignity she could muster. Gathering her shattered poise about her, she forced a smile to her stiff lips.

"Do please come in," she invited in a voice that came out sounding a bit high-pitched and as stiff as her lips felt.

She kept the smile plastered on her face in an attempt to disguise her shock at seeing the balding store owner here of all places. While she'd certainly known that Mr. Peabody was friends with Belle Wilson, she'd never expected him to . . .

Quickly, Kate cut the rest of her thought off

when she felt her face heating with a blush. She certainly wasn't in any position to begrudge any of Belle's clients. Their business was paying her salary.

This was her new job, she reminded herself, she wouldn't ruin it. Smile pretty, she ordered herself, like Belle had told her earlier.

Howard Peabody stared back at her in open-mouthed astonishment. He gripped his hat so tightly in his hands that the brim bent.

"Ah, ah," he gulped, snapping his mouth open and closed like a turtle she'd once seen.

"Please come in," she invited again. Her own voice threatened to fail her if he didn't comply soon. She couldn't take much more of him staring at her in obvious amazement.

Kate opened the door wider in an invitation, hoping he'd step into the house. When he still didn't move from the spot, she reached out and slipped her hand into the crook of his arm and eased him inside, resisting the urge to propel him into the nearest chair. He moved stiffly, like a child's toy being pulled into place.

She half-led, half-dragged the silent Howard Peabody through the room, not pausing until they reached one of Belle's brightly colored sofas. She thought for a moment he was going to bolt for the door, and she wasn't about to allow him to do that.

The poor man looked terribly uncomfortable. She supposed it was because he was so surprised at seeing her.

She grimaced, for he wasn't any more shocked than she'd been to open the front door to someone she knew. For the life of her, she couldn't think of anything more to say to help put him at ease. He insisted on standing there and staring at her.

"Please be seated." Kate forced the polite invitation out. "I'll tell Belle you're here."

In spite of her efforts, Howard Peabody remained silent and standing in the same spot.

Running dangerously short on patience, Kate placed one hand on his shoulder to guide him into sitting down. Howard jumped back at her touch, almost falling onto the velvet sofa. She gave him a not-so-gentle push that helped him the rest of the way down, and he landed on the seat with a soft whoosh.

"Belle will be with you shortly," Kate announced, politely avoiding looking directly at the store owner's flushed face. "If you'll excuse me, I'll go and tell her you're here."

"Kate," Howard Peabody finally choked out her name, then fell embarrassingly silent.

"Yes?" She turned back to him with the same smile she'd plastered to her face when she'd opened the door to reveal his presence.

Her smile was becoming strained with the effort it took to keep it in place. She was still dazed at finding him here. Heaven knows, she hadn't expected to greet anyone she knew.

At least not on her first night.

"What . . ." Howard cleared his throat and started again. "What are you doing here?"

"Working."

"Here!" He swallowed back a sudden spasm of coughing, and his spectacles slid farther down his nose.

"Yes. Belle was nice enough to hire me," she informed him in a curt voice. "So, you see, in practically no time I'll be able to pay you back that money I owe you for Miss Sally's, ah," she paused in delicate embarrassment, "her special order."

"Forget about that." He raised both hands and waved off her words, starting to stand to his feet. "You don't have to do this."

"Oh, no." Kate placed a hand on his shoulder, forcing him back down onto the sofa.

Belle Wilson wouldn't like it if she thought she'd chased off a potential customer. Not about to lose this job, she rushed to calm him. "I intend to repay you in full. I—"

"Surely not by . . . working . . . here?" Howard insisted. His voice held a distinct note of entreaty and a little bit of desperation.

"Why, yes."

"Kate, this is a—," he paused and nervously smoothed his hand over the dark fringe of hair rimming his head. "It is a—"

"I know."

"Then you—"

"Not doing that." She stiffened her back in affronted dignity. "I help out."

"Help out?" Howard threw a nervous glance around the lavishly furnished room, then pushed up his spectacles with his index finger. "What exactly are your duties here, Kate?"

"Why, first I'm supposed to greet the guests at the front door with a nice smile. Like a hostess would do back home in Boston."

"Kate, this isn't exactly Boston—"

"You're telling me! Why, people would never come calling at a home this late in the evening in Boston," she announced.

"And this isn't exactly a home," Howard fell silent, as if he were suddenly at a loss for words. He pushed up his spectacles again.

"Oh, I know that," Kate assured him.

"I wonder," he muttered.

"Wonder what, Mr. Peabody?"

"What you're doing here." His voice raised with each word.

"Shh." Kate put a finger to her lips. "I don't think Belle would appreciate you shouting in her business establishment.

"Ha!"

"Mr. Peabody."

"Kate," he asked with rising exasperation. "Exactly what are you doing here?"

As she opened her mouth he raised a hand to stop her. "Don't say working. I want to know what kind of work you've been hired to do."

Kate could have sworn that Howard Peabody actually winced at his last words. As she stared at him, she saw a red flush creep upward from his collar to tinge his neck with color.

"I'm to greet the guests. See that they are comfortably seated." She ticked each item off on her fingertips.

"And?"

"And I'm not supposed to serve the drinks. Not to anyone."

She glanced over her shoulder to a round mahogany table that gleamed richly in the lamplight. A prominent display of golden sherry in a sparkling decanter surrounded by crystal glasses was set atop the silver tray gracing the center of the table.

"It seems that Belle doesn't trust me to pour," she noted with a hint of injured pride.

"After last night—"

"And," Kate interrupted, having no desire to hear a single word more about the night's brawl and her part in it, "then I inform Belle or one of her ladies that they have a guest."

"Is that all?" Howard asked.

"Oh, I also sweep up."

"Kate, you don't have to do this," he attempted to reason with her.

"Yes I do. I have to earn money some way."

Howard shifted his hat from one hand to the other. "Perhaps if you asked her nice like, Miss Sally would let you work for her—"

"The woman hates me."

Kate had no doubt as to the truth of her statement. Why, when she'd met the restaurant owner earlier that morning in front of the hotel, Miss Sally had crossed the street to avoid her. And almost got run down by a horse-drawn buggy in the process.

Why, Kate swore her ears were still ringing from the woman's loud shriek and the litany of extremely colorful phrases that poured from her lips. Phrases no lady would dare utter according to Mrs. Parker.

"Miss Sally's not really a bad person, once you get to know her. She's . . . ," Howard Peabody paused at a loss for words.

"A mite outspoken," Kate put in, repeating his earlier description of the woman. "Believe me, I'm aware of that fact."

Howard's face flushed, and he ducked his head. "You two just got started off wrong."

"She tried to take a swing at me at your horse trough—"

"Miss Sally is a mite touchy over having people see her personals in public."

Kate supposed that by "personals" he meant her long red woolen underwear.

"Did I truly ruin them?" she asked tentatively.

"I think maybe they'll be all right." He paused to add, "Eventually."

Kate winced.

"But I ordered her another set to smooth her ruffled feathers," he admitted.

Ginger! Her hopes plummeted. That meant she still owed him for a new set of long underwear, Kate thought in dismay. She'd hoped maybe the red long johns would be fine, and she wouldn't have to pay for them on top of all her other debts.

"Kate?" Howard drew her wandering attention. "It never hurts to try a bit and smooth over things like that whenever you can. You might want to remember that." He offered her the piece of fatherly advice with a kindly smile.

"Thank you." Kate patted his shoulder. "I'd better let Belle know you're here."

"Then you're staying on working for her?"

"Yes."

A deep frown creased the store owner's face. Kate didn't understand what the fuss was all about.

Howard shook his head. "When Brannigan hears of this, he will— "

"He'll nothing." Kate tossed back her hair. "What I do is none of his business."

He'd made his intention perfectly clear to her. All he was interested in was collecting the debt she owed him— any way he could. But now she'd found her own way to pay him back his all-important money.

Once the money was paid, he'd probably have nothing more to do with her, Kate thought to herself. A sharp pain followed the thought, and it persisted in staying with her even as Belle swept down the staircase to welcome their guest.

* * *

Brannigan rapped on the door of Buck's room.
A gruff bellow greeted him, and he swung open
the door and stepped into the room.

"I'm a mite surprised to see you tonight." Buck
turned away from the window and sat on the bed.

"Sorry I didn't get by to see you earlier today."
Brannigan sank tiredly into the straight-backed
chair without being ordered into it first like usual.
"I've been kept busy all day what with cleaning
up after last night's fight."

"Heard tell it was more of a brawl," Buck noted
with a gleeful chuckle. "Dagnamit. Sorry to have
missed that one."

"Count yourself lucky. Over half the town is
either sporting a black eye or a limp." Brannigan
rubbed the back of his neck. The persistent knot
of tension at his neck was beginning to be a habit,
ever since Kate Danville had arrived in Deadrange.

As if he'd read his mind, Buck asked, "How's
Kate doing?"

Brannigan shook his head in amazement. "She
didn't even get a scratch on her. I swear that
woman could survive anything."

Buck roared in laughter. "Told you that gal was
sturdy, didn't I?"

"Trouble is what she is. Frank's still totalling up
the damages."

"And you'll pay 'em."

It was a statement, not a question.

"Yup."

"I suppose that's what kept her outta jail?" Buck
asked with a smile.

Brannigan groaned. "The last thing I need is
Kate in my jail."

"Might be that's exactly what you need." Eyeing him closely, Buck quickly changed the subject. "Hear tell that young Hank Granger has sworn off women. Something about him meeting up with the wrong end of a whiskey bottle."

"Thanks to Kate," Brannigan added.

Buck slapped his leg and chortled with glee. "That young rascal has had it coming for a long time. Past time some gal put him in his place."

"That's not why she did it," Brannigan bit off the rest of what he'd been about to say.

"Oh?"

He met the old man's question with marked silence.

"Come on, boy. Out with it." Buck leaned forward in anticipation of his answer. "Why'd she do it?"

"She said that he was going to hit me."

Buck reached out and slapped him on the shoulder. "Well, I'll be damned."

"Probably."

Chuckling, Buck sat back and rubbed his jaw. He eyed Brannigan for another minute, then stroked his jaw with long, measured movements.

"You don't seem at all in a hurry tonight, I'd say," Buck noted, his grin fading as Brannigan continued to sit calmly in the chair. "To get someplace else," he added with emphasis.

"It's a quiet night. Seems that most everyone is either resting up, or nursing bruises from last night." He leaned back in the chair, stretching out his legs and shifting to a more comfortable position on the hard wood seat.

"So?" Buck prodded.

"So, I have some time to sit here with you." Brannigan was beginning to get irritated with his

Wish You Were Here?

You can be, every month, with Zebra Historical Romance Novels.

AND TO GET YOU STARTED, ALLOW US TO SEND YOU

4 Historical Romances Free

A $19.96 VALUE!

With absolutely no obligation to buy anything.

YOU'RE GOING TO LOVE GETTING
4 FREE BOOKS

These books worth almost $20, are yours without cost or obligation
when you fill out and mail this certificate.
*(If the certificate is missing below, write to: Zebra Home Subscription Service, Inc.,
120 Brighton Road, P.O. Box 5214, Clifton, New Jersey 07015-5214*

4 FREE BOOKS!

Yes! Please send me 4 Zebra Historical Romances without cost or obligation. I understand that each month thereafter I will be able to preview 4 new Zebra Historical Romances FREE for 10 days. Then, if I should decide to keep them, I will pay the money-saving preferred publisher's price of just $4.00 each...a total of $16. That's almost $4 less than the publisher's price, and there is no additional charge for shipping and handling. I may return any shipment within 10 days and owe nothing, and I may cancel this subscription at any time. The 4 FREE books will be mine to keep in any case.

Name _____

Address_____ Apt. _____

City_____ State_____ Zip_____

Telephone ( )_____

Signature _____ LF1195
(If under 18, parent or guardian must sign.)

insistence that he should be elsewhere. He thought
his old friend would be happy to share his company tonight.

Buck pursed his lips into a silent whistle. "Is
that so?"

His old friend's quizzical behavior was making
him decidedly uneasy. "Well, what is it?" Brannigan asked tersely.

"Nothing." Buck looked casually around the
room, then pointedly glanced from the door to
Brannigan. "Jus' thought you might be in a bit of
a hurry to get yourself over to Belle Wilson's place
tonight."

"Nope."

Brannigan wondered what was going on. He
could sense his friend watching his every move.
He felt like a rabbit cornered by a coyote. It was
a decidedly uncomfortable feeling.

"Why do you think I'd be in a hurry to go to
see Belle?" As he voiced the question, his skin
cooled in the telltale manner he'd grown used to
when something was very wrong. "Is there a problem at her place?"

"Not yet."

Trouble was definitely brewing. It was only a matter
of time before he learned its source. Brannigan
shifted in the chair.

"You truly not in a hurry, boy?" Buck asked,
suddenly deadly serious. All trace of his earlier
laughter had left. Disbelief screwed up his face,
turning his frown into a grimace.

"No, I'm not in a hurry."

"You're taking things mighty calm, don't you
think?" Buck asked. Accusation coated his words.

"I guess, if you say so."

Buck sat up straight, then leaned forward, staring hard at him. "You don't know, do you?"

The skin on Brannigan's arms broke out in chill bumps. "Know what?"

His question was met by several seconds of silence as Buck stared at him. The tension in the room increased to a tangible level, so real that he could swear he could almost taste its bitterness.

"Kate's gone to work for Belle," Buck announced in a hoarse voice.

The words fell into the silence like rocks thrown onto the surface of a glass-still pond. They shattered the quiet.

"What?" Brannigan surged to his feet, his hat toppling to the floor.

"She's working for Belle," Buck repeated.

"Hell and damnation," Brannigan muttered.

In the next instant, he grabbed up his hat, turned on his heel, and slammed out the door.

Buck's low chuckle followed him. "Now that's more like it."

Eleven

Brannigan burst into Belle Wilson's house without even bothering to knock or wait for the door to be opened. He kicked the door closed behind him, then strode through the parlor.

Belle met him halfway into the room. "Good evening, Marshal."

"Where is she?"

A smile tilted the tips of Belle's lips, but she quickly subdued it. "That depends."

"On what?"

Brannigan was in no mood to barter for Kate or her favors.

"On who you're asking for," Belle answered, her smile slipping free.

"Where's Kate?" He bit the words out.

Belle tapped one slim finger against her bright lips. "Let me think."

Too frustrated to put up with her usually good-natured teasing, he spun away from her and headed for the stairs. He had one booted foot on the bottom step when she stopped him.

"She's not up there. So, don't you go disturbing my paying guests."

"Where is she?" He ground the question out.

"Belle, what's all the shouting—" Kate rounded the corner and stopped in mid-step at the sight of

Brannigan in the front parlor. Her face paled when he turned his anger at her.

"Hell and damnation, lady. Do you have any idea what you're doing?"

"Of course, I do." Kate raised her chin in indignation at his implied insult.

"Then would you mind explaining it to me?"

His terse tone of voice said plainer than any words could that he had no intention of listening to anything she had to say.

"Yes, I think I would," she answered, turning her back on him and dismissing him with the stiff pose of her spine.

Brannigan wasn't about to let her get away with it. He reached out a hand, caught her by the elbow, and swung her back around to face him.

"Would what?" he asked.

"Would mind explaining to you." Kate enunciated each word clearly, giving the deliberate impression that she was speaking to a child or a very obtuse adult. She rebuffed him with a shrug of her dainty shoulder.

Brannigan felt his temper rising with each carefully spoken word she uttered. He released his hold on her arm. Kate Danville could raise his ire quicker than a jail full of outlaws.

Here she was spitting at him when he was trying to rescue her from working in a brothel! It completely confounded him. Didn't the fool city woman have a lick of sense?

"Kate." His voice was low and held a gut-deep warning to it.

She instinctively took a step backwards closer to the table.

"You're coming with me," Brannigan ordered

in an overly calm tone that warned her better than
a long speech could have done.

"No, I don't think so. I'm working."

She took another step back, slowly inching her
way around the side of the round table set in the
center of the room. She was careful not to touch
the highly polished table. It was Belle's pride and
joy, and held the place of honor in the parlor, as
well as a tray of her best sherry and glasses.

"Kate, you're coming with me," Brannigan repeated.

"No, I'm not."

Kate raised her chin a notch higher and faced
him in open defiance. The barrier of the gleaming
wood table between herself and Brannigan gave
her the courage to defy him.

"Kate." He advanced a step.

She held her ground. Resting one hand on the
edge of the tabletop, she met his glare with one
of her own.

"I'm working. Leave me alone."

"Like hell I will."

He slammed his hands down on the edge of the
table and leaned forward. The crystal glasses rattled, and a drop of sherry spilled over the decanter
rim.

"Excuse me, folks." Belle reached out and picked
up the silver tray displaying her prize sherry decanter and glasses. "I'll be out of your way in a
moment."

Her footsteps and soft chuckle signalled her departure from the room.

"Brannigan," Kate said his name firmly in warning.

He took a quick step to the right. Kate responded by moving in the opposite direction. A slow smile tipped the corners of his mouth.

Darn the man, he was enjoying himself, she thought in a rush of irritation. His smile widened.

Kate watched him closely. His eyes gleamed with an underlying emotion, almost imprisoning her, holding her firmly in place. She almost felt as if he were already touching her.

His gaze never leaving hers, he stepped to the left this time. Kate inched away. The distance between remained the same, but she had the definite feeling that it was shrinking. Fast.

She gripped the edge of the table, watching for his next move. He slid a long, slow step to one side, decreasing the distance separating them. Kate anticipated him, quickly taking two steps. The distance between them evened again.

His low chuckle reverberated along her nerve endings. She began to wish that Belle's fancy mahogany table was a whole lot bigger.

He lunged to one side; she parried, moving quickly to her left. They fenced back and forth, each refusing to leave the advantage of the table. Suddenly something changed. Brannigan was no longer smiling. Not even a bit.

Kate wished that Belle had left the decanter and glasses. At least then she would have had something to throw at him, and then maybe she could make a run for another room. As it was, she knew if she left the safety of the table that separated them, he'd catch her in a flash.

She glanced wistfully over her shoulder to the next room. It had both a sturdy door and a secure lock. Dare she chance it?

The giveaway sound of Brannigan's boot heel on the polished wood flooring warned her, and

she turned her full attention back to him, jumping
to the left just in time to stay out of his reach.
They faced each other across the protective width
of the table. Kate could swear it was shrinking for
certain this time.

Brannigan faked to the left, then lunged to the
right, closing the distance between them. Kate let
out a startled yelp. In desperation, she turned and
ran for the next room. He had her before she'd
taken two steps, catching her firmly around the
waist in a viselike grip and drawing her back
against his body.

She struggled, kicking out and attempting to
wiggle free, but soon realized the futility of her
efforts. Nothing she did loosened his grip in the
slightest. He held her hard and tight. She was
caught as surely as a prisoner in his jail cell.

"Kate," he growled in a low voice that reeked
of anger barely held in check.

She swallowed and the next instant felt herself
being spun around to face him. Before she could
even make another attempt to escape, Brannigan
shifted his hold and swung her up and over his
shoulder. The breath left her in a rush as her
stomach slammed against his shoulder.

He turned and hauled her back through the parlor as if she were of no more consequence than a
sack of flour that had been misplaced. Anger
fumed in Kate, rising up and almost choking her
with its intensity. Words tumbled through her
mind, struggling to get past her lips, but first she
had to be able to get enough air drawn into her
lungs to speak.

Kate sucked in several shallow breaths in rapid
succession until the tightness left her chest. With
each breath, her temper rose. Brannigan had no

right to treat her this way, no right to carry her anywhere.

"Brannigan!" she shouted as loudly as she could manage, not giving a whit about disturbing Belle's guests.

"Shh," he shushed her.

Kate felt his chest rumble beneath her stomach. She wished she could reach around and slap him. Anything to make him put her down.

"Brannigan," she said his name even louder.

He ignored her and simply continued across the room with long strides. Kate saw the round table, Belle's prized possession, teeter as they passed it. From her upside down position, she watched in horror as the mahogany table slowly tilted to one side.

She bit her lip waiting for the crash. Instead, she saw Belle grab the table barely in time to save it from toppling over. If only the woman could save her, she wished, but Belle would likely as not rather save her prized table.

Kate slammed her fists against Brannigan's broad back. It felt as if she'd struck solid wood. Her hands stung from the impact; but even worse, her actions seemed not to have the slightest effect on him. He merely shifted her and continued walking.

"Dammit, Brannigan," Kate yelled, completely forgetting Mrs. Parker's rule about ladies never raising their voices in a public place.

His steps didn't even falter.

Kate planted her hands on his back and pushed herself up until her mouth was even with his ear. Drawing in a full breath, she released it with a scream.

His shoulder jerked under her, and for an in-

stant Kate thought he was going to drop her. He
steadied his hold on her and rubbed his right ear.
She smiled in satisfaction.

Drawing in another breath, Kate readied to re-
peat her performance.

"Don't even think about it," Brannigan threatened.

"Then put me down," Kate said with affected
sweetness. "Or, I'll scream the place down."

"One more sound and I'll take you upstairs instead of outside."

His threat gave her a moment's pause. He
wouldn't dare, would he?

"Will you be needing a room then, Marshal?"
Belle inquired with a chuckle from her protective
stance beside her table.

"No," he answered curtly.

"No!" Kate echoed.

Brannigan spun around to face Belle, making
Kate dizzy with the movement. She shook her head
as the floor swung in a crazy arc. Damn the man.

"Kate just quit!" he shouted to Belle.

Kate shut her mind against the dizziness and
plummeted his back furiously with both fists. "I
did not!" she shouted to Belle as loud as she could
manage from her awkward position against his
back.

Brannigan swung back around and headed for
the door. Once again, the floor tilted crazily in front
of Kate's eyes.

"If you keep this up I'm going to be sick," she
warned him. "And it would serve you right," she
pushed herself up and added in his ear.

"Will I see you tomorrow night or not, Kate?"
Belle called from across the room. A slip of laugh-

ter passed her lips, but froze the instant Brannigan turned around to face her.

"No!" he shouted.

"Yes!" Kate rushed to answer as the room spun again.

She opened her mouth to say more, but Brannigan stepped out the front door, and the impact of his booted heel striking the wood-planked boardwalk sent the breath whooshing out of her, making it impossible for her to utter a single word.

"No!" Brannigan called back over his shoulder with finality.

As he stepped into the street, Kate poked his broad back with her fingertips. "Do you think we could continue this conversation in another position?" she asked in a voice dripping with sarcasm.

"Don't tempt me."

"Brannigan, I'm getting dizzy."

He muttered something that sounded remarkably like, "Serves you right."

"Dammit, Brannigan, put me down."

"I thought ladies didn't swear."

"Who do you think you are? Mrs. Parker?" Kate bit out the question.

"No, I'm the man who's going to put you to bed."

Kate opened her mouth, then shut it just as quickly. How did one respond to a remark like that one?

Before she could think of what to say, Brannigan strode up the steps and into the hotel. His boot heels clicked in a sharp staccato on the hard floor.

"Marshal? Miss Danville?" Tommy Tyler called out from behind the desk, jumping to his feet.

"Good evening, Tommy," Brannigan greeted the young man as if nothing was out of the ordinary.

Kate was certain that her face blushed bright red as she heard Tommy rush out around the desk. Thank goodness her hair concealed her cheeks from him. She knew this event would be all over town within the hour. She shuddered at the thought.

Brannigan would pay dearly for this humiliation, she vowed.

"You can put me down now," she ordered him.

He acted as if he hadn't even heard her, and strode right for her room. Once there, he kicked the door shut behind him and sat her on her feet.

Kate shoved her tangle of hair out of her eyes and faced him. She was so mad at him she didn't know what to say first.

She needn't have concerned herself with that, he had his speech all planned out and launched into it within seconds of her feet touching the floor.

"Did you get hold of a batch of loco weed?"

Kate blinked her eyes. What would she want with something called loco weed?

"No, I—"

"Hell and damnation," he cut her off, tossing his hat down onto the washstand.

A dark curl brushed his forehead and suddenly she found herself aching to brush it back. She called herself a fool for even entertaining the thought. She was angry with him—angrier than she'd ever been in her life.

"Lady, don't you have the sense God gave a goose? That was a brothel you were working in. Do you realize what could have happened to you?"

As Brannigan continued his tirade of scolding, she decided that she was tired of being dictated to by a man. First her father, and now Brannigan. Well, she'd had enough.

Stepping forward, she jabbed him hard in the chest. "Get out."

The two words stopped him in mid-sentence.

"Lady, I just rescued you from heaven knows what," he informed her.

"Did I ask to be rescued?" Kate shouted, not caring a whit who might hear. "Did I?"

"No, you didn't have the brains to."

Kate gritted her teeth. "Me, why— "

"Hell and— "

"I know," she interrupted him, "and damnation."

"Kate!"

"If I were a man, I'd— "

"If you were a man, then we wouldn't have this problem."

"What problem?"

"Of me having to rescue you," he fired back. "Did you ever think of the trouble you could have gotten into? I swear that's your middle name. Did you even consider the danger?"

Kate laughed aloud at this. "Sweeping floors? What was I supposed to be afraid of? Getting a splinter?"

"No." He took two steps forward and pulled her into his arms. "Of this."

He lowered his head and took her lips in a hard, thorough kiss.

It started out as a warning, a lesson to prove his point, but it misfired as surely as an old, rusted pistol. Desire flared between them, hotter than the Nevada sun at noon time. It blazed up, catching them both off guard and enveloping them.

Brannigan shifted one hand from her shoulder

and brushed back her hair, burying his hand in
its lushness, and drawing her closer against him.
The rasp of the day's growth of stubble on his
chin rubbed against her cheek and sent a tingling
throughout every nerve ending of her body.

Kate knew she should resist, should push him
away, but instead she found herself linking her
arms around his neck and pulling him closer.
Brannigan kissed her until she thought he'd ab-
sorb her very breath. Then, instead of releasing
her when that kiss ended, he slanted his mouth
more fully over hers and kissed her again.

Kate's knees turned weak from the feelings
coursing through her. So, this was desire, she
thought for an instant. No wonder it was whispered about at night at Mrs. Parker's School.

So, this was love. The thought rocked her all the
way to her dainty toes. She was in love with Brannigan. Hopelessly, wonderfully, totally in love. Really in love this time.

Brannigan drew back a moment, giving her one
last chance to deny him. Kate couldn't have forced
the words out in that instant, even if she'd wanted
to do so. She was still reeling from the surprise of
learning of her love for this man.

Instead of answering him with words, she did it
with action. She cupped her hands behind Brannigan's neck and drew his head down until her
lips met his.

She was sure the wooden floor rocked beneath
her feet with something akin to an explosion, so
overwhelmingly powerful was their next kiss. She
held tightly to the corded strength of his neck beneath her hands.

Brannigan drew her closer, their bodies pressing
together, melding into one. He pressed his hard-

ness against the cradle of her thighs. She gasped
at the unknown intimacy, but he swallowed the
sound with his very next kiss. He ran his hands
down her back, with a touch that was both rough
and tender, molding her body more completely to
his.

Kate thought she was going to nearly swoon
from the feel of him stroking her skin through the
silken fabric of her gown. Never had she been so
pleased not to have a corset on.

Brannigan's loving touch made her feel secure,
loved, and hot. She could scarcely breathe for the
heat surrounding them, and wondered for the
space of an instant if a fire had been lit in a fire-
place nearby by accident. She returned his next
kiss, forgetting the heat, forgetting to breathe or
even think. The pressure of his embrace thrilled
her, aroused her as she hadn't thought possible.

It shouldn't feel so good. But, ginger, it did.

She met his kisses eagerly, her arms wrapped
tightly around his powerful body.

Oh, how she loved him.

Releasing a ragged breath of need against her
lips, Brannigan caressed her back, the touch of his
hand threatening to melt away the fine fabric of
her gown. He ran his hands up and down the
length of her back, pausing at her waist, then sliding his palms lower to curve over the swell of her
shapely derriere.

Exquisite sensations flooded over Kate. Richard
had most definitely never made her feel like this.
She knew that no one except Brannigan would
ever be able to make her feel like this.

Brannigan dragged his mouth away from her
lips and swung her up into his arms. He carried
her to the bed uttering tender words against her

ear. Kate missed the sweet pressure of his lips
against hers and drew his head lower until she
could brush a kiss across his firm mouth.

Brannigan lowered her to the bed, and she felt
the feather mattress give beneath their combined
weight. Funny, the usually lumpy mattress didn't
feel the least bit lumpy now. It felt like a soft cloud
in a little piece of heaven.

Without giving a thought to her actions, she
tugged at his shirt, loosening its fastenings. The
skin it revealed was warm beneath her fingers.
She longed to run her hands over him, exploring
the firmly muscled contours laid bare to her eyes.

She gave into the temptation, skimming her
hands down his powerful shoulders, across his
broad chest and down his flat belly. Her hair whispered across his skin in the wake of her hands.

Brannigan thought he would go crazy from her
touch. She started out tentative, seeking to dis-
cover, and ended up setting him afire.

She felt so right, so damn right, in his arms.
However, he couldn't tell her this. He didn't de-
lude himself— she'd return to Boston as soon as
she could. And he would be free to go back to his
life. Oh, but he didn't want to. He wanted to hold
her forever. Love her forever.

Brannigan ran his hands down, skimming his
fingers over the tempting silk of her gown. He
could feel her curves beneath his hands. A smile
tipped his lips. Kate wasn't wearing a corset.

Surprise combined with pleasure made him
draw back until a scarce few inches separated their
mouths. He gave her a smile of pure satisfaction.

"Why, Miss Kate Danville of Boston, you're not
wearing your corset," he said in mock shock.

Kate giggled at him. She'd never been so happy

to be without that particular garment in her entire life.

"No, Marshal, I'm not. Are you going to arrest me for that?"

His eyes twinkled. "No, ma'am. I'm going to love you for it."

Kate's breath got lost somewhere between her lips and her throat.

Together, they moved as one to free her from the remaining garments that separated her from his full touch. Brannigan drank in the sight of her.

Kate blushed under his perusal. Gently, tenderly, reverently he rained kisses from her pink cheeks, to the slim column of her throat, to her breasts. There he paused to worship them with loving tenderness.

Kate was fired with sensations she'd never known were possible to experience. She clung to him, digging her fingertips into the firm muscles rippling along his back. How she loved his strength, and his tenderness.

She gave freely of herself, her touch becoming bold in return as she brought her hands around to his stomach and then followed his tight muscles downward.

He eased himself between her legs, whispering reassuring endearments against her mouth. Her breath was sweet against his lips, so sweet.

Gently, lovingly he increased the pressure until he had made her his. Completely.

Kate arched beneath him, her body acting on its own accord. She clung to him tightly, following his lead, unable to do anything else.

Under his loving, something in her spiraled up, higher and higher as if reaching for the stars themselves. Then, suddenly in a burst, the stars seemed to be all around her, surrounding them with heat and beautiful, sparkling light.

Twelve

The sun streamed through the curtained window, trailing a path of silken rays across Kate and Brannigan's entwined bodies. Stretching like a contented cat, she raised her arms over her head. The thin gown she'd donned sometime in the middle of the night rode up with her movement, sculpting itself to her body.

Brannigan turned on his side, propped himself up on his elbow, and watched her. A smile tipped Kate's lips as she met his leisurely gaze.

"Morning." He drawled the greeting out, giving it the sexiest sound Kate thought she'd ever heard in her life.

Her stomach performed a flip flop in an instant response, and her smile suddenly turned shy.

"Morning," she answered back, lowering her arms from over her head.

Brannigan returned her smile with a rakish one of his own and slid his arm across her midriff.

Life was wonderful, Kate thought to herself.

The day was perfection itself—sun shining warmly, a gentle breeze stirring the curtains, and waking up in the arms of the man she loved.

Brannigan ran a finger down her bare arm, stirring goose bumps of pleasure in his wake. Kate's happiness grew like a flower blossom opening to the sun. He cared for her. He loved *her*, not her money. Especially since she hadn't any money now. And her papa had nothing to do with their love. In fact, money didn't enter into it in the slightest, she assured herself.

Kate didn't know when she'd felt so wonderful in her entire life. For the first time in her life a man loved her for herself. Not her father's money!

The bed shifted as Brannigan rose. "Sorry, honey, much as I'd love to stay right here with you, I've got a job to do."

"Umm."

She turned on her side, rested her head on the feather pillow, and watched Brannigan as he crossed to the washstand. Sighing softly, she allowed herself the luxury of imagining a bright future as shiny as the sunlight streaming through the nearby window. Why, Brannigan would ask her to marry him, of course. And she'd accept. Of course.

The picturesque future spread out before her. They'd live in his little house at the edge of town, and she'd make it a perfect home. Or, maybe they'd return to Boston. How she'd love showing him off. He would be a . . .

The picture faded before her. Somehow, no matter how hard she tried, she couldn't picture Brannigan as anything other than what he was—a lawman.

Just then he turned around to face her, and all thoughts of Boston fled her mind. He was gorgeous. Dressed only in his pants, he fulfilled any dream she could conjure up. His bare chest rippled as he shifted position, and the muscles flexed with his movements.

Tossing back the sheet, she sprang out of bed

and crossed the cool wood floor to brush her lips
across the firm skin of his shoulder.

"If you persist in doing that, honey, I'll never
finish getting dressed," he noted in a low drawl
that stroked her as surely as if he'd touched her
skin himself.

At the thought of spending the day abed in the
unladylike pursuit of lovemaking, Kate felt a
heated blush steal up her cheeks. Such thoughts
had never even entered her mind before this man.
Her cheeks heated once again, practically burning
with her blush.

Brannigan's soft chuckle only made it worse. He
slipped his arms into his shirt, but didn't fasten it
yet.

"Keep looking at me like that, honey, and I won't
make it to the jail. And if we do that, my deputy
will be pounding on our door soon." He glanced
over to the window and the bright sunshine outside. "I've never been this late in my life."

As memories of exactly why he was late filled
her mind, a fluttering sensation started below her
breasts and raced lower as if a butterfly had suddenly taken flight within her body. She'd never felt
so unladylike. And so womanly.

Confused at the opposing sensations, she hurriedly turned away to scoop up his coat from where
he'd tossed it last night. As she shook it vigorously
to try and dislodge the wrinkles, a folded piece of
paper slipped from an inside pocket and fluttered
to the floor. It landed face up on the wood flooring.

Without thinking, Kate bent to pick up the paper. She recognized it as a telegram. A telegram?
A shiver of premonition mingled with fear skittered its way up her spine.

Curious, she held the paper between her fingers, debating whether to read it or not. It crackled with impending doom. Slowly at first, she straightened the creases with her fingertips, then gave into temptation and scanned the words.

As each word penetrated her mind, her earlier happiness fled until not even a vestige remained. Shock and pain swept over her. The pain buried itself deep like an arrow striking the heart of its target. She curled her fingers over the edge of the paper, crushing it. Shock surged through her, then receded to be replaced by anger, that turned into blind fury. She reread the missive, each word of it branding itself in her heart.

Keep an eye on his daughter for a fee, of course. Her father's words stared back at her . . . taunting her . . . destroying her.

Brannigan was being *paid* to take care of her by her father. By her father's money. Fury and pain brought clarity to her shocked mind. Money. There it was again. That explained why Brannigan always appeared when she got into trouble. He was doing a job— for her father.

Keep an eye on her! Kate narrowed her eyes.

For a fee! She stomped her bare foot. Brannigan was accepting payment to watch her!

"Damn you," she murmured. The words came out scarcely above a whisper.

At that moment she was incapable of uttering another sound. She didn't know which man the curse had been aimed at— Brannigan or her dear papa.

Brannigan had been bought and paid for by her father. Paid to keep an eye on her.

White hot anger caught her up in its grasp, stealing the breath from her throat. How could

her father stoop this low? Even worse, how could
Brannigan do this to her? She'd loved him. Pain
shot through her, stabbing each nerve ending with
fiery pinpricks. She wrapped her arms across her
midriff. She'd given herself to him. Shame welled
up in her.

Fool! Fool! Fool! she told herself. Shouldn't she
have known better?

She'd done it again. She'd fallen in love with
another money-hungry man. Only this time, that
man was Brannigan, and he'd bargained away her
love. She bit her lip so hard she tasted the bitter
sting of blood. She wondered how much love sold
for nowadays. One hundred dollars? Two hundred? Or more? Her father could be very generous
when he wanted to be.

She swallowed down the lump that rose in her
throat, threatening to choke the breath out of her.
She stared at Brannigan's broad back. How could
he have made love to her so beautifully and completely last night, and then coldly collect his fee
from her father?

His fee. The realization struck her with a knee-
buckling force. She meant nothing more to Brannigan than a means of making easy money. And
if she knew her father, it would be a hefty sum.
Bitterness welled up in her, blotting out everything
else.

She almost let the acid laughter slip free at the
irony facing her. She meant nothing to Brannigan,
while he had become her life. He had been inching his way into her life since the moment she first
encountered him. Last night had completed that,
making her completely his.

Fresh bitterness arose as she watched Brannigan
casually dry his hands on the thin towel hanging

on the hook by the washstand. He was totally un-
affected by the very thing that had shattered her
happiness. Well, not any longer he wasn't.

Kate closed her fist over the hated telegram. It
crumpled against her skin, the paper as harsh
against her flesh as the words had been to her
heart. Clenching her teeth, she took great pleasure
in throwing the balled up paper at Brannigan. It
bounced off his shoulder, and he whirled around
to face her.

"What in— "

At the expression on her face, he stopped in
midsentence. The look she sent him could almost
freeze hell itself. While her eyes cut straight
through with a cold glare, the ramrod stiffness of
her body warned of fury waiting to be unleashed.

What had happened?

Where moments before had been a loving,
blushing seductress, now stood an inferno ready
to erupt. Surely she wasn't suddenly angry about
what they'd shared through the night?

"Kate?" He took an hesitant step towards her.
His open shirt fluttered with the movement.
"Honey?"

"Don't you take another step," she threatened,
her voice as chilled as a snow drift.

"Kate?"

Brannigan reached for her, but she knocked his
hands away.

"Don't come near me!"

Ignoring her order, he took a broad step. She
kicked him soundly on the shin.

"Hell and damnation!" he yelled, hobbling
backwards.

"Don't swear at me." She crossed her arms over

the top of her thin nightgown in an unconsciously defensive gesture. "And don't call me honey."

He stood back and returned her glare of anger. "What put a burr under your saddle?"

Kate clenched her hands into impotent fists and began counting silently to ten in an attempt to hold back her soaring temper. If she let loose now, she'd plummet him. So help her, she would.

"Three, four," she whispered, gritting her teeth. "Five."

That's as far as she made it.

Her voice started out low, but raised with each word. "You no good, conniving rattlesnake!"

"Me?"

"You should climb back under the rock you crawled out from. You lowdown— "

"Now, what's this all about? I'm not going to apologize for last night."

"Apologize?" Her voice rose on the single insulting word.

Kate crossed her arms over her chest again and turned her back on him to keep herself from striking him. She blinked back the sudden, unwelcome sting of tears. As if a mere apology would make everything right She grabbed for her anger and wrapped it around her like a shield to hold the pain at bay.

At the sound of Brannigan's footfall on the wooden floor, she spun back around. "Don't you dare touch me."

He stared at her, disbelief clouding his blue eyes. "What— "

"You deceiving scoundrel— "

"What the— "

Cutting him off as if he hadn't even spoken, she

continued her tirade. "Worthless, money-grubbing, son of a—"

"Dammit, Kate." Brannigan reached out and caught her, effectively clamping her arms to her side.

She kicked out, but he quickly dodged back out of the range of her feet. Then, before she realized what he was doing, he spun her around, crossed his arms over her stomach, and pressed her back up against his chest, pinning her to his muscled body. She couldn't move, and could scarcely breathe. Dampness from his freshly washed chest seeped through her thin gown.

"You—"

"I think we've covered what you think of me quite well," he noted. "But now I want to know why."

Kate thought she detected hurt in his voice, but pushed that possibility aside instantly. Why would he be the one hurting? He'd used her. And made a fine sum of money doing it!

Anger rippled through her in waves, strengthening her resolve. She struggled against his hold, not wanting to feel his touch on her a second longer.

In spite of her outrage, she could feel the traitorous heat seeping through her back from his broad chest. She knew exactly how wide that chest was, she'd memorized every inch of it through their passion-filled night.

Shame coursed through her, replacing all heat and any vestige of softness she might feel for him. Her throat burned, and she tried to swallow down the gagging bitterness.

"I hate you."

Her words fell into the silence of the room. They echoed off the walls and pierced her. And him.

The pain rose up to almost choke her. She'd thought that this time it was really love. Only once again it was the seductive lure of her papa's money. Couldn't any man look past the dollar signs and see her?

She now knew that Brannigan couldn't. She had to get out of here. It hurt more than she'd ever known it was possible to hurt; she had to get away from Deadrange and Lucas Brannigan, even if she had to work her way to Boston one town at a time.

Why didn't he want her? The question cut through her like a hot poker straight to her heart. Refusing to give into the pain, she straightened her spine ramrod stiff and raised her chin, although it took every bit of latent acting ability she possessed and then some to act as if she wasn't hurting inside. Pain, so bad that it almost ripped the breath from her lungs, coursed through her.

"If you'd kindly release me, I'd like to pack." Her question was the epitome of politeness.

"What?" Brannigan shouted.

"I'm leaving."

Her statement had the effect of shocking him enough that he dropped his arms to his side. Kate walked away from him with her head held up in disdain. It was the most difficult thing she'd ever done in her life.

"Like hell you are," he bit the words out.

Kate refused to turn around. She crossed her arms over her chest in an attempt to hold herself together, fearing that if she dared let go she'd shatter into a pile of pieces on the bare wood floor, like a china doll that had been destroyed.

"Why? Are you afraid that you'll lose money if I leave?" She bit the question out.

"Honey, you've already cost me a month's pay by being here!"

"Then have my dear papa reimburse you!" Her words held all the bitterness she felt at his betrayal.

"What are you talking about?"

His voice had lowered with a hint of trepidation, and Kate knew she had her answer. If she'd harbored any doubt of Brannigan's innocence, his tone effectively killed it at that moment.

She clenched and unclenched her fists, then whirled around to point at the damning telegram lying in a crumpled ball on the floor. Brannigan bent to pick up the paper, and she watched the tanned skin across his cheekbones pale.

"Where did you— ," he stopped.

"It fell out of your coat. Keep it. It's been paid for. Like me."

"Kate." Brannigan stepped toward her, but one glance at her face stopped him.

"You take one step closer, and I swear I'll break that pitcher over your head," she threatened in a tight voice that testified to her seriousness. Stepping to the side, she came within arm's reach of the washstand.

Brannigan stayed where he was.

"All right, I admit I probably should have told you I got the telegram— "

"Told me!"

"I meant to throw it away, and— "

"I'll just bet you did."

"How was I to know it'd put such a burr under your saddle?"

"Oh, yes, why ever would learning that a man had been *paid* to keep an eye on me upset me?

Why would learning he'd made love to me for money 'put a bur under my saddle,' as you called it?" Her voice dripped with intended sarcasm. "You son of a—"

She grabbed up the water pitcher and threw it at his head. He ducked, and it missed him. Instead the pottery crashed against the far wall, shattering as surely as her heart.

"Now, Kate, I admitted I may have been wrong—"

"Wrong?" Kate interrupted. "Wrong? You may have been *wrong*? Why ever would I think that?" Bitterness covered her words like dew on early morning grass.

"Dammit, Kate. I never took any money from your father."

"Ha!" She choked on her laughter.

She forced out another laugh, so he wouldn't see the tears that burned and lurked just beneath the surface. He'd never see her cry. No one ever saw her cry.

"Liar!" Kate fired back. "In my world, *nobody* turns down money."

"I do."

"Are you trying to make me believe you're different from every other man I've met?"

"Damn right."

"Give it up, Marshal." Kate sighed. "I'm long past believing in your innocence. You're no different than Richard Hale, or any other man."

She ignored his quickly indrawn breath. There was no way she was going to believe that her words had any power to hurt him.

"Just answer one question." Kate raised her chin a notch for the courage to continue. "Were you keeping an eye on me?"

She held her breath while she waited for his answer. At that moment she realized that she was still hoping against hope for something to prove him innocent.

"Yes."

His answer pierced her, killing and burying any hope she'd foolishly clung to. Her knees quivered beneath her thin gown. She felt the unquenchable need to lash out, to hurt him in return.

"But, Kate, last night I—"

"You think that meant something to me?" She forced a harsh laugh past lips turned stiff from anguish. "Don't flatter yourself, I only did *that* to get back at my dear papa for not sending me money. Can you imagine his dismay when he learns I spent the night in the company of a mere marshal?"

Bile rose up at her lies, and she forced it back, almost choking on the taste.

"Be sure you tell Papa *how* you took care of me. Maybe he'll even pay you extra." She stopped and tapped a fingertip over her tight lips. "Oh, perhaps you better not. He might not pay you at all."

"Kate, I—"

"Get out," she ordered quietly, wanting to scream it at him, but not having it in her. "I have nothing else to say to you."

Brannigan yanked up his coat and his black Stetson. He faced her squarely, meeting her gaze for the space of a heartbeat. He slowly fastened his shirt.

Kate was half-afraid he'd refuse to leave, and half-afraid that he'd leave and she'd never see him again. She didn't know which was worse.

"I'll be back. When you're ready to listen. But don't take too long." He rammed his hat on his head and slammed out the door.

He didn't have to worry about that. She'd be

gone. Long gone. As far away from Deadrange as she could get, even if she had to walk.

Brannigan forced himself to keep walking down the hallway and not turn back and return to Kate's room. It was about the hardest thing he'd ever had to do. Every part of his being told him to go back, to catch her up in his arms and make her listen to him.

He took the stairs two at a time and strode through the hotel lobby without looking anywhere except straight ahead. He knew if he even glanced to the side, he'd turn around and go back up those stairs to Kate.

What he wanted to do was take her in his arms and kiss her into silence. Kiss her until she listened to what he had to say.

She hadn't been willing to hear his explanation for her father's telegram. *Hell and damnation,* he swore. She hadn't even been willing to give him a chance; instead she'd dismissed him like a servant.

If she thought she was through with him, Miss Kate Danville of Boston had a lot to learn. She was far from through with him.

As soon as they'd both had time to cool off, he'd be back. And she'd listen to what he had to say this time. He wasn't about to let her leave town.

Kate wouldn't leave like Elizabeth. He'd see to that.

"Damn that woman." Brannigan strode into Buck's room and kicked the door closed behind him.

"I take it we're talking 'bout Kate?" Buck chuckled and pointed to the straight-back chair. "Sit."

Brannigan sent his friend a look that clearly said "no" better than a week of talking could have done. He slammed his hat onto the chair and crossed to the window with angry strides.

"I figured you two'd already patched things up over her working for Belle." The old man scratched the growth of beard that was starting to fill in along his jawline. "Leastwise since you was seen carrying her into the hotel last night," he paused, "and not seen again till this morning. Figured that meant things was fine."

"You don't miss a thing, do you?" Brannigan asked in irritation.

"Not much, boy. But it appears that I've missed a plenty. What's she done that's got you madder than a rained on rooster?"

"She won't even listen to me. She threw a pitcher at me." Anger and hurt tinged his words, making them sound stiff and stilted.

Brannigan paced the width of the room, pausing to rub the back of his neck. His persistent headache was back. Compliments of Kate.

"And said I'm the same as Richard Hale," he finished with a snort of disgust.

"That scoundrel who abandoned her? What'd you do give her that idea, boy?"

"She thinks I can be bought."

Buck burst into laughter at that.

"She's serious." He turned to face his old friend and sighed raggedly. "She believes I'm on her father's payroll."

"What for?"

"For doing my job!"

Buck's lips twitched, but he stilled them. "And what would that be?"

"Watching out for her." Brannigan rubbed the back of his neck again. The ache remained.

"You been doing plenty of that, I'd say."

"But not for her father's money."

Buck sobered. "Now what in blue blazes gave her a fool idea like that?"

"She found this." Brannigan took the crumpled telegram from where he'd crammed it in his pocket and handed it to his friend.

After a minute, Buck let out a long, low whistle. "I'd say you done been found guilty by that little gal. What'd you tell her?"

"Nothing she was willing to listen to."

"So?"

"I left. I'll give her a chance to cool down and go see her tonight."

"Got a temper, has she?"

Brannigan crossed to the chair, moved his hat, and sat down. "Don't tell me you've missed out on hearing about that?"

Buck chuckled. "Told you she was plumb full of sand and fighting tallow, didn't I?"

Brannigan shook his head.

"Likely that's the reason folks are taking to her," Buck stated like a proud papa. "Seems they want to see she's taken care of and all."

Brannigan threw him a disbelieving look.

"Dagnamit, boy, she kinda grows on folks."

"On you?"

"Well, a mite." Buck had the grace to at least look a bit sheepish with his admission.

"Has she been to see you?" Suspicion colored Brannigan's voice, giving away far more than he intended for it to do.

"Every day," the old man announced with a grin, revealing his secret at last. "Except today."

"Well, I'll be—"

"Boy, that gal's got a heart on her as big as all outdoors. When are you gonna accept that?"

"I know that." Brannigan sighed and rubbed the back of his neck again. "She's also mule-headed and unreasonable."

And the one woman he wanted to hold in his arms again.

Thirteen

Kate dressed in one of her best gowns, a silk confection of pale lavender, to fortify herself for what she had to face the rest of the day. She grabbed up her lace parasol to shield her from the sun and prying eyes on her walk to the telegraph office. The first thing to do was notify her father that she was leaving Deadrange.

Fleeing was a more accurate description, her conscience nagged. She buried it with a harsh laugh.

"Well, Papa, you certainly got your money's worth when you bought the marshal," she whispered bitterly to the empty room.

Oh, yes. Brannigan had gone above and beyond what her papa would consider his duty to him. Brannigan had done his job well. Too well. In fact, she'd never guessed that he was "keeping an eye on her." Her father's words still stung her.

What a fool she'd been. She'd honestly believed that Brannigan had cared for her. Loved her.

How many times was it going to take for her to learn her lesson? First Richard Hale, and then Brannigan. Men were a lot more interested in her papa's money than in her. In the end it all came down to money, exactly the way her papa had tried to teach her.

The thought of the hated word "money" recalled her debts to her mind. She couldn't very well leave Deadrange without paying them. But she refused to stay a moment longer.

The debts she'd ran up would have to wait for repayment until she reached Boston. Right now, she knew that her very sanity depended on getting out of town as rapidly and quietly as possible.

She had to get away from Lucas Brannigan before he decided to return to talk to her. She had about as much resistance to his particular brand of charm as he had to her papa's money.

But dammit, she loved the man.

The fact stared her in the face as surely as if she'd scrawled it on the wall. In spite of what he'd done, she still loved Lucas Brannigan.

"Oh, ginger!"

She'd never felt worse in her entire life. Her feelings for Richard Hale paled to nothingness compared to how she felt about Lucas Brannigan. She'd never loved Richard; she could see that now. Richard had been attentive and pretended to care for her, and she'd been so happy and flattered by his attention that she'd convinced herself that her gratitude was love. How she'd fallen for the lies she had needed so desperately to hear.

The thought of lies brought her mind back to Brannigan. How could he have deceived her? And worse, how could she have fallen for the same old lies all over again?

She loved him and hated him all in the same breath. No, that wasn't true. In spite of what he'd done by working for her papa, she still loved Brannigan. Even worse, she knew deep inside that she'd always love him.

What was she to do about the situation? The question taunted her. What was she to do?

Not a damn thing.

She wanted to shout the words out, setting them free. There wasn't a dadblammed thing she could do. Brannigan didn't love her in return— he only loved her papa's money. Long ago she'd learned that you couldn't make someone love you no matter how hard you tried.

Remaining in Deadrange was out of the question. The only solution, no matter how temporary it might be, was to leave the town. Leave Marshal Lucas Brannigan.

Tears stung the back of her eyes and burned her throat, but she forced them away. Sitting here in a dingy hotel room crying would accomplish nothing, and she wasn't about to do that.

She had to get out of here. Scooping up her reticule, she dumped its contents atop the unmade bed and counted out the wages that Belle had insisted on advancing to her. The funds totaled enough for a telegram and some left over, if she watched her words to her father. It wouldn't take many words to say what she intended to tell him.

Once she sent the telegram, she'd look into renting a buggy or a horse— both things she feared with every bit of her existence. She still remembered the only time she'd been on one of those hairy beasts with a shudder. Why, the smelly thing had promptly tossed her to the ground and then tried to bite her!

Well, she drew herself up, as Papa said, "Desperate times call for desperate measures."

She'd even ride a horse to set herself free of the town of Deadrange and Marshal Lucas Brannigan.

Resolute, she dumped the contents back into her

reticule, secured it to her wrist, and stormed out
the door with her parasol over her shoulder for
courage. She only hoped she didn't meet Brannigan on her walk. Her newfound fortitude against
him wouldn't stand a chance if confronted with
his beautiful blue eyes.

She kept reminding herself of her determination all the way down the seemingly endless walk
to the telegraph office. She half expected Brannigan to jump out at her from every building and
alley along the way.

Passing a glass-fronted store, she caught a
glimpse of her reflection. The lavender color reflected in the glass made her pause, suddenly recalling to mind the first time she'd seen Brannigan.
She'd been wearing a similarly colored gown that
day. Immediately she remembered vividly the day
of the foiled stagecoach robbery; the day he'd rode
in to rescue her, and been stopped by her mistake.

She spun away from the reflection and the memory, putting both out of her mind. If she stopped
now, she feared she'd never leave Deadrange.
Catching up her skirt, she hurried on her way to
the telegraph office, as if she were being pursued
by some unknown force.

At last she reached the relative safety of the
small telegraph office. Jerry, the operator, was reassuringly in residence. He sat behind his desk, an
unlit cigar clamped between his teeth exactly like
the last time she'd been in the office.

"Morning, ma'am." He rolled the cigar to the
other side of his mouth and gave her a lopsided
grin.

Kate forced herself to smile in return. The last
thing she felt like doing was smiling.

"Good morning, Jerry. I need to—"

"Oh, no! I bet you're here to pick up that telegram of yours." He jumped to his feet and began rummaging through the stack of papers atop the desk.

"Telegram—"

"I know I put it here somewhere."

"A telegram for me?" Kate asked in puzzlement.

"Came a day or so ago," he muttered. "Now where . . ." He let the words trail off as he pulled open a drawer and withdrew a handful of papers.

He bent over the desk, all his concentration focused on the papers in his hands. After rifling through half the stack, he tossed one paper onto the desktop and shoved the rest of the papers haphazardly back into the drawer. Walking over to where she waited, he handed the message to her.

"Here it is. I'm right sorry, ma'am. With all the ruckus going on the last day or so, I plumb forgot about it until I saw you walking through that door."

Kate stared at the telegram in her hand. Slowly, she unfolded it and read the message. She swallowed, and tears burned behind her eyes.

Her father had relented. He'd sent her money to return home to Boston.

Too late.

She shook her head in denial. If only he'd done this earlier. If only she'd received the telegram before last night. If only . . .

If only she hadn't given herself to Brannigan and learned the truth of his deception. Pain coursed through her, becoming as much a part of her as the blood in her veins.

She blinked back the tears of remorse that threatened to spill over. Instead of giving in, she stiffened her spine up straight until she thought it would snap with the effort.

If onlys are useless, she reminded herself bitterly. What had happened, had happened. It was over and past. Nothing she could do now would change that no matter how hard she might try. She had to face up to that and move on with her life.

"Move on and out of Deadrange," she muttered under her breath.

And the sooner the better. Before Brannigan got it into his head to come and see her, and attempt to talk to her. She knew her heart— she'd listen to whatever he had to say. And if the love that still held her captive won out, she might even believe his lies.

She couldn't allow herself to do that. She wouldn't allow it.

The obvious answer stared her in the face. She had to leave Deadrange before that possibility had the chance of occurring. She had to leave today. Now.

She crumpled the telegram into a tight ball and dropped in back on the desk. "Please dispose of that for me, Jerry?"

She wished she could dispose of the memories of Lucas Brannigan and the town of Deadrange as easily, but somehow she knew they would stay with her for a lifetime.

"Ma'am," Jerry asked, concern written on the wrinkles lining his face. "I'm right sorry about not getting that message to you sooner."

"It's fine," Kate lied, wanting to reassure him that she didn't blame him. He looked so contrite, she couldn't let him feel guilty.

Loving Brannigan had been her act. Her decision. Her folly.

"Ma'am, you want to send an answer back?"

His question jerked Kate's thoughts back. She shook her head, then spoke with finality. "No. No answer."

Right now, the words she wanted to say to her father weren't printable in any telegram. She'd wait until her anger with him cooled before she wrote a message to him . . . until she'd put the dust of Deadrange, Nevada and Marshal Lucas Brannigan far behind her.

Holding her tattered pride about her like a worn-out cloak, Kate left the telegraph office and headed straight for the only bank the town had to offer. Straight for the bank and her money

Kate paused outside the small building to take a look around. It was similar to the banks back home in Boston, but on a much simpler scale. No opulence here. But this bank possessed one thing that no place else held at this moment. Her money to get home!

Jerry waited until Kate disappeared inside the bank, then he slipped out the door. He headed straight for the marshal's office at a run.

"Marshal?"

As Brannigan turned, Jerry skidded to a halt on the worn wooden floor. He clutched his customary cigar in one hand, and his chest with the other.

"Marshal!" Jerry paused and sucked in several shallow breaths.

Brannigan jumped up from where he'd been sitting at the desk, his sudden movement sending the chair crashing to the floor.

"What's wrong?" He reached Jerry's side in an instant.

"Miss . . . Miss . . ." Jerry paused to cough.

"Gotta tell you . . . Sorry, shouldn't have rushed so."

Brannigan tried to restrain his patience, giving the other man the time he needed.

"Kate," Jerry finally choked the name out, then went into a spasm of coughing.

"Kate?"

Fear clutched Brannigan's heart, and he grabbed the other man by the shirt front, hauling him upright.

"I shouldn't have run all the way here, I guess." Another cough took Jerry's breath. "Sorry, Marshal."

Brannigan led him to the chair. Pausing to set it upright, he eased the man onto the seat.

Jerry smiled his thanks, then waved him away. "Be all right in a minute. Getting too old for all this rushing around."

"What's wrong with Kate?" Brannigan pushed for an answer to still the fear clutching at his gut.

The other man waved aside his worries. "Nothing. She was fine when she left." He shoved the cigar back to its customary place between his teeth.

"Left?" Brannigan's throat closed on the word.

Kate was gone. He hadn't acted in time to stop her. Just like Elizabeth . . .

"Yeah, she left my office right before I headed here. Pretty as you please, too, with that fancy parasol of hers." He coughed. "Soon as she left, I got here quick as I could." He removed his cigar and gestured to the open door to the office.

"Jerry, what in blazes are you talking about?" Exasperation roughened Brannigan's voice to a low roar.

"Why, Marshal, I was only trying to help you."

Jerry stuck his cigar back in his mouth and chomped down on it with his teeth.

Brannigan felt like he was caught in a whirling dust storm. He couldn't make the least bit of sense out of what the telegraph operator was saying. The man had never been this disjointed before.

He bit back the anger that threatened to sink its claws into him, and offered Jerry an apologetic smile.

"Why don't you start over?" Brannigan suggested, striving to keep his voice calm.

The more upset he allowed himself to get, the more confused Jerry sounded. What was it about Kate Danville that threw the whole town into an uproar?

"About Kate," he prompted the operator.

Jerry rolled his cigar around in his mouth and breathed in deeply. "That's what I came here to tell you, Marshal. She got a telegram from her pa. It came a couple days back, and I forgot all about it. She was mighty forgiving about that, too, I tell you."

"What about the telegram?" Brannigan barely kept himself from shouting out the question in an attempt to bring the man back to the subject of Kate's message.

Jerry took the cigar out of his mouth a moment, then replaced it and shoved his hands in his pockets. "Got it here somewhere. I'm sure I do."

Brannigan held onto his waning patience with an effort of will as he watched the other man rummage in first one pocket, then another.

"Ah, here it is, Marshal." Jerry held out a wadded up roll of paper. "Read it for yourself."

As Brannigan straightened out the telegram and scanned the words, Jerry interrupted, "Rushed

right off to the bank she did. Said something
about moving on, getting out of Deadrange. And
she didn't even take time to send back a reply."

Brannigan shoved the telegram back at Jerry.
"Where is she?"

"That's what I've been trying to tell you, Marshal. She's headed to the bank to collect that there
money. Then she's . . ."

Brannigan didn't wait to hear the rest of what
he had to say. He grabbed up his hat from the peg
by the door and slammed out the door.

Joe Crocker looked up and down the main street
of Deadrange, then stared hard at the door of the
bank. Two of his men were already inside. He slid
his hand between his bulging shirt buttons to
scratch his belly. Dang thing always itched whenever he got excited.

Right now he was plenty excited. A vision of a
stack of money sitting on a soft bed in a fancy city
hotel room teased at him. Fun times were jus'
awaiting him and Bobby in St. Louis.

The only thing that could stop him now was that
lawman, but soon he'd be putting a bullet into
him. Then he'd be rid of Marshal Brannigan once
and for all. He could just about reach out and
touch his revenge on that lawman if he wanted to,
it was that close.

He'd get the fool town's money and the lawman,
too. His fingers twitched with the urge to pull the
trigger and see Brannigan fall. A grin covered his
face, and he eagerly glanced back down the street.
He hadn't seen Lawman Brannigan yet. But he
would soon. Soon he'd have him in his gun sights.

Joe could feel the anticipation burning a hole

in his gut, building higher and higher. It made
his belly tingle and itch.

"What're we gonna do, stand here all day waiting?" Bobby asked in a cross tone, coming up beside him.

"Shut up until it's time."

"Ain't turning yellow, are you?" Bobby kicked a
clod of dirt with the toe of his dirty boot.

In a split second, Joe had his hand reaching for
his gun. He stopped the instant before he drew.
Bobby was his brother—a man didn't draw down
on kin.

Besides, Bobby didn't mean nothing by his care-
less words. His mouth always ran away with him
when he got all churned up over getting to use
his gun.

"Now, don't go shooting anybody in the back
this time," Joe ordered. "Townspeople don't cotton much to that."

"Ah, Joe, you know that's how I like to do it."
Bobby's childish pout turned into a wide grin in
the blink of an eye, and he added, "They present
a better target that way."

"Shut yer yap and come along with me."

Joe led the way across the street, not waiting to
see if his brother was following him. He would be.
Bobby most always gave in to his orders. Especially
if there was going to be gunplay.

Just shy of the door to the bank, Joe pulled up
short and turned to his brother. "Don't draw that
gun of yours yet," he ordered in a low voice. "And
don't forget to cover your face."

Joe reached down and yanked up his soiled kerchief to hide the lower half of his face. Bobby followed his lead, pulling his own up to cover the

wide bridge of his nose. The excitement and blood lust shone from his eyes peering above the fabric.

"We ready, Joe?" Bobby's voice quivered with an inner tenseness that almost scared his older brother.

Joe shook off the uneasy feeling, and stepped forward. "Let's get this over and done. Then I can kill me a lawman."

"Yeah, and I can help."

"I done told ya before, Brannigan's mine."

Bobby stepped back a footfall at the vehemence from his brother. "Anything ya say, Joe. You're the boss."

"Damn right. Don't you forget it."

Joe paused at the door to the bank building. Sometimes he had to make his men understand he was the one in charge. Bobby had a way of forgetting that at times when he got too churned up.

"Don't waste no time," he ordered. "We want to do this fast."

He and his boys needed to get the job over with and get outta here. Hanging around too long could get them caught. Or dead.

"Sure, Joe," Bobby answered.

He shoved open the door to the bank. It was nearly empty, jus' like he'd figured it would be. The hour was nigh on noon, and he'd watched one teller leave for lunch a scant few minutes ago.

He sauntered into the bank, Bobby on his heels. A rapid-fire glance around showed that the little bank had only one customer— a lady with a right fancy parasol dangling over her shoulder.

An uneasy feeling crept over Joe, but he shrugged it off. Nobody had even looked up at them when they entered the small bank. Things couldn't be going better.

Joe grinned beneath his kerchief. He inclined his head to the left to signal his brother to cross to that side of the room, while he sauntered up to stand behind the lady customer talking to the teller. He wanted to be close enough to her in case he might need to use her as a shield. One never knew when things might go wrong.

He kept his head lowered behind the lady customer's purple bonnet and feathers. His grin widened. The fool teller wouldn't even see him until he shoved his gun in the fool's face.

He bit back a harsh laugh. Hell, the fool teller couldn't even see him thanks to the lady's fancy feathered bonnet.

Getting restless, he stared at the lady standing in front of him. She was dressed mighty fancy for a town lady. He eyed her closer. She was too skinny for his tastes; he liked his women taller, too. The purple color of her showy dress tickled the back of his memory, jogging something unpleasant to his mind.

Uneasiness blanketed him again, and he ran out of patience. Maybe he'd hurry the little lady up some himself. He withdrew his pistol . . .

Kate held her breath without even realizing it as she watched the teller count out her money. Every muscle of her body was strained with tension. Here was her way out of Deadrange.

Just as she reached for her money, someone grabbed her by the shoulder and spun her around. A gun barrel was pointed directly at her face.

She screamed.

"Shut up!" the gunman growled at her. "Boys, get to work."

Kate saw that to the side stood two more men, guns drawn. They rushed forward to scoop up bills from the teller's shaky hand.

A robbery!

No! She wanted to scream out her denial. She reached for her money again anyway, determined to get it before the robbers could do so. She enfolded the money in her hand and hung onto it. She wouldn't let them have it. No matter what.

This was her money and no thieving bank robber was going to take it away from her without a fight. She would *not* be left penniless in this broken-down town again.

"Gimme that!" the armed outlaw ordered.

"No!" Kate closed her fingers tighter around the bills in her palm.

In a swift move the man reached out and grabbed her hand. Before she could stop him, he yanked open her hand and took the money from her grasp. She lunged for the bills, trying to grab them back.

A sudden commotion at the door stopped their struggle, and they both turned their heads toward the door.

"Let me in!" a high-pitched voice ordered.

Kate cringed in recognition of Miss Sally.

"The bank's closed for the day!" Bobby yelled from his position beside the door.

He reached out and flipped the closed sign outward, so it could be read through the beveled glass door panel.

"Hell's fire, boy, this bank has never closed before noon."

"It is today," Bobby said in a flat voice.

"Willis?" Miss Sally called out. "What do you think you're doing, closing up early and turning away your good customers?" she demanded in a loud voice that carried even to the far side of the room.

Ignoring the dirty young man attempting to shut the door in her face, Miss Sally slammed her hand against the door, pushing it open. She swept past the man blocking her path with her nose up in the air.

"You'd best mind your manners, young man," she told Bobby, "or Mr. Willis will send you packing."

Bobby laughed a harsh cruel laugh. "I don't think so."

He caught Miss Sally by the shoulder and shoved her across the room. She stumbled and fell against Kate, who reached out to steady her.

The young man strode across the room after her. Kate watched in horror as he raised his hand holding the pistol and began to swing. She shoved Miss Sally back, hopefully out of the range of his fist.

"No!" Kate screamed, ramming her body into the young robber's in the split second before he could strike the older, helpless woman.

Bobby caught nothing but air. He roared in fury.

Kate had succeeded in saving Miss Sally, but she'd turned the outlaw's full wrath on herself. He yanked her sideways and swung.

Sharp, stinging pain slammed against the side of her face as the pistol barrel caught her cheekbone. Kate couldn't hold back her outcry.

He raised his gun hand to strike again, but Joe grabbed his arm. "Let it be. Get the money into the saddlebags. And don't leave none behind either."

As Bobby scooped up the money from the teller's cage, Joe turned to examine the ladies in front of him. The old bat cringed against the wood counter, but the young woman faced him squarely. Fury glared from her eyes. A red welt streaked the pale skin of her cheek.

In that instant, Joe recognized her. Oh, he remembered her well. This was the same fancy lady who'd shot him during the stagecoach robbery!

"You!" he screamed at her.

A chill snaked its way down Kate's spine. She knew that voice. In spite of the kerchief concealing his features, she recognized the familiar hated voice.

Before she thought about what she was doing, she yanked the kerchief down in a swift move. Her breath froze in her throat. She knew this man. As she stared up into his exposed face, she saw his eyes narrow. Hatred spewed from his dark eyes.

"You," Kate whispered in dawning recognition.

As Joe reached for her, she swung her parasol with all her might, catching him full on the shoulder. The blow sent him sideways, and she caught up her skirts and raced for the door. She hated leaving Miss Sally behind, but somebody had to get help. If she didn't the robbers were going to make off with not only *her* money, but that of all the hard-working people in Deadrange. She couldn't stand meekly by and allow that to happen. She couldn't.

Determination gave her more speed than she'd known she was capable of achieving. Her feet fairly flew across the spur-scarred wooden flooring of the bank.

She almost made it. Mere steps from the door, Joe Crocker caught up with her. Reaching out his meaty fist, he grabbed Kate's shoulder, spinning her around and slamming her into the wall.

For the first time in her life, Kate saw stars, or at the least brilliant spots before her eyes. She blinked them away.

"Kate!" Miss Sally called out, concern in her old-sounding voice.

"Shut yer yap, woman!" Joe ordered.

"Hey, Joe!" Bobby yelled. "That there lawman is coming this way."

"Damn," Joe swore. "Let's get outta here."

"I got the money right here," Bobby informed him with a sneer of laughter.

Joe planted his hand on Kate's shoulder and whirled her toward the door. She attempted to pull back, to escape him, but he tightened his hold, pinching her shoulder until she cried out in pain. He pushed the barrel of his gun tight against her ribs.

"You're coming with me, sugar," he spat at her.

Kate's blood froze in her veins. No! This couldn't be happening.

Joe Crocker yanked the door open and shoved Kate forward out the door in front of him, using her body to shield his own. He pushed her forward again as he stepped out onto the wood-planked boardwalk.

She stumbled and would have fallen if he hadn't hauled her back up straight again. The cold steel barrel of his gun prodded her in the back.

She battled the trembling that threatened to steal the strength from her legs. She knew as surely as she breathed that if she fell, he'd shoot her.

"Hey, lawman!" Joe called out.

"Right here," Brannigan answered in a cool voice. However, his body's stiffness betrayed the tension that gripped him. He carefully held his gun aimed directly at Joe Crocker— and Kate.

Brannigan couldn't believe what he was seeing. Crocker had Kate positioned directly in front of him.

Using her as a shield.

Fourteen

Brannigan's heart slammed hard within his chest. He felt as if the air was being forced out, as if a hand had closed around his chest.

Crocker had Kate.

It seemed as if everything else in the world ceased to exist in that moment. Only one horrible fact remained. The outlaw was holding a gun on Kate. His Kate.

Brannigan swallowed down his fury and the surge of possessiveness that rose up to practically choke him. He tightened his grip on the pistol in his hand and stood his ground.

"Step away, lawman!" Joe Crocker shouted with a sneer in his voice. *"Now."*

Kate let out a cry of alarm as the gun barrel jabbed her ribs.

"Ya heard that, lawman?" Joe challenged. "That's the last sound she'll make if ya don't do as I say."

Behind her, Joe laughed aloud, his spurt of sound carrying across to Brannigan like a shot.

Brannigan stepped back slowly, one step, then another. He never took his eyes off the man. Or Kate.

"Crocker," he called out. "You know I can't let you go."

A harsh laugh from the outlaw brought a chill along Brannigan's spine.

"I don't see where you got a choice, lawman. If you don't do as I say, she's dead."

Brannigan swallowed and waited.

"And ya know I'll do it, lawman!"

Kate stared at him, her eyes filled with fear, something he'd never yet seen her reveal. Brannigan felt his stomach clench into a tight knot as he was forced to stand and watch.

He felt the frustration rise up, and he inhaled deeply to squelch it back down. He had to remain calm, ready to move at a second's notice.

Crocker stepped off the boardwalk, being certain to keep Kate's body directly between him and Brannigan. Bobby Crocker sidled up behind them, a wide grin splitting his face.

Brannigan had never known true fear before in his life, but he knew it now as he was forced to watch Joe Crocker and his brother, Bobby, back away with Kate. A cold, hard fist of dread coiled in his gut like a restless snake. He tightened his fingers around the pistol in his hand; the gun practically burned in his palm. He ached to pull the trigger, but he knew he couldn't dare to fire. Not with Crocker using Kate as a shield.

He couldn't, wouldn't, risk Kate's life—no matter what.

Joe Crocker was deriving enjoyment out of the power he wielded, and Brannigan could sense it. He knew for certain that if he pushed the outlaw now, Kate could well end up dead.

"Lawman!" Joe Crocker yelled across the distance separating them, taunting him. "Jus' you let us ride out and I'll release her."

When Brannigan remained silent, he called out, "Ya hear me?"

Brannigan heard him all right. The outlaw's promise did nothing to assuage the fear coiling and uncoiling in the pit of his stomach. No matter what he did or didn't do, he had no assurance that Crocker would keep his word and free Kate unharmed.

Joe Crocker took another step back, dragging Kate along in his wake. Two more steps and he neared the post where two horses were hitched.

Bobby stepped away and pulled the horses' reins free. He slowly eased up onto the saddle of one of the horses, keeping his gaze on Brannigan the entire time. Grinning, he whirled his mount around and rode away to join two other men farther down the street.

As Joe tugged Kate another step closer to the horses, Brannigan could sense her fear, but he knew Kate would never show it. Crocker met his gaze with one of pure hatred.

Was the outlaw going to keep his word?

Waiting for that question to be answered, he'd never felt so powerless or such fury before in his life. Both ate at him with equal intensity.

The question seared Brannigan's soul. Chances were that Crocker's word was worth about as much as the outlaw. Was he right in letting the men ride out of town unchallenged?

One glance at Kate was all the answer he needed. Her face was ashen; he could tell that even from where he stood. Several loosened tendrils of hair curled about her cheeks, the copper color vibrant against the whiteness of her skin. A red welt discolored the starkness of her face, and he had to force himself not to rush toward her.

The outlaws would pay for hurting her, he vowed silently. They would pay if it was the last thing he ever did. Brannigan stiffened with suppressed fury as he watched Joe Crocker drag Kate ever closer to the horses. He wanted to cry out "No!"

Kate came to a halt the moment she spied the horses. The beasts were tied to a railing, and one horse stomped its hooves menacingly at her. She dug her heels into the hard-packed dirt of the street, then began to inch back out of instinct.

Joe pushed her closer. She gulped and felt herself pushing back. Her body couldn't have been any stiffer if she'd been a board, she thought. There was no way she'd ever get on one of those beasts willingly. Never.

"Go on!" Joe shouted at her.

Relief rushed over Kate in waves. He was telling her to go. She was free. She could scarcely believe the wonderful words.

He was letting her go.

Her legs sagged weakly and she had to blink back the tears that sprang to her eyes. Her ordeal was over. A sigh escaped her lips, and she turned away from the horrible man and his gun.

Before she'd taken one step, Joe grabbed her arm and yanked her back against his bulging stomach.

"Jus' where do you think you're sneaking off to?" He spat the words out at her.

"You said I could go," she answered with a hint of her usual defiance.

"Like hell. Now get moving where I say."

Kate knew that beneath her skirt, her legs were shaking, but she'd never let this outlaw know it. Right now she was certain that her outward bravery was all she had on her side.

Crocker shoved her harder, careful to position both himself and her behind the lone brown horse. The animal acted as a shield between them and Brannigan.

Kate sought out Brannigan, needing even a glimpse of his reassuringly broad form. He'd do something, she knew he would.

"Crocker!" Brannigan called out. "That's far enough. Now let the woman go, and you can ride on out like we agreed."

Harsh laughter crackled in Kate's ear, sending a chill of foreboding racing through her tense body.

"Sorry, lawman." Crocker clamped a hand on Kate's shoulder, holding her in place in front of him. "I think maybe I better keep sugar here with me."

"No." Brannigan clenched his jaw so tight that it hurt.

Crocker's laughter rang out again. "Yup, I figure maybe I'll live longer if I keep her. You look like you'd jus' love to shoot me dead. About as much as I'm aching to kill you."

"Crocker, you got my word that you can ride out. Unchallenged—"

"Lawman, your word don't mean spit to me."

Brannigan knew without a doubt that if he so much as moved a muscle, Kate would be dead. He forced himself to wait and bide his time.

"Go on." Joe Crocker pushed Kate closer to the one brown horse.

She stared at the huge beast. It snorted, and she thought she'd jump out of her skin. It was the biggest horse she'd ever seen.

"I can't," she answered in a wooden voice.

He shoved her again. "I said get up there."

Kate shook her head, her eyes never leaving sight of the horse. As she stared at it, it seemed as if the beast grew several more inches.

"Get up there," he snarled in her ear.

"I can't." Kate's husky voice came out in a sound just above a whisper.

"What d'ya mean you can't? If you don't get on that horse, I'm gonna shoot you right here." He jabbed the gun into her back for emphasis.

"I can't ride," Kate responded in a flat voice.

"What?"

She stiffened her back and raised her chin in defiance. "I said I can't ride!" she shouted the words at him.

He grabbed hold of her by the waist and almost threw her atop the horse. Kate screamed and clutched at anything to keep herself from falling off the other side and plummeting to the ground beneath the horse's feet. She caught a clump of the hair on the horse's neck. It felt coarse between her fingers, but she held to it as tightly as she could.

Joe Crocker swung up behind her. Leaning forward, he snarled into her ear, "Sugar, you jus' had your first riding lesson."

Kate jerked away from the touch of his body pressing against hers.

He laughed harshly at her movement.

"You got reason to fear me, sugar," he snarled. "You cost me killing that lawman. And you're gonna pay for that."

A chill coursed its way down Kate's spine in spite of the bright sunlight beating down on her head.

"You'll pay real good. And that's my promise."

The threat echoed over and over in her mind,

and she sent up a silent plea for Brannigan to come after her and rescue her.

Brannigan stood and watched the outlaws ride off— with Kate. Fury coursed through him until he thought he'd choke on it. He forced himself to wait and do nothing until they were almost out of sight. Then he swung into the saddle and rode after them.

For once he didn't give a hang about saving the town or the people's hard-earned money. All he cared about was Kate.

The only thought pushing him on was to save Kate from the horrible fate that surely awaited her at the outlaws' hands. He spurred his horse on, following in the outlaw gang's wake.

The ride seemed endless to Brannigan. He stayed only as far back as concern for Kate's safety would allow him. He longed to send his mount galloping into the midst of the outlaws, but held himself and his horse back.

Time stretched on, as the hours passed in morbid slowness. The ride was hard and long. Too long. It gave him plenty of time to think. With a sheer effort of will, he shut out the images of Kate and the outlaws that persisted in haunting him.

Brannigan refused to even consider the possibility that he wouldn't be able to rescue her. It seemed that rescuing Kate had become a habit with him, and it was one he didn't intend to stop. Not now. Not ever.

The thought shot through his consciousness that he was coming to care too much for her. He shoved it aside. There was no way he could have possibly fallen in love with the troublesome, irritating city woman. No way.

Brannigan pulled his hat lower as if warding off the persistent thought. Kate Danville was exactly the type of woman he didn't need in his life. As a matter of fact, Kate Danville was the last woman he needed in his life.

And she was the one woman he couldn't live without.

A chill of fear washed over him. He had to get to her in time. He had to rescue her. Or die trying.

He'd wait only long enough for the outlaw band to make camp, settle in, and drop their guard before he made his move.

The outlaw camp was even worse than Kate had expected it to be. There was not a stream or even a drop of water in sight to wash off the dust of the hard ride. The barren camp was bleak, with nothing to offer comfort but scrub brush and rocks. It abounded with these.

As soon as they dismounted, Joe ordered Bobby to tie her up. With a derisive sneer, the younger outlaw tied her hands roughly behind her back and shoved her down against a rock. It jabbed into her back, but she faced him unflinchingly.

Joe Crocker was in a foul mood and said little. Retreating to his brother's side, Bobby pulled out his sweat-soaked shirttail and fanned his dirt-stained stomach with complete disregard for Kate, sitting less than a foot away from him.

"Damn it all! Did we have to ride that hard, Joe?" he complained in a whiny voice that reminded Kate of a petulant child.

"What d'ya think, you fool kid. We had that marshal hot on our heels."

"Yeah, and all because you had to bring *her* with us," Bobby fired back.

Joe swung around to look at Kate. "Damn bitch, you're 'bout more trouble than you're worth."

A shiver raced its way down her back and she struggled to retain her outward composure. Something told her that the first sign of fear she showed these men might well be her last.

She knew beyond any shadow of a doubt that Joe Crocker would derive great enjoyment out of watching her die.

Joe Crocker's mood worsened as Bobby's complaints continued. The longer they were in the camp, the more orders and curses flowed from his lips.

Joe's two underlings, Pete and Jensen, took the brunt of his temper as he insisted they work to make the camp look as if they'd all been there at least a week undisturbed.

"Now get busy," Joe Crocker ordered his men. "Get those clothes stretched out on the scrub brush. Make it look like we've been here awhile. A long while."

"Sure," one man answered, tossing a shirt over a tangle of brush.

"And hurry it up, too."

Joe barked out orders to the men in the camp. They hopped to do his bidding. All except Bobby, who sat with his back against another rock, sipping on a bottle of whiskey and watching the activity around him with sullen disregard. The saddlebags of money lay close beside him.

Finally the camp was set to Joe's satisfaction. A shirt and several old rags hung across two bushes, while a crusted black pan sat beside an old burned-out campfire. Kate couldn't believe the transformation. She feared that anyone coming upon the camp would believe exactly what the outlaws wanted them to believe. It appeared for all to see that the campsite had indeed been in use for several days.

Afraid of being found, Joe Crocker had ordered that no campfire be lit. Kate longed for the warmth of a fire, even a small one, to ward off the approaching chill of the evening. A torn strip of lavender silk blew against her neck with the breeze, reminding her that her expensive gown lay in tatters. The fine material hadn't been designed for use as a riding habit and was much the worse for wear after her ride. The rips and tears in the shoulder of her gown offered little warmth against a chill.

Her skin turned cool, and she wished again for a campfire. She needed it to dispel the greater chill that had settled deep within her.

As she fought back the shivers, Kate's stomach growled with hunger, and she pressed back against the rock in an effort to still the hunger pangs. She'd had nothing to eat that day. Glancing over at the outlaws, she was relieved to see that they continued to ignore her. The last thing she wanted to do was call any attention to herself, or the fact that they'd forgotten to retie her hands again.

Her stomach clenched into a cramp, and she didn't need to be reminded that the hunger was through her own fault. After untying her hands, Bobby Crocker had grudgingly offered her a turn at the cold can of beans, but after she'd seen him dip his grimy fingers into the mixture, all she could manage was a weak "no, thank you."

Her polite refusal had amused him and he'd taunted her by sticking the can under her nose and warning her how eager she'd be for food come morning. While she knew it to be true, there had been no way she could have forced down a single morsel from the tin he held under her nose.

She turned her gaze to the area stretching away from the camp. Nothing stirred. Darkness was fast approaching with the setting sun, and her optimism sank with the sun.

No one was coming after them, the thought pierced her mind. With an effort of will, borne out of sheer preservation, she tamped down the fear that threatened to rise up and overcome her. Someone would come. They had to.

She'd welcome anyone who strayed into the camp to offer assistance. Why, she'd even welcome Marshal Lucas Brannigan about now. In truth, she'd especially welcome Brannigan.

Where was he? She refused to believe that he'd simply forsaken her. Her papa was paying him good money to take care of her, and right now he wasn't doing a very good job of that.

Brannigan paused to listen for any giveaway sounds, but the area surrounding him remained quiet. He kept his sigh of relief locked tightly inside. It was far too soon for that.

He resumed his plan of attack. Inching along the ground, he reached the area where the gang of outlaws had tied their mounts. He loosened the horse that stood farthest from the camp and gingerly led it away.

Once he'd reached the area he'd set up for himself, he tied the outlaw's mount near his own. Turning back, he retraced his steps to the outlaw

camp. It took only minutes to accomplish his task
of setting the remainder of the horses free.

They stood ready and waiting for the first sound
of gunfire to send them galloping off, leaving
Crocker and his men on foot. Smiling, Brannigan
crawled back to his lookout spot and peered at the
outlaw campsite. Everything appeared to be the
same as when he'd left.

Keeping to the shadows, Brannigan observed the
outlaw camp. He'd counted four men—Joe
Crocker, his brother, Bobby, and two hirelings. The
Crockers were the ones to be concerned about.

At the first sign of gunfire, the other two out-
laws would likely as not hightail it out to safety.
But the Crocker brothers would stand and fight.
They'd even enjoy it. It was a known fact that
Bobby Crocker, in particular, derived a perverse
pleasure out of killing.

As if that thought had communicated itself
across the distance separating them, Bobby staggered to his feet and swaggered over to where Kate
sat against the rock.

Brannigan's heart rose into his throat, threatening to choke off his breathing. He watched with
a sense of helplessness as the outlaw stopped in
front of Kate. Tensing, he clamped one hand over
his gun. If the younger Crocker so much as
touched her . . .

Bobby Crocker stared down at her, his very
stance a challenge. Brannigan only hoped that
Kate would resist this particular challenge. He
should have known better.

As Bobby leaned forward, Brannigan could see
his lips move, but was unable to hear his words.
However, it was evident that Kate had no such
problem. She raised her chin, then kicked the

young outlaw soundly in the knee. He howled in
pain and slapped Kate soundly across the face.

Brannigan scarcely stopped himself from burying a bullet in the outlaw then and there. The only
thing that prevented him from doing so was the
knowledge that the first bullet the outlaws would
fire in return would most surely be aimed right at
Kate.

He drew in a breath to calm himself and give
himself a moment to plan. If he rushed in without
thought, he'd likely get Kate killed. However, he
could stand no more. Right time or not— he
wouldn't be able to stand by and give the outlaws
another chance to hurt Kate.

Bobby stood over Kate for the space of a heartbeat, then spun on his heel and crossed back to
the other men. This time Brannigan released the
ragged sigh of relief that caught at his throat.

The time had come to make his move.

Fifteen

Kate ignored the faint rustle of sound when she first heard it. She'd stopped flinching at every rolling rock and coyote howl long ago. Now she kept her attention on the true danger—Joe and Bobby Crocker.

The second time the noise came, she glanced up, but saw nothing amiss. The four outlaws were either engrossed in low conversation or drinking from the bottle of brown liquor being passed around.

She knew better than to count on the outlaw band drinking themselves into a stupor and allowing her to freely escape. However, she still intended to escape them. Somehow.

All she needed was one opportunity.

The third time the same peculiar rustling noise sounded, it brought with it a light shower of pebbles raining down across her arm and shoulder. As the pebbles struck her arm, she barely caught back her cry of "ouch" in time.

Glancing around the area, she spotted a figure crouched on the ground, partially hidden by scrub brush. Lucas Brannigan.

Kate opened her mouth, and in the next instant snapped it closed. She'd almost given him away. He didn't need to put his finger to his lips to silence her, she'd already cut back any possible sound.

Brannigan jerked his head to the side, and Kate didn't need to be told twice to follow his lead. Pushing herself away from the rock, she started forward.

Sharp shards of pain ran up her legs at the movement after sitting in one place for so long, and she bit her lip to hold back any sound. Between the long horseback ride and the time sitting on the cold ground, her muscles had tightened up into bindings of steel.

Sucking in several deep breaths, she forced herself to ignore the pain and crept forward. She'd only gotten a few feet when a cry of alarm sounded from behind her. Ducking her head, Kate surged up and ran toward Brannigan and safety.

Shouts followed her, leaving her in no doubt of what the outlaws would do to her if they captured her again. She didn't intend for that to happen.

In the next instant, the sharp report of a pistol sent a rush of terror through her. She ducked lower to the ground and forced herself to keep running. She would not be recaptured.

She only prayed she wouldn't be shot in the process.

Brannigan returned the outlaw's fire, carefully keeping his attention fixed on Kate's progress. One slender man stood and fired. The bullet came dangerously close to striking Kate.

The cry of warning lodged in Brannigan's throat as Bobby Crocker turned his gun and aimed again— this time at Kate's back. Without hesitation, Brannigan pulled the trigger.

Bobby Crocker jerked with the impact of the bullet. His body lurched backwards, and he staggered, then raised his gun again.

Brannigan fired again.

The second shot caught Bobby full in the chest. He buckled, grabbing for the nearby rock and missed. He was dead before he hit the ground.

Joe Crocker's scream of fury echoed through the night, mingling with the howl of a coyote. It sent a chill of terror racing down the full length of Kate's spine. She forced herself to keep going and resist the impulse to turn back and look.

Instead, she detoured sharply to the right. She had one more thing to do before she fled the camp.

Pausing only an instant, she grabbed up the saddlebags of money where Bobby had left them before he'd joined the other outlaws and their whiskey. She wasn't about to let the gang of outlaws keep either the townspeople's money, or her own money. Not as long as she could do anything about it.

Dodging back to the left again, she increased her pace and kept running toward Brannigan and safety.

"Hell and damnation, Kate!" Brannigan shouted. "Hurry up."

While she'd been running, he'd swung up in the saddle of his mount and now rode towards her. As he drew even with her, he reached down and scooped her up alongside him. Swinging her up, he deposited her across his lap. Kate held tightly to the saddlebags from the robbery.

For once she didn't mind being tossed about like a sack of flour.

She could hear the outlaws shouting behind her as well as the loud pounding of horses. From the corner of her eye, she saw three riderless horses gallop away. Realization hit her full force. The outlaws were on foot. She smiled at Brannigan's ingenuity.

The next instant, the smile fled as rapidly as the horses as she distinguished Joe Crocker's voice.

"You're both dead. Ya hear me!" he screamed. His voice echoed and re-echoed in the night.

Kate shivered from the vehemence in the outlaw's voice.

"Dead! I'll get you!" Crocker swore in rage. "I'll kill you for Bobby."

Kate didn't doubt the determination behind his threat. Feeling Brannigan's body stiffen, she knew that he didn't doubt it either.

Brannigan swerved his mount, angling to the left. As Kate wondered what he was doing, he drew near where another horse stood. Reaching out, he caught up the reins from a bush, yanked them free, and pulled the second horse along after them.

Kate had a moment of hesitation. She wasn't sure which was worse— riding slung over Brannigan's lap like a bag of Mr. Peabody's flour or facing the prospect of riding a horse all by herself.

The decision was taken out of her hands minutes later. Brannigan drew both horses to a stop. Gently he eased Kate down until her feet touched the ground. Her knees threatened to buckle under her, but she caught hold of the saddle stirrup and steadied herself. The leather saddlebags slipped from her grasp to land with a soft thud on the ground.

Brannigan swung down from the horse and caught Kate close against him. "Are you all right?"

Before she could utter even a single word in answer, he bent his head and crushed her lips be-

neath his. Kate released her hold on the stirrup
and clasped her arms around Brannigan.

One kiss turned into two, then three. Brannigan
held her tight against him. Kate had no complaints, instead leaning against him. Her arms
wrapped around his waist, and she clung to him.

Finally, Brannigan set her from him and drew
in a ragged breath. He gazed down at her, taking
in her tangled hair, teary eyes, and the bruise that
was beginning to discolor the fair skin of her
cheek.

Gently, he brushed a thumb across the welt.
"Who did this?"

"Bobby Crocker," she whispered the hated name.

Brannigan's hand tightened into a fist. "If he
wasn't already dead, I'd kill him for this."

The next instant, he swept her close and kissed
her as if it might be the last kiss ever. Kate gasped
at the intensity of his emotion, reveling in it.

Perhaps he cared after all, she thought to herself, grabbing onto the possibility and hanging on
even tighter than she was to Brannigan's waist.

Shuddering, he drew back, then set her away
from him. Kate felt a chill at the action and tensed,
waiting for what she wasn't certain.

"What in the name of heaven were you doing
back there?" he shouted at her, worry adding an
edge to his voice. "When you took off running to
the side, I was certain I'd lost you."

Kate bit her lip. "I had to."

"Had to what?"

"Get these." She bent and scooped up the saddlebags, heavy with the bank money.

Brannigan's jaw dropped, and he stared at the
bag in her hands in disbelief.

"I couldn't let them keep the money," she stated earnestly.

A chuckle crossed Brannigan's lips in spite of his efforts to hold it back.

Kate shrugged one dainty shoulder and handed the saddlebags over to his keeping.

"Joe Crocker will be coming after this," Brannigan stated.

"And us," she added.

"We've got to ride, Kate." Brannigan reached out and gently brushed a wayward curl away from her temple. "There's no telling how long before Crocker will be after us."

Luxuriating in the feel of his fingers against her skin, all Kate could do at that moment was nod in silent agreement.

"If he catches one of the horses . . ." He left the remainder unspoken.

Kate swallowed down the sudden surge of fear the half-spoken thought had brought with it.

"Ready?" Brannigan asked.

Kate tore her gaze from his beloved face to stare at the horse. She gulped.

"Kate?"

She swallowed a breath for courage and faced him. "Well, let's get going."

"That's my girl."

Brannigan's words brought a thrill to her heart. If only she were "Brannigan's girl."

"Take my horse," he told her.

She glanced from his tall roan back over to the smaller horse from the outlaw camp. "I'd rather have this one," she said tentatively.

Truth was, she didn't want either of them. But there didn't seem to be any other choice. They weren't going to outrun the outlaws on foot.

"No." Brannigan stopped her as she turned toward the outlaw's horse. "Take mine. He's saddled."

At her unspoken question, he rushed to explain, "It'll be easier for you to ride."

Kate sent him a scathing look of doubt.

"I promise." He bit back the threatening smile, but not before she'd glimpsed it.

Sighing, Kate stepped toward his horse. "It better be," she muttered under her breath at him.

The horse swung his powerful head around to stare at her. Kate took a quick step back, hopefully out of range of his teeth. Her gaze fixed on the horse's mouth. The animal shifted, and she scrambled away.

"He won't bite," Brannigan teased.

"He better not."

A smile pulled at his lips again. "Here, let me help you up."

Kate raised her chin with pride. She hadn't missed the smirk of laughter Brannigan had tried to hide. Laugh at her, would he? Well, she'd show him.

"No, thank you." Kate refused his offer with a customary swish of her skirts. Even torn and tattered, the action had dignity and the distinct air of dismissal.

Brannigan had to admire her. Even though his pride stung from her too-polite, Boston rebuff.

Damn the woman, she had too much pride by a long shot, he decided.

"Kate—"

She stiffened. "I said no thank you. I know how to climb onto a horse. Thanks to that disgusting group of outlaws."

Brannigan resisted the impulse to correct her.

One didn't "climb onto a horse." But, wisely, he kept this information to himself.

Kate raised her foot up to the stirrup and gingerly eased the toe of her slipper in. The horse sidestepped, almost sending her toppling over backwards. Gritting her teeth, she tried again, this time grabbing the pommel firmly with her right hand.

Taking a deep breath for courage, she swung herself upward with all the strength she possessed. Her stomach hit the hardness of the leather saddle, knocking the breath and her courage right out of her.

"Kate?" Brannigan called. "Are you all right?"

"I'm fine."

She slid back down until her feet safely touched the ground.

"Kate?"

Grumbling to herself, she reached for the saddle again and levered herself upward, swinging her left leg over with a burst of determination.

This time, she kept going, her body's momentum carrying her up atop the horse and on over the other side. She hit the ground in an undignified heap of petticoats and bare limbs.

"Kate? Are you hurt?" Brannigan called out.

She shoved her hair out of her eyes and glared up at him.

"I'm just fine," she bit out.

Muttering dire threats to the horse, she circled around and tried again. Grabbing hold of the protruding saddle horn, she counted to three and swung herself up. As she felt herself sliding, she wrapped both arms around the saddle horn and pulled herself back to the center of the saddle. After a few seconds, she pushed herself upright, straightening her spine with all the dignity she could muster.

"Kate—" Brannigan began.

"Yes?" she asked in a slightly breathless voice.

"We should hurry up."

"Oh, ginger," she muttered. "Well, then, let's get going."

She held the reins with her fingertips, watching the horse closely for any sudden moves he might make. Surprisingly, the horse dipped his head and began to munch on a sparse growth of grass.

"Pull up the reins."

At Brannigan's order, she yanked up the leather, one rein in each hand, until the brown leather strips were at eye level. Her mount sidestepped to one side then the other. She grabbed hold of the saddle horn, yanking the reins back in the process.

"Ease up on him," Brannigan warned in a voice terse with worry.

Too late.

The sorrel turned sharply to the side, then as Kate seesawed on the reins, he whirled a full circle in the other direction.

She let out a yelp and held on for dear life. The beast was going to kill her, she just knew it. She'd escaped murder at the outlaws' hands only to be killed by a damn horse!

Hugging the horse's neck firmly in both arms, she breathed in several deep, smelly breaths.

"Straighten up."

"No." She only held tighter to the horse.

"Kate, let go," Brannigan ordered.

"Not on your life," she gritted out.

"Hell and damnation." Brannigan swung down from the other horse and approached Kate.

As he touched her leg, she reared back her leg

and kicked at him. "Let me be." Her face was almost buried in the horse's mane.

"Damnation, woman!" Brannigan yelled. "If you
don't let go of that horse, he's going to bolt."

"Bolt?" she squeaked out.

"Yes, bolt." Brannigan caught the reins and held
to them tightly.

Kate peered over at him. "Is it safe now?"

Brannigan didn't know where to shake her or
laugh at her. He decided not to do either.

He reached out and drew her upright. Placing
the leather reins in her hands, he proceeded to
instruct her how to guide her mount.

After what seemed like hours of aimless riding
to Kate, Brannigan finally deemed it safe enough
for them to stop and make camp. He helped her
off her horse before she even had the chance to
refuse him.

Little did he know that refusing his assistance
had been the furthest thing from her mind. She
honestly didn't know how she was going to manage
climbing down off the beast by herself.

The constant bumping up and down of the
horse ride and the day's events had combined to
drain the last of her energy. Tiredness seeped
through her body, melting into every pore.

She stretched her sore back. Why, she didn't
know when she'd ever been jostled and bounced
so much in one day in her entire life. She ached
from head to toe, and knew that not an inch of
her body felt unbruised.

She hobbled over to a nearby flat rock and sat
down. Even that hurt and she winced. Seeing this,

Brannigan sent her a smile of sympathy. Too tired
for politeness, she didn't return it.

Kate didn't think she could take another step,
even if her life depended on it.

"Here." He tossed the saddlebags, a bedroll, and
a canteen onto her lap.

"What am I supposed to do with this?" Kate
asked, sitting upright.

"Make camp while I tend the horses."

Kate dropped the items onto the ground. "No,
thank you, I— "

"Would you rather take care of the horses?" he
asked with deliberate slowness.

Kate gritted her teeth. "I'd rather— "

"I thought so," Brannigan cut her off. "Lay the
bedroll out over there." He pointed to a bare spot
several feet away. "Oh, and don't forget to smooth
out the rocks first."

"I— "

"When I come back, I'll make the fire. Unless
you'd rather . . . ?" He left the rest unspoken.

"Fine," Kate snapped back at him. She was too
tired to argue. After all, how long could it take to
lay out a bedroll?

Practically forever, she thought several minutes
later as she continued to struggle with the bulky
pile. She reached underneath and yanked out another rock. Closing her fist over it, she lobbed it
in the direction she'd seen Brannigan take.

It would serve him right if . . .

A surprised yelp stopped her thought instantly.
Oh, no! She closed her eyes tightly, then slowly
opened one eye, then the other. She heard footsteps, and the sound spurred her into action.

Quickly, she pulled the bedroll into place and
scurried back over to the large flat rock. She was

safely sprawled atop the flat surface when Branni-gan entered the campsite. She smiled at him in attempted innocence.

"Next time, you get the horses," he informed her, tossing a blanket at her feet.

Kate sighed in bliss at the pure wonder of going to sleep.

"Come on, Kate," Brannigan called to her, step-ping away.

She snapped her eyes open. "What?"

"Let's go."

"Go?" She shook her head vigorously. "No, thank you. I'm perfectly comfortable right here. In fact, you can even have that bedroll thing. If you'll just hand me that blanket—"

"Kate, we've got work to do."

"Speak for yourself," she informed him with a haughty lift of her chin. She was well past tired, and becoming more irritated with him by the min-ute.

"Kate," Brannigan's voice was hard with deter-mination. "We don't have time for this. Let's gather up rocks and fill the bedroll."

She turned her head and blinked at him in con-fusion and disbelief.

"I'm not sleeping on any rocks," she informed him in a voice that was every bit as determined as his had been moments before.

"Neither am I." He dragged his hand through his hair and proceeded to explain. "The rocks are the best thing at hand. We need to make it look like we're sleeping in that bedroll."

"What—"

"We aren't sleeping here. We're moving."

"Not me." She crossed her arms over her chest.

"We're both moving," he stated.

"The bedroll—"

"The hell with the bedroll. We're leaving the campsite," he snapped in a low voice that brooked no arguments.

"Speak for yourself." She glared over at him. "I am not budging from this spot until I'm good and ready."

The next instant, Brannigan reached down and pulled her to her feet. "Now you're ready," he informed her.

Kate opened her mouth to refute him, but he placed his palm across her lips.

"Not another word," he lowered his voice and leaned closer. "If Crocker succeeds in tracking us here, we could be trapped. And I have no doubt that you left plenty of tracks for any tenderfoot to find and follow."

"Me—," she attempted to mumble around his hand to no avail.

"Yes, you. Understand this, I am trying to save your very expensive hide. We are moving. Now."

Brannigan removed his hand and pulled her along in his wake. Kate didn't know when she'd been so furious.

Her expensive hide! There it was again— money. She just bet he'd realized that if something happened to her, he wouldn't be able to collect his fee from her father.

She blinked back the sudden moisture that insisted on filling her eyes. She wasn't crying. It was merely dust bothering her.

Dust, and Marshal Lucas Brannigan bothering her. How dare he think he could treat her this way. Much less after what she'd been through today.

"I'm hungry," she leaned forward and growled in his ear.

"We'll eat when we set up our new camp."

"I'm not making another camp," she informed him with a toss of her head.

Brannigan rubbed the ache at the back of his neck. He knew exactly where it originated from this time, and she was standing two feet behind him.

Brannigan led on until they had reached a tiny outcropping of rock overlooking their old campsite.

"We'll camp here." He drew to a halt, dropping the lone blanket onto the ground.

Kate watched it fall. "Is that all we have to sleep on?"

"Yup."

"The ground's hard."

"It'll have to do." He threw a cautious glance around, then focused his attention on their former campsite spread out below them.

Kate kicked a large pebble out of her path with the toe of her stained slipper. Even her pretty lavender slippers were ruined, while her expensive gown was a complete loss. No amount of stitching could repair the damage. She'd started out the day looking so nice. And so properly every inch the lady. Why, Mrs. Parker would have been proud of her pupil.

Added to all of that, Brannigan now expected her to ignore the perfectly laid out campsite that *she* had worked to set up, and instead to sleep on the rock-strewn ground with only a thin blanket to share between them. She wrinkled her nose in distaste. That blanket probably smelled like one of the horses.

At a sudden gust of wind blowing through the area, Kate wrapped her arms around her midriff and shivered. "I'll be cold."

She knew she sounded like a petulant child, but she no longer cared. She was hungry, tired, achy, and getting madder by the minute with Brannigan's high-handed attitude towards her.

"Don't worry. I'll keep you warm," he stated.

"When a particular place freezes," she fired back.

"Dammit, Kate." He rubbed the back of his neck. "Sit down and shut up."

She sat down and did as he ordered, but glared at him. So much for his kisses. So much for his earlier tenderness. And here she'd thought that perhaps he truly cared for her. Ha!

Sixteen

Joe Crocker took a long swallow from the half-empty whiskey bottle. It burned down the full-length of his throat, firing his hatred and doing little to quench his thirst for revenge. His mood matched the growing dark around him.

Staggering to his feet, he squinted his eyes and sighted down the barrel of his pistol. He squeezed the trigger and a branch of a nearby scrub brush flew into the air.

Damn, he wished it had been Brannigan.

He ached to kill that lawman now. Squeezing the trigger again, he ground his teeth in frustration.

Everything was ruined now. Bobby was dead. The money was gone. And so were his good times in that fancy St. Louis hotel he'd been planning on for so long.

That lawman was as good as dead. He'd killed Bobby for no good reason. All Bobby had been gonna do was get rid of the bitch. She deserved it anyhow. Bobby didn't deserve what Brannigan did to him. The damned lawman hadn't had to kill him.

The gal hadn't been worth it. He owed her— owed her big. And he was gonna repay her in full.

She was nothing but trouble— had been since the

moment he'd first laid eyes on her, too. He
scratched the persistent itch in his belly.

Damn blazes to hell! She'd caused too much
trouble to be allowed to go on drawing breath.

If it hadn't been for her ruining their robbery
of that stagecoach, they likely wouldn't have had
to rob the bank in Deadrange. Then, he and
Bobby and the boys would have never met up with
her again. But, they had, and she'd brought even
more trouble down on them.

It was her fault that they had the law after them.
If she hadn't been there, he could have killed Lawman Brannigan back in town like he'd planned on
doing.

Joe continued to tally up her offenses. He
faulted her for their trouble with the bank robbery,
for that lawman coming after them, and for Bobby
getting himself shot and killed.

A twinge of pain ran through his foot, and he
remembered to add shooting a hole in his boot to
her list of transgressions. Now he couldn't even
afford to buy himself that new pair of boots he'd
been counting on buying for his feet. Not without
the money from the bank robbery he couldn't.
And she'd made off with that, too.

She'd had no business taking their money.
They'd earned that money. It was theirs.

And he intended to get it back.

His gaze strayed over to where Pete and Jensen
were skulking by the newly laid campfire. The two
men had their heads bent low together, and he
knew they were planning something.

"The first one of you to try and slip away gets
a bullet in the back," Joe Crocker called out to
the two men who were now trying to ease their
way out of the campsite real quiet like.

His threat succeeded in freezing the other men in their tracks as he'd been sure it would. Obedient to his wishes, Pete and Jensen crossed to stand alongside him in uneasy silence.

"We gotta bury my brother," Joe informed them, taking another drink from the bottle.

"But it's dark," Jensen noted. "Can't it wait till morning?"

"That's my brother laying there in the dirt. He ain't waiting."

The other two men stared at the dead corpse of Bobby Crocker. Both knew that the chances were if they stayed with Joe Crocker they'd end up the same way.

"You!" Joe pointed to Jensen. "Get to digging." He rested his gun hand on the butt of his pistol to ensure he hurried at it.

The outlaw opened his mouth, then closed it exactly like Joe knew he would be prone to do. Neither of the two men left would cross him.

He always made sure when he picked out his men to ride with him, he chose the ones who were a mite chuckleheaded. They followed orders and didn't go getting ideas to cross him like the smarter men might be apt to up and do.

He turned and jerked his thumb at Pete. "You, get moving and go find those horses. Don't come back without 'em."

As the man stared at him in disbelief, Joe added, "And don't go telling me it's dark. I got eyes, don't I? You'll jus' have to look harder for those horses."

He caressed the barrel of his gun with his other hand, and watched with enjoyment as the two men lowered their eyes from his gaze. Yup, they'd do as he said.

As both of his men scurried off to do as he'd

ordered, Joe crossed over to lean against a rock
and do some thinking. Sliding his fingers between
the gaping buttons of his shirt, he scratched his
exposed belly. He always thought better when he
was scratching.

By the time Pete returned with the horses, Joe
had his thinking all done. Yup, his plan was sure
to work. He called his men over to him.

"Now, listen real good. We're gonna kill us a
lawman tonight."

He ignored the look of unease that passed from
Jensen to Pete. Neither of the men had the guts
to either cross him or disobey his orders. He'd
made sure they knew for certain that he'd kill
them if they tried anything except obedience.

"We owe it to Bobby!" he yelled to them, staring
down at the freshly filled grave.

Joe continued to gaze down at the hastily con-
structed grave. He felt like he ought to say some
words over his brother, but he couldn't think of
anything to say. He tossed another rock onto the
pile to protect his brother's body from any scav-
enging creatures and abruptly turned away.

As Jensen shifted from one foot to the other,
Joe settled his voice some and added, "Ya two want
your share of the money, don't ya?"

When they both answered with yes, he let a slow
smile settle across his face and slid his fingers between his gaping shirt buttons again.

"Boys, it'll be as easy as stealing a fresh pie from
a farmer," Joe assured the two men.

They joined readily in his laughter just like he
knew they would.

"I got me a plan. Besides, we got him outnumbered. That lawmen won't last as long as a fat

grasshopper in a full chicken yard. Now, listen up to what ya two gotta do.''

Yup, he had a surefire plan. A plan to kill both Brannigan and the woman.

Joe Crocker leaned back and scratched his belly. A smile settled on his face.

Kate shivered and drew the thin blanket tighter about her shoulders. For the tenth time in as many minutes, she chided herself for thinking that Brannigan had cared for her.

Why, he hadn't said a dozen words to her since they had moved from the camp and argued. Whenever she'd tried to start a conversation, he had been distant, even distracted. His attitude reinforced what she'd feared. He hadn't cared about her. He'd only been assuring himself of his payment from her father.

She clenched her hands into fists and thought about what she'd do to Brannigan once they made it back to Deadrange.

Why, she'd leave him and the dust of that town so far behind that . . .

Suddenly, a hand clamped across her mouth. Terror took possession of every one of her senses, and she fought against the restraint, flailing her arms and kicking out against her assailant.

Her efforts at freeing herself didn't do any good. Panicking, she leaned forward, opened her mouth as wide as she possibly could against the hand holding her, and bit down. Hard.

"Hell and damnation," Brannigan growled in her ear.

Kate froze at the familiar voice and too-familiar

words. She squeezed her eyes closed as if that could reverse what she'd done.

He muttered several other remarks in her ear before he sucked air in through his teeth and withdrew his hand from her mouth. Kate nibbled on her lower lip and tilted her head back to look up at him.

Brannigan swore under his breath and shifted position so that he was beside her.

Morose at what she'd done, guilt swept over her. She'd never intended to bite him. "I didn't know it was you," she started to explain. "What in— "

Abruptly, Brannigan leaned forward and clamped his other hand over her mouth, silencing her immediately. Kate forgot all about feeling sorry for what she'd accidentally done to him.

"Not a word," he whispered hoarsely in her ear.

Kate glared at him in response.

Brannigan inclined his head to their former campsite below. Kate looked but didn't see anything in spite of the moonlight bathing the area. She shrugged her shoulder, and it brushed against his thigh which was far too close for comfort.

Brannigan mouthed the word, "Crocker."

All thought of how Brannigan was too close to her fled her mind. She knew her eyes widened, and she turned her head back to search the area again. Fear ate at her, coursing through her veins and threatening to envelop her. The next breath caught somewhere between her mouth and her throat, wrapping itself around her tongue and threatening to choke off any further breathing.

As if sensing her fears, Brannigan slid his hand from her mouth to cup her shoulder. The warmth of his palm was strangely reassuring to her, and Kate began to breathe evenly again.

Somehow she knew most assuredly that Brannigan would not allow Joe Crocker to recapture her.

A faint hiss of sound drifted up from the camp below, drawing both of their attention. Kate felt Brannigan tense beside her, and she stiffened when she noticed the rifle in his hand.

The moonlight glinted off the blue-black barrel. It hadn't been there moments before. She sucked in her breath at the speed and silence with which he'd produced the rifle.

What did he intend to do? Instantly, fear for Brannigan's safety overwhelmed her. The outlaw gang surely outnumbered them. It would be Brannigan against three armed men. If he attempted to stop the outlaws, what would happen to him? Her heart thudded in her chest.

She wouldn't lose him. No, she'd do anything she had to do to keep him safe and alive.

Suddenly, the sound of gunfire erupted from below, shattering the silence. Brannigan shoved Kate to the ground, throwing his body atop hers to protect her. She raised her head and peered down, looking into their former campsite.

Three dark figures were silhouetted in the moonlight. As several bullets tore into the bedroll, she couldn't help but flinch with each and every shot.

If Brannigan hadn't made them move, they would have been asleep in that bedroll when the outlaws ambushed the camp. They would most assuredly be . . .

She cut the remainder of the thought off. As more shots rang out, she realized that the danger to them was far from over.

Joe Crocker's scream of rage echoed out from below. "Brannigan?"

A shiver of fear inched its way along Kate's spine. In spite of the warmth of Brannigan's body stretched protectively across hers, she felt suddenly cold.

Kate knew that having learned their camp was empty, Crocker had worked himself up into a red rage. He was not going to give up until he killed them.

"Lawman?" Crocker screamed into the darkness. "I'm gonna kill you for Bobby."

Brannigan tensed at the vehemence in the outlaw's voice. In the next instant, gunfire rang out throughout the clearing below. Even though he knew they were out of range of Crocker's pistol, he instinctively hugged Kate's body, shielding her from any possible harm.

He leaned up and returned fire into the clearing. A slight movement to the left of the camp below alerted him seconds before two figures swung their mounts around, riding hell-bent for leather away from the deserted camp. It seemed as if Joe Crocker's men couldn't get out of there fast enough.

"Get back here!" Joe Crocker shouted. He whirled around and fired after the two riders, winging one and missing the other.

The two men continued riding away from Crocker and the campsite. With a scream of fury, Joe Crocker ran to his horse and followed after the men.

Brannigan knew a moment of relief; however, it was short lived. Joe Crocker wasn't going to give up. He'd be back, perhaps when they were less prepared for him.

His skin cooled in spite of the warmth of Kate's

body against his. More trouble was brewing. Brannigan knew it as sure as he breathed.

If he didn't pursue him and capture the outlaw, Crocker would continue to trail them until he'd succeeded in killing them both. He also knew that he dare not wait until the light of morning to track the outlaws. They now knew where he and Kate had made camp, and they could return at any time in the night, under the protective cover of darkness and use it to their advantage this time.

Pursuing Crocker was the only way to keep Kate alive.

Brannigan eased himself away and rolled to Kate's side. He had no doubt that she wasn't going to like what he had to tell her.

"Kate? I want you to stay here and not move from this spot. I have to go after Crocker. I'll be— "

"I'm not staying here alone," Kate informed him, standing to her feet in a lightning fast movement of swirling petticoats and skirts now that she was certain that the outlaws were gone.

Brannigan opened his mouth to protest, then realized that she was right. She couldn't very well stay alone. He couldn't risk leaving her here alone and unprotected. What if Joe Crocker or either of the other two outlaws circled back?

Kate faced him, both of her dainty hands balled into fists and planted on her hips. Waiting.

He didn't have a choice. He had to go after Crocker and his men. Or the outlaw band would be back to attack again.

"Dammit, Kate," he spoke in a low voice. "You can come with me, but you have to do exactly as I say."

When she continued to stare up at him, he knew

there wasn't much chance of her doing as he said. No, not much chance at all.

"Yes."

Her soft spoken answer startled him.

"What?"

"I said yes," she snapped at him.

That was a first, he thought to himself. And, somehow he knew he was going to regret taking her with him. He just knew it.

An hour later, Brannigan knew he'd made a mistake.

It wasn't that Kate had done anything on purpose. She was just being Kate, he thought with a wry smile at the irony of their situation. Here he was attempting to give chase after the outlaws and capture them so that he could keep Kate safe and alive. Meanwhile, she was inadvertently helping those same outlaws at every turn.

He couldn't believe it.

"Brannigan, slow down," Kate called out from several feet behind him.

Pausing for her to catch up with him yet again, he pondered the probability of Crocker escaping clear into the next territory before he could reach him. It seemed that riding at anything above a trot was an impossible feat for her.

Brannigan had long ago lost count of the number of times he'd heard her soft voice ask for him to "slow down."

He turned and watched her approach with amazement. She bobbed up and down on the saddle like a child's top. He'd never known a person to still ride that way after several hours in the saddle.

Usually a person's body adjusted itself to the horse's gait. At least to some extent. But not Kate.

He'd never seen the like. She continued to ride in exactly the same manner as when he'd first watched her on a horse. It was the strangest thing he'd ever seen.

Kate Danville and horses simply didn't mix.

"Kate," he called out to her. "Move with your horse— "

"What do you think I'm doing?" she snapped back, her voice coming out jerky with the jarring movement of her ride.

Brannigan barely stopped himself from shaking his head at her in disbelief. She sat ramrod straight in the saddle. He decided to try again.

"Relax some— "

"What?"

"Don't sit so stiff," he instructed. "Lean forward."

Kate obediently slumped forward, her feet swinging outward, then landing with a solid whack against the horse's side. Her mount reared up, then bolted.

Screaming, Kate grabbed the saddle horn with both hands and hung on for dear life. She passed Brannigan in a blur of movement.

Brannigan rode hard after her. Fear clutched at his chest. He was certain that she'd tumble to the ground at any second.

Drawing even with her, he reached out and grabbed the reins, then slowed both horses to a trot. Kate bounced alongside him, her hands tightly gripped around the saddle horn. He shook his head.

As soon as he'd stopped both mounts, he handed the reins to her. "Are you all right?"

Kate glared over at him. "Do I look all right?"

Relief washed over him at her snappy remark. She was obviously fine.

"I think it's about time we made camp," he suggested to her.

At the rate they were traveling, they would be safer making camp than continuing to ride out here in the open at the pace they were proceeding—thanks to Kate. The best thing to do was make camp, get some rest, then get Kate back to Deadrange as fast as possible.

With the way she rode, it would likely as not take them at least two days to reach Deadrange. Thanks to Crocker's attack and their subsequent pursuit of him, they'd traveled even further away from town.

"Camp?" Kate echoed hopefully.

"Yes."

"I'm not doing all the work," she informed him with a haughty toss of her head.

The action almost unseated her. Brannigan decided that they couldn't make camp fast enough for his peace of mind. If he didn't get her off the horse soon, she was likely to break her pretty little neck.

"Don't worry. I'll take care of everything this time," he volunteered.

"Good."

If possible, she sat up straighter on the horse.

Brannigan uncapped the liniment he always carried in his saddlebags. He was particularly thankful he'd had it along this time.

Kate lay stretched out on the tattered remains of his bedroll. The blanket covered her back. Once she'd dismounted from the horse, she'd been too sore from riding to dare try and lay on her backside.

A grin pulled at Brannigan's lips. She had grit, he'd give her that. Or as Buck was prone to say, "Full of sand and fighting tallow."

Right now, he was certain that every inch of her "sand and fighting tallow" hurt plenty. In uncharacteristic behavior for her, she hadn't complained once they'd made camp. They'd eaten the provisions he'd brought along, packed away in his saddlebags, then Kate had fallen strangely silent for her.

"Kate?" he called out softly, not believing that she'd actually fallen asleep yet.

"Umm?" she mumbled, then winced.

"I've got some liniment for you."

As he strode near, she got a whiff of the scent from the bottle and sat upright.

"Get that smelly bottle away from me," she ordered, grabbing for her aching backside.

"Kate, it will help," he said.

She shook her head.

"Hell and damnation, woman."

"No," Kate said firmly.

"If you don't let me use it on you, you're not going to be able to stand up in the morning," he shouted at her stubbornness.

Kate wrinkled her nose again. "Are you sure it will help?"

Brannigan could tell that she was considering the liniment now. "Definitely."

"Oh, all right. But just a little."

Brannigan felt his lips twitch. There was no such thing as a little liniment for aching muscles. But he wisely kept that information to himself.

Kate turned her back to him and waited.

"You'll have to ease your dress down for—"

"I will not," she snapped, stiffening her back. "Ouch, now look what you've made me do."

Brannigan's soft chuckle stroked the air between them. It had the effect of warming her back like a roaring fire.

He sat down behind her and reached out to gently touch her shoulder. Unfastening her gown, he eased the torn lavender fabric down her back. The fine silk slid down to pool on the bedroll in a ripple of soft color in the moonlight.

He sucked in his breath sharply and forced himself to concentrate on pouring the liniment in his hands, then rubbing them together to warm the liquid. Now was not the time, he told himself over and over again. It did little to convince his body of that fact.

As he spread the soothing liniment across Kate's back, her skin warmed beneath his touch. She sighed as her aches eased beneath his practiced fingers. The liniment even began to smell rather nice to her.

Brannigan stroked lower, rubbing her shoulders and down along her spine. He eased his fingers around the curve of her waist and lower.

"Brannigan?" Kate murmured in a husky whisper.

"Yes?" his voice came out ragged.

"Thank you—"

"I knew the liniment—"

"No," she stopped him. "I meant for saving my life. If you hadn't made us move, we—"

"Don't think about it."

"But—"

"Think about this instead." He slid his hands

up to her shoulders and along her collarbone, then rubbed down to her hips again. "Let the liniment soothe—"

"The liniment and your hands feel wonderful." Kate sighed and snuggled against his hands.

"Kate," Brannigan warned, sucking his breath in through clenched teeth.

"Umm?" She wiggled against his hip.

"Kate, you don't know what you're doing."

"Umm, I think I do."

"Kate—"

She snuggled closer, pressing her body against his hip. "The question is, do you?"

"Dammit, Kate, I can't take much more—"

"Then don't." She rolled over to face him.

Reaching up with her arms, she caught his neck with her hands and drew him down to her.

"Are you sure?" he asked in concern.

"Yes," she answered truthfully. "Are you?"

"Oh, Kate." He drew her closer against his body, enveloping her with his embrace. "I could have lost you today—"

"Not a chance," she whispered against his ear, brushing the hair back from his forehead.

Brannigan surrendered his self-control with a ragged sigh of need against her lips. He closed his mouth over hers, both giving and taking at the same time.

Kate sighed against him, all thought of soreness brushed away from her senses by the heated touch of his hands on her bare skin.

Brannigan kissed away the sigh, catching it up with a brush of his tongue against her lips. With his next kiss he claimed her, as surely as if he'd spoken it aloud.

Kate returned his kisses, surrendering to him

completely, totally, lovingly. Giving him her very soul. She wrapped her arms around his neck, hugging him to her. She longed to be loved by him. Truly loved.

Brannigan eased her back onto the bedroll and obliged her. He cradled her in his embrace and loved her with all his heart.

Later, cushioned in his loving embrace, Kate drifted off to sleep.

Seventeen

The next morning, Kate knelt on the bank of the nearby creek; a smile of contentment lifted both her lips and her spirits. Giving into the temptation the cool water offered, she plunged her hands into the crystal clear water until it reached her elbows.

With a gasp at the cold temperature, she pulled her hands back out. Sunlight reflected off the droplets of moisture splashed across on her forearms, and she tilted her head back, enjoying the sun for a moment. As memories of the night in Brannigan's arms washed over her, she could feel her cheeks heating to match the sun.

The clear water beckoned to her again, tempting her with the promise of cooling her blush-stained cheeks and removing the grime from her travel-weary body. For a split second, she pondered stripping off her torn, dirty clothing and wading out into the tempting freshness of the cool water.

Kate could almost swear she heard Mrs. Parker's gasp of horror that such a thought had even dared cross her pupil's mind.

Whatever was happening to her since coming out West? Kate wondered in disbelief. She was certain that she was becoming less of a lady day by day. At a memory of her most assuredly unladylike behavior with Brannigan, her cheeks heated again. This time though they warmed with a blend of embarrassment for her brazenness and recalled pleasure of his tender lovemaking.

Why, before he'd finished, the liniment had been spread equally over both their bodies. She wrinkled her nose at the scent, but had to admit she was becoming accustomed to it. Perhaps it wasn't so bad after all. The concoction had definitely taken away most of the soreness, exactly as Brannigan had said it would do.

Kate leaned back on her heels and dipped her lacy handkerchief into the water. The poor cloth was most bedraggled, but it would have to do, although she knew the tiny square wouldn't begin to remove all the travel dust from her body. Or the liniment.

She had to smile at the remembered feel of Brannigan's hands administering the potion. By morning she'd actually gotten rather used to the smell of the liniment, blended the way it had with the scent of Brannigan on her body. It brought along such wonderful memories of the night and their lovemaking with it.

Tilting her head back and closing her eyes from the bright sunlight, she wiped the wet, lace-edged handkerchief across her face. The creek water felt wonderful. It was clear and fresh to her warm skin. She sighed in contentment.

As a hand closed over her mouth, she tensed, and a fissure of fear ran along her spine. Then, she remembered the number of times Brannigan had done this over the last two days. Didn't he ever believe she was capable of hearing a soft-spoken shush?

Kate resisted the instinctive impulse to fight,

and decided to surprise Brannigan in return. She leaned back against him in a pretense of meek surrender.

It wasn't until she felt the bulging stomach against her back and the disgusting smell of a long-unwashed body stung her nose that she realized her mistake. Only by then it was too late.

Her mind screamed the name Joe Crocker and ordered her to flee. The warning came too late as well.

Her arms were roughly pinned to her side, and before she could manage to do one thing to stop him, Joe Crocker shoved a dirty kerchief in her mouth, pulled her arms forward, and wrapped a harsh, stiff rope about her wrists.

Kate thrashed and attempted to cry out for help, but neither did a bit of good. Her screams were silent pleas for help that no one could hear. She was well and truly caught.

She was Joe Crocker's prisoner.

She tried to call out around the dirty kerchief in her mouth and almost gagged with her effort as the horrible taste of only heaven knew what assailed her.

"Now come along nice like, sugar," Crocker growled in her ear.

Kate surged to her feet and attempted to swing out at him with her bound arms. She only succeeded in unbalancing her body and tumbled back to the ground. Joe Crocker laughed at her ineffectual efforts.

She would not go along meekly, she swore to herself.

As he jerked her to her feet, she kicked out at him. He jumped back scarcely in time to avoid her well-aimed attack.

"You'll pay for that, sugar." Crocker yanked her to his side with enough force to send her stumbling backwards to the ground.

He pulled her back up, then jerked his thumb toward a lone saddled horse tethered not far away. "Now move. Get going."

Kate knew if she got on the horse with him this time, she was as good as dead.

Where was Brannigan? she questioned fate.

Perhaps if she could stall the outlaw long enough, Brannigan would come to see what was taking her so long. Perhaps she could . . .

As she hesitated, Joe Crocker gripped her arm tighter until she visibly winced. "Do you want me to kill you right here and now?" he growled at her with a sneer.

Kate knew her face paled at his threat, but she couldn't help herself. Fear ate at her, stealing away her courage bit by bit.

"Or I could jus' sit back and wait until your lawman friend comes here looking for ya, and shoot him in front of you." He hissed the threat in her ear. "Would ya like that, huh, sugar?"

Kate wanted to scream out "no" but not a word passed the gag in her mouth. Her limbs froze in fear at the possibility of harm coming to Brannigan.

No! She couldn't let the outlaw do as he'd threatened. Brannigan wouldn't be expecting danger right now. He'd be unprepared for the vicious outlaw's gunfire.

She couldn't, wouldn't allow Crocker to kill Brannigan. Not while she could do anything to prevent it.

Perhaps if she went along willingly with Crocker, she could manage to catch him off guard and escape. Or something. Anything but allow him to ambush the man she loved.

"Well, sugar, what's it gonna be?" Crocker grinned at her with chipped, stained teeth.

Inwardly, she cringed, but outwardly she nodded her acquiescence.

She was far from willing or meek, but Crocker didn't need to know that. Yet.

Brannigan pushed back his hat and looked in the direction of the creek. What on earth could be taking Kate so long?

He'd determined to give her time alone to wash up and take care of her needs, but how on earth could any woman take so much time? he questioned.

Well, whatever she was doing, she'd spent long enough at it, he decided then and there. He resettled his hat on his head. It was long past time they were riding out— if they had any chance of reaching Deadrange before tomorrow evening.

Irritated, he strode toward the creek bed where he'd escorted her earlier. Much earlier.

"Kate?" he called out.

No answer.

"Kate?" he called again, louder.

Silence greeted him in return.

His first warning was the sight of the white frilly handkerchief laying discarded on the stream bank. As he drew nearer, he took note of the trampled footprints marring the area.

A cold lump of fear wrapped itself around his throat, nearly choking him. An accompanying chill snaked its way down his back.

Kate was gone.

And from the evidence on the bank of a struggle, she hadn't left alone, or willingly.

He knew without a doubt that Joe Crocker had her, and that he intended to kill her. But not until he'd used her as the bait to lure him along.

Brannigan swore softly to himself, calling himself every kind of a fool for leaving Kate alone. He'd left her unprotected and vulnerable to the cold-blooded outlaw's attack. How could he have allowed this to happen after he'd sworn to keep her safe? Crocker would kill her unless he stopped him in time.

For an instant, a memory of Elizabeth passed through his mind. He would not let Kate die like he had Elizabeth.

He wouldn't.

He'd track the man to hell and back if need be to save Kate. There was nothing for him to do but follow the trail that Crocker wanted him to follow.

Within minutes, Brannigan had shoved what he'd needed into his saddlebags, caught up the pouch of money from the robbery, and saddled his horse. Swinging up onto his mount, he rode after Kate.

His Kate.

And she was *his* Kate, Brannigan knew deep within his heart. For the first time he let that realization flow over him and seep into his heart and soul. He loved her. He loved her more than life itself. And if need be, he'd give his life for her.

No way in hell was he going to let Joe Crocker escape this time.

Crocker had taken Kate in order to force his hand. The wily outlaw wanted to choose his location for their showdown. Well, so be it. At least as long as Crocker thought he had him under his control, Kate would remain alive.

Brannigan clenched his hands on the leather reins, jerking back. Yes, Kate would stay alive as long as Crocker thought he had a use for her, and as long as she didn't cross him.

Kate, don't cross him, Brannigan begged her, wishing he could send the prayer across the distance separating them. She had to hear him, she had to.

Double-crossing Joe Crocker was the utmost thing on Kate's mind. She didn't know how much longer she could stand his meaty hand clamped across her stomach.

Not only that, Crocker smelled, he scratched, and he persisted in uttering threats in her ear. She bit her lip to force herself not to respond to his taunts.

She scooted forward in the saddle and stiffened her spine even more than it already was, if possible.

"Dammit! Will you relax some!" he yelled at her. "You're gonna get us both thrown."

If only she could manage that, Kate thought, she might even kiss the horse for cooperating with her.

As if he'd read her mind, Joe Crocker leaned forward and hissed, "And if you do, I'll gut shoot ya. Ya hear me? Do ya?"

Kate merely nodded, not able to speak with the gag still in her mouth. However, even if she could have spoken, she didn't trust herself to open her mouth to answer him. Heaven only knew what she'd end up saying to the man. Fear and anger warred in her. It was a toss up which one was going to win out.

Thirst gnawed at her, turning her mouth and tongue into dry cotton. It was as if the disgusting kerchief in her mouth was sucking all the moisture from her. What she wouldn't give right now for a glass of chilled champagne or even a tall glass of cold water.

She forced herself to concentrate on figuring out a plan to get herself out of this situation. Alive.

Where was Brannigan? she wondered again. She refused to give up hope that he would rescue her. He'd always seemed to sense when she needed him before.

If she could only let Brannigan know what had happened or where they were going. She bit down on the gag in frustration. She couldn't make a sound. She couldn't leave any marks behind. She . . .

A recollection of Brannigan's earlier remark after he'd made them move their camp that he "didn't doubt that she'd left plenty of tracks for any tenderfoot to find and follow" drew her disparaging thoughts up short. That was her answer. She'd leave a trail anyone could follow. Especially Brannigan.

She racked her mind for what she could use. Thoughtfully, she twisted the torn edge of her lace cuff between her fingers. If only she wasn't bound. If only her hands were free. If only . . .

If onlys are useless, she reprimanded herself. *Instead, do something.* She jerked her bound hands in frustration, and a small strip of the lace ripped off in her hand.

Kate stared down at the brightly colored trim between her fingers, and she managed to smile around the gag in her mouth. Most assuredly nature out here produced nothing that even resembled purple lace. It would stand out in the barren countryside like a gas lantern on a cobblestone street.

Cautiously, hardly daring to breathe lest Crocker notice what she was doing, Kate eased her hands to the side and let the pretty lavender lace flutter to the ground. She waited, holding her breath to see if he would react or say anything.

Silence, except for the clop-clop of the horse's hooves on the dirt. She made herself count to twenty before she eased another piece of lace loose and let it slip through her fingers to the ground. From the corner of her eye, she saw that the purple trim landed on a scraggly piece of scrub brush and embellished it perfectly.

Working her fingers together in careful silence, she ripped off another piece of lace. It soon followed the path of the first two strips. And there was plenty more where that came from, she thought with glee.

Her ruined lavender gown was thoroughly trimmed in matching lace. The finery edged each cuff, her waist, the neckline, and one flounce. She was equipped with enough lavender lace to spread from here to San Francisco.

There was no way Brannigan could miss seeing her trail. For his information, she was leaving a trail even a tenderfoot could follow.

When Brannigan spotted the lace the first time he didn't even stop to think that it might be Kate. All his energies were concentrated on following any kind of tracks left by a lone mount carrying two people.

Fear for Kate threatened to overcome his judgment, and he had to keep reminding himself that nothing would happen to her. He would not allow it. He couldn't allow it. She was his life.

Another strip of lavender lace caught his eye, and he drew his horse up. Reaching down he pulled the fabric free for a closer look.

It couldn't be, he thought to himself, not daring to believe what his eyes were telling him. The fancy lace edging was the same color as the gown that Kate had been wearing— exactly the same.

Hoping against hope that the lace had been torn by her on purpose and not by Crocker while attacking her, Brannigan urged his horse on. This time he kept his full attention focused on searching for any more pieces of lavender spread among the scrub brush and dust.

When he spotted the third strip of lace dangling from a sharp edge of brush, a grin eased his set features.

"That a girl, Kate," he muttered.

He wanted to shout for joy, but he knew it was too soon for that. Far too soon. He still had to find her and rescue her before Crocker made his move.

Nudging his horse forward, he continued following Kate's carefully laid trail. Several paces farther along he found another torn strip of lace. He hoped she didn't run out of the fancy stuff before Joe Crocker got to where he was planning on stopping.

Relief and fear surged up in Kate with equal measure as Crocker drew the horse to a halt. They'd been steadily going up for the last few minutes. The flat area had fallen away to rock-strewn hills and barely visible caves.

"We're here, sugar," Crocker informed her.

Her heart lunged for her cramped toes. For a second, she'd feared that he'd noticed her trail of lavender lace. She'd almost ran out of the lace edging that she could reach without drawing undue attention to herself.

Kate didn't know a person could be so happy to climb down off a horse, and yet be so unhappy that the journey was over. Fear clutched at her tightly, practically suffocating her the second the full realization of what Crocker had said reached her.

What did he plan now?

Would he kill her now, or wait?

She threw a glance around the site, looking for any chance of escape to freedom. Escape was nearly impossible— one side of the area he'd chosen fell off sharply to end in a cluster of jagged rocks, while another side presented a sharp incline that she couldn't hope to navigate with her hands tied.

"If you're so intent on ripping your clothes off, sugar, you can finish it here," Joe Crocker stated in a flat, passionless voice.

Kate knew her eyes widened, giving her guilt away.

Crocker laughed a harsh sound that carried little humor in it. The cackle echoed off the surrounding emptiness. A chill raced from the nape of Kate's neck all the way to her toes.

"Damn blazes to hell! Did ya think I'm a fool?" he screamed at her.

Kate wisely resisted the impulse to nod her head in the affirmative.

"I know ya been leaving a trail of those purty frills that any fool could follow." He reached out and tore away a remaining strip of lace.

As Kate stepped back a step instinctively, he grabbed her arm and jerked her closer until she was only a breath away from his face. He sneered down at her, not even attempting to mask the hatred in his gaze.

"And that's jus' what I wanted. Ya see, sugar, you're gonna lead that lawman right into my trap."

Kate shook her head back and forth. No! She couldn't have helped him. She couldn't have helped Crocker trap Brannigan.

Joe Crocker laughed in her face. He shoved her away as if he couldn't stand the sight of her any longer.

"That lawman's as good as dead. And you right along with him. First, for Bobby, then for sticking your nose in where it don't belong."

Crocker shoved Kate backwards. Caught off guard with the suddenness of his act, she stumbled and fell to the ground.

"Now stay out of my way and I jus' might kill ya quick and outright. Otherwise, sugar, I can make it real slow." Crocker pulled his rifle from its scabbard and waved it at her. "Slow like I'm gonna kill Brannigan."

Kate clenched her hands into impotent fists. She fought back the fear that threatened to paralyze her. She had to do something. She couldn't let this happen.

Suddenly, Crocker spun around, searching the area below them. With a cackle of crazed laughter, he turned back to her.

"Now, ya stay real quiet like, sugar," Crocker whispered to her.

Kate mumbled around the gag in her mouth. Joe Crocker turned and grabbed her by the elbow. For the first time, she noticed the insane glint in his eyes. The man had lost his mind. He was even more dangerous than she'd dared to think about.

He pulled the gag out of her mouth. "What, ya wanting to apologize for what ya done, sugar? Well, it's too late for that." Unexpectedly, Crocker shoved her away as if he'd been burned. "Get on over there and sit down," he ordered.

Kate eyed the spot he pointed to, and shook her head. If she sat there, she'd be boxed in on three sides by rocks without any hope of escaping.

"No, thank you," she answered primly, hoping to distract his thoughts with her prudish act. She'd barely been able to speak for the dryness of her mouth, but at least the hateful gag was gone. Now she could scream for help should anyone appear. "I—"

"What, ya don't cotton to my company?" Crocker's voice held a definite note of insulted pride.

Kate fought back her smile of success. He hadn't replaced the gag, and he wasn't forcing her to sit where he'd ordered her. It was working.

She strove for the same prim tone. "Precisely."

"Well, sugar," Crocker sneered, "perhaps you'd rather I turned over a few stones and found you a rattler or two to keep you company instead?"

He kicked a rock down into the rock-strewn pit below, and Kate heard what sounded like a bunch of dry seeds rattling in a wooden bowl. She recognized the distinct giveaway sound of rattlesnakes. Her stomach clenched into a knot of fear.

"Angry-sounding creatures, aren't they?" He

laughed at her reaction. "Now, sugar, what do ya
have to say about you and—"

Crocker suddenly fell silent in mid-sentence. He
jerked his head back and forth like a chicken looking for feed. Before Kate could take more than
one step away, he yanked her back and shoved the
kerchief in her mouth.

"Somebody's coming," he said in a voice that
came out hoarse with excitement. "It's him. It's
that lawman Brannigan, I know it is. Now I get
him and the money, too."

Yanking her forward, he placed her directly in
front of his body, using her as a shield.

"Now, sugar, if he shoots, guess who gets it
first?" Crocker grunted against her ear, then
added, "It doesn't much matter. You're both gonna
die for what ya did to my brother Bobby."

Kate winced at the threat. Frantically she
searched the area for any sign of Brannigan. She
had to warn him somehow.

Crocker's whole attention focused on the area
spread out below them. He released his hold, and
Kate eased a step to the left, then another. Her
foot caught a rock, sending it toppling over the
edge to crash alongside the rock Crocker had
thrown earlier. The angry hiss and rattle of snakes
carried up to them, alerting Crocker to her movement.

He snaked out his hand and caught her foot,
yanking it out from beneath her. Kate tumbled to
the ground, scraping her arms in the process. She
only prayed she didn't end up over the edge.

"Now, ya stay where I put ya this time, or I swear
I'll shoot ya first, sugar." Crocker shoved her into
the corner he'd ordered her to earlier. Jabbing the

rifle barrel into her ribs, he glared at her. "Now, stay!"

Sidling to the left, he eased away from her, while keeping his rifle pointed squarely at her chest.

Kate froze in place. She honestly didn't know if he was going to pull the trigger right then and there or not. Blocked in on three sides by the large rocks, she had no place to escape to if he decided to shoot her.

Crocker glared his hatred for the space of a second, then angled away from her and positioned himself against a rock. Kate knew that he could see her every move as well as any movement below.

She sensed the instant Crocker spotted Brannigan. A certain light of madness came into his eyes, and he tensed like a bow drawn tight. He aimed his rifle straight at Brannigan.

Frantically, Kate reached up with her bound hands and tugged on the gag, but couldn't loosen it. Desperate to do something, she stepped forward, not caring if Crocker knew it. She wasn't going to stand by meekly and let him kill the man she loved.

Brannigan came into her view, and Kate did the only thing she could think of doing without being able to cry out a warning before Crocker fired. She lowered her head and slammed her body into Joe Crocker's tensed body.

In the next instant, the roar of Crocker's gun sounded in Kate's ear seconds before the impact of her body sent them both rolling over the ledge.

Eighteen

"Kate, no!" Brannigan's hoarse cry of alarm went unheeded and too late.

He watched in paralyzed horror as she shoved Joe Crocker, and he heard the rifle shot as if from a far distance.

The rest happened in a blur of confusion and movement. Kate and Joe Crocker disappeared over the side of the embankment at almost the same time that the impact of the bullet tore into his side.

"Kate!" he cried out again before the blackness swirled over him, taking him down. Down . . .

Kate heard Brannigan's voice calling her name as she grabbed for anything to stop her fall. Rolling downward, she screamed against the gag in panic and felt a branch jab her in the back. Snatching at it, she missed. She rolled one more time, then came to a jarring halt against an outcropping of brush.

Joe Crocker's bellow echoed through her mind. She cringed and held to the brush as if her very life depended on it. All around her, rocks rained down, tumbling to the pit below. The rattling noise rose up from below in a fierce commotion that struck terror into her very being. She closed her eyes tight against the images the sound brought.

Moments later, it fell silent around her. She opened her eyes and saw that she had only rolled a short distance. Luckily, the brush had stopped her body's downward momentum before the ground sloped too steeply. She'd been saved from the horrible snakes below.

Could rattlesnakes climb? The question pierced the numbness that was threatening to settle in her limbs. She didn't know the answer for sure, but wasn't about to wait around and find out. The thought of the vicious-sounding creatures climbing up the pit after her spurred her into action.

Pushing with her feet, she scooted and clawed her way back up to the flat ground above. Once there, she rested her cheek against the earth for a moment, but a sense of urgency spurred her onward. She might not be safe from the snakes yet.

Or from Joe Crocker. Her panic of the snakes below had chased all thoughts of the outlaw from her mind, but now her equal fear of him returned. He could be only inches behind her. Heaven only knew how close he might be to where she rested at his very moment.

She could only hope that Joe Crocker wasn't too near, and she still had a chance at escape. She dared not hope for more than that right now.

Once she'd managed to scramble to her feet, she gathered up her shattered courage and peered back down over the edge, searching for the outlaw. Below her the ground sloped away in a steeper decline than she'd realized before, coming to an end in a narrowed pit. At the bottom of the pit lay the crumpled body of Joe Crocker covered by the rock slide and the slithering rattlesnakes.

Kate turned away from the horror below and ran for the far side of the small clearing. With her bound hands, she yanked at the gag in her mouth, finally freeing it. She was going to be sick.

She kept her gaze from straying to the direction of the pit, although it pulled at her with a gruesome force. When her stomach was empty, she turned around, careful to focus her eyes on her feet. A sharp rock near her right foot snagged and held her attention. It angled to a sharp point—sharp enough to cut through the rope binding her hands.

Bending down, Kate rubbed the rope back and forth over the rock's edge. One thought consumed her mind. She had to get away from this place. Brannigan was waiting for her.

Desperation ate at her, and she couldn't get away fast enough. She sawed at the rope with renewed fervor, and finally the frayed edges of the rope snapped. Grabbing up her tattered skirt and petticoat, she began to run back down the path. The slight incline slowed her descent, and she chafed at the slow speed she was forced to go to navigate her way down safely. The only thing that restrained her was concern over falling and breaking her neck in the process.

At last, she reached the flat ground below and skidded to a halt. She'd expected Brannigan to meet her, but there was no sign of him. Her heart raced, and her next breath lodged in her throat.

Had something happened to him? She brushed her foolishness aside. He must have taken cover at the first gunshot and hadn't seen her scrambling down the rise yet. That had to be it. He couldn't know that Joe Crocker was dead.

"Brannigan!" she called. "It's over."

Waiting for his response, her nerves stretched to the tautness of a violin string. Where was Brannigan?

"It's over," she repeated. "Crocker's dead."

The finality of her words struck her, and she stopped, unable to say another word. Nausea caused her stomach to lurch, and she fought it down. It was over, she told herself. Think of that. Only that.

Shading her eyes against the sun, Kate scanned the area for any sign of Brannigan. She nibbled on her lower lip out of habit, worrying. To her left she finally spotted his horse and sighed in relief.

Brannigan was nearby. He was . . .

Then, she saw him. Her heart raced, then thudded in her chest. Brannigan lay crumpled on the ground, deathly still. Recollection of Crocker's rifle shot rang through her mind, and she knew with absolute certainty that he'd hit Brannigan.

Kate bit back her sob of terror. No, he had to be all right.

She ran towards him, offering up a premature prayer that he was alive. Clenching her hands tightly in her skirts, she kept repeating her prayer over and over. He *had* to be alive.

When she reached him, he was lying on his side, his head turned away from her. Hardly daring to breathe herself or even swallow, she knelt down beside him and rolled him over. Her hand came away red with blood, and she bit back the scream that lodged in her throat.

Blood, so much blood. It covered her hand as well as the side of his shirt, seeping around even to the front of the fabric.

Horror washed over her anew. Oh no, he was . . .

She couldn't even finish the thought.

A low moan sounded, and at first she didn't know who had made the noise— herself or Brannigan. It sounded again, and she realized it was Brannigan.

His eyelids fluttered a moment, stilled, then he opened his eyes and gazed into her terror-filled gaze. His deep blue eyes mirrored his concern for her, and Kate felt like weeping at the wonderful sight.

He was alive.

The cold fist of fear that had clutched her heart began to melt and release its iron-clad grip on her. She blinked back the tears of joy and reaction that burned behind her eyes.

Brannigan stared into her teary gaze for a moment. Time itself stood still while she offered up a silent prayer of thanks.

Thank you, God, she repeated, *thank you.*

At a low moan of pain from Brannigan, her prayer stopped in mid word. What was she supposed to do now? How did one start to take care of a bullet wound?

Mrs. Parker's Finishing School back in Boston had never covered this in any of her classes. The instructor had never even mentioned to her students what to do with a wounded, bleeding man.

"Oh, Brannigan, what do I do now?" she asked him.

His eyelids fluttered closed, and Kate's mouth dropped open in surprise.

"No, don't!" she called out. "Don't you dare pass out on me!"

His eyes opened at her commanding shout, and a faint smile graced his lips. Kate smiled back in relief.

"Well?" she prompted. "What am I supposed to do?"

Brannigan tried to smile but winced instead. "Got to stop the bleeding."

He slid his hand across his stomach and gritted his teeth as he checked the wound. His breath whistled out between his tightly clenched teeth.

"What?" Kate leaned forward.

"Bullet's gone. It only creased me."

Thank heavens there was no bullet to deal with. She didn't know how she would have done it. Or even what she would need to do to start. Mrs. Parker most assuredly hadn't covered bullets and their removal in her lady's decorum class.

Kate searched her mind for the best source of information on the subject of bullets— her forbidden novels she'd sneaked into her room at the school. Yes, one in particular had elaborated on the wounded gunfighter's injuries. First, they'd cleaned the wound and then bandaged it tight, wrapping it first with damp cloth then dry.

Feeling more secure in her knowledge, she sent Brannigan a reassuring smile. "Leave everything to me."

She could have sworn she heard him groan. But of course a wounded man would do that.

Speed would be of importance, she thought to herself and hurried over to Brannigan's horse where she retrieved his canteen. Once she reached his side again, she started the task of getting him bandages.

Tossing aside futile modesty, she hiked up her skirt and ripped off the ruffle of her lavender petticoat. The fine, expensive material would make an excellent bandage, although her papa would be horrified if he knew the use to which she'd put the garment this day.

Seconds later, another strip followed the first. When she thought she had enough material, her fancy petticoat was half gone.

She wet a strip from the water in the canteen and gathered up her courage. Using both hands to grip the soggy material, she wiped it across the bloody area on Brannigan's side. When she heard his breath hiss out between his teeth, she halted, sure there was no way that she could continue. But she knew she had to. There was no one else to do it.

Gripping the cloth even tighter, she resumed her task. There was so much blood. If this was only a crease, it was one hell of a crease.

She folded another long strip, making it into a thick pad, then placed it over the wet cloth, pressing against the wound. Biting her lip, she forced herself to continue holding it tightly against his side, even when she saw him wince and grit his teeth.

If Crocker wasn't already dead, she'd like to stomp up there and shoot him for doing this to Brannigan.

The vehemence of the thought startled her. She'd never experienced this surge of protectiveness toward another person in her entire life It was an earthshaking emotion, she realized.

With a sigh, she grabbed up the torn ruffle to her petticoat and wrapped the dry material around Brannigan's side and chest. Around and around she passed the cloth until he was wrapped in lavender.

Finished, she sat back on her heels. "Anything else?" she prompted.

"Need to get out of the sun," he spoke with difficulty. The strain of his injury and her nursing was beginning to show.

Kate tilted her head back and gazed up at the bright ball of sun in the sky. Its brilliant rays bounced off everything around them, heating the ground beneath them and radiating heat from the rocks around them. Now just how was she supposed to accomplish the feat of finding them a precious patch of shade?

As if he'd sensed her question, Brannigan added, "There's a cave back a ways. Passed it on the way here." He drew in a rough breath.

Kate placed her fingertips gently across his lips. "Don't say anymore. I'll find it."

She recalled passing several caves on the way here with Crocker. Intent on checking where her strips of lace were landing, she'd observed much of the surrounding scenery at the same time. All she had to do was follow her trail of lavender lace in reverse, and it would lead her to one of those caves.

However, first she had to get them both on the horses. Definitely not a job she relished. Easing away from Brannigan was one of the hardest things she ever had to do. She ran a hand over his forehead a moment before she turned and headed for the horses.

Glancing back at him, she realized there was no way she was willing to risk his riding alone and possibly sliding off should he lose consciousness. That meant they'd have to share one horse. Now how on earth was she supposed to get them both up on one of those beasts?

Kate retrieved the horses, all the while searching her mind for a solution, while carefully tying one horse a short distance away. She had no intention of dealing with more than one of the beasts at a time.

As she led the saddled mount back to where Brannigan lay, he attempted to lean up. Kate thought she might faint with relief. Now she didn't have to figure out how to lift him on the horse.

It took two tries before Brannigan was seated on the horse, but they'd finally accomplished the task together. Breathless from the exertion, Kate stepped back, panting. Now all she had to do was climb on as well.

The prospect was daunting to say the least. She eyed the tall animal and tried to mentally measure the distance from the ground to the stirrup which had Brannigan's foot in it. Well, cross that possibility off the list, she thought to herself. She'd have to find another way up.

Spying a large rock with a flat edge, Kate kept one hand on Brannigan's leg and led the huge horse over to the side of the rock. She only hoped that the beast would at least cooperate in some small measure.

Sure enough he didn't; the instant she grasped the back of the saddle, the beast sidestepped. She pulled the horse back closer to the rock again.

"Easy, there. Easy," she muttered, not sure if she was attempting to calm the horse or herself.

Once the huge animal settled back down and stood still for a minute, she told herself it was time to get it over with. Stepping up onto the rock, she slung one leg over the horse's rump and grabbed hold of the back of the saddle to pull herself in place. To her immense relief, the horse stopped moving, and she found herself safely aboard and seated behind Brannigan.

Kate released her breath in a ragged sigh. While it had certainly been easier than hauling herself up with her foot in the stirrup, it was not something she'd ever like to try again. She'd been certain the beast was going to kick her or stomp on her at any second by the uneasy way he kept shifting around.

She hadn't been certain if she was going to end up on the horse or under it. Actually she shuddered at either one. Someday a brilliant person was going to invent a mode of transportation that didn't require one of these creatures. At least she hoped they would.

This time she remembered to gently nudge the horse's side with her heels, and they set out at a slow walk. As they passed the second horse, Kate leaned over and grabbed up the reins. It was working, she thought in amazement and a hint of pride.

However, before long both emotions fled with a vengeance. She soon learned that one horse didn't automatically follow the other out of some sort of horsey instinct like she'd expected it to do. By the time they reached the cave, Brannigan was sagging against her, Kate was exhausted and had never hated a horse more in her life.

The chore of dismounting was accomplished with a great deal of huffing and puffing. Kate even used a few of the choice words she'd learned from Miss Sally.

Once she half-carried, half-dragged Brannigan into the cave and got him settled on the tattered bedroll, she returned outside to the horses. Somebody had to tend to the animals, and she appeared to be it.

Recalling watching one of the outlaws take care of the band's horses in the camp, she followed what she remembered him doing to remove the saddle. First, she felt around under the horse's stomach until she finally located a wide band. Sensibly, this must be what held the saddle on, she reasoned. It took her several minutes before she worked the strap free.

She paused to dust her hands off on her skirt and suck in a deep breath, then she reached up for the saddle. At her sudden movement, the horse sidestepped. She jumped back out, biting back her scream. Blasted creature, what was he trying to do? Scare her to death?

"You do that again," she threatened in a low voice, "and I'm leaving that thing right where it's at."

Almost as if he'd understood her warning, the horse settled back down and stood still. Kate reached out again, cautiously keeping her eyes fixed on the animal for any sign of movement. He remained still. She clamped her hands tight on the saddle and pulled. It came free, sending her tumbling to the ground with the saddle and blanket atop her.

"Oh, ginger!"

Kate shoved the heavy thing off her legs and scrambled to her feet.

"I should have let you keep the damned thing," she grumbled to the horse.

He nickered in response.

"Don't you dare laugh at me," Kate snapped back.

She picked up the blanket and gave it a vigorous shake. Horse hair flew into the air, sprinkling down like tiny bits of snow. Promptly, she erupted into sneezes and dropped the blanket.

Heavens, the thing smelled.

She fanned the air with her hand, while giving another sneeze into her other hand. Clamping her thumb and fingers over her nose, she backed up several feet.

Once the air had settled, she gingerly picked the blanket back up from the ground and, holding it as far away as possible, she crossed to a nearby bush. She tossed the blanket across the bush like she'd seen the outlaws do with their items in the camp.

Feeling quite proud of herself, she dragged the saddle over to the bush and kicked it in place beside where the blanket hung down. Next, she retraced her footsteps back to the horses.

A small bush stood near the animals. It was small enough not to interfere with their movement during the night. Yes, she thought, it looked perfect for the task. Smiling, she carefully looped the leather reins around a branch.

Standing aback to survey her work, she pronounced it commendable. Even Mrs. Parker couldn't complain with either her neatness or efficiency.

Wouldn't Brannigan be surprised at what she'd done?

When Brannigan awoke the first thing he noticed was that they were in a cave. The second thing was that he was wrapped up like a Christmas package. All that was missing was a bow.

He stare down at the pretty strips of lavender criss-crossing over and around his chest. Lavender? He shook his head. Thank goodness Buck couldn't see him now.

"Brannigan?" Kate whispered across the short distance separating them.

He turned his head and spotted her curled up on a blanket, her feet tucked under her. Shimmering copper curls tumbled about her shoulders in the disarray he was coming to expect. Her fancy gown was definitely far worse for wear this time, and for once her parasol was missing.

As he stared at her, he realized that the strips of cloth around his chest matched the color of her gown, but they definitely weren't silk. He rubbed his thumb across one corner of the fabric and realized with a jolt that he was wearing her petticoat.

"What in heaven?" he asked, easing himself up on his elbow. Pain shot through his side like a hot poker.

"You were shot," Kate answered. "Don't you remember?"

"I meant this." He gestured to the colorful strips binding his chest.

"I stopped the bleeding like you said, then bandaged you."

"With your purple petticoat?"

"It was all I had available." She shrugged one dainty shoulder.

"The lace you left me to track was purple too," he observed in a dazed voice. His head was beginning to hurt.

"Um huh."

"Does everything you wear match?" he abruptly asked in disbelief.

Kate looked affronted. "Of course."

"Why?"

She simply blinked at his question. "Because . . . ," she paused. "Well, because it's supposed to. Now go back to sleep."

His lips twitched at her response. Ah hah, she didn't know why either. Satisfied, he closed his eyes.

The next time Brannigan awoke it was nearing dusk. He blinked at the dim light filtering into the cave and searched for Kate.

She sat less than two feet away, her head leaned back against the side of the cave. Her eyes were closed, and he simply enjoyed looking at her for a minute.

Soon, realization of their situation brought him up short. She was alive and safe, but with no thanks to him. He hadn't done a very good job of protecting her. Guilt gnawed at him like a persistent creature seeking satisfaction.

He'd almost cost Kate her life. The same as Elizabeth.

He must have made some sound because Kate sat upright with a start. When she saw him watching her, she sent him a tentative smile.

"How are you feeling?"

"Like a horse that's been rode hard and put away wet."

She smiled at his answer. "Hungry? I found some food in your saddlebags."

At his look of disbelief, she gestured to where both sets of saddlebags were propped against one wall of the cave as if it were a common everyday occurrence.

Kate crossed to the bags and withdrew the provisions, chattering the entire time. "There's some meat, I think it's what Buck calls jerky. And some biscuits, but they appear awfully hard. Oh, and I

found your matches, so there's some coffee outside
on the fire."

Brannigan heard the words, but he could
scarcely believe them. Less than two months ago
she never would have considered searching out
food for them. Miss Kate Danville of Boston would
have simply assumed that food would naturally appear whenever and wherever at the proper time
when she became hungry. And she didn't even
complain at the hard biscuits or stringy meat jerky.
Although he wasn't sure he wanted to even dare
to try her attempt at coffee.

He smiled at this. Oh, Kate was still spoiled,
never doubt that, but she was becoming quite love-
able. And damned near irresistible.

Nineteen

The next morning, Kate stepped outside the cave. A beautiful, sunny day greeted her. She inhaled the fresh air and stretched in the sunshine. Glancing around herself, she suddenly felt a chill of dread and disbelief run down her spine.

Both the horses and the little bush she'd tied them to were gone.

She raced to the spot and saw the small clump of dirt that had held the bush in place. Oh, no. Shading her eyes against the sun, she searched the area that stretched out around her as far as she could see.

No horses.

Kate squeezed her eyes shut and swore, "Hell and damnation."

Brannigan and she were stranded. On foot. And days out of Deadrange.

"You did what?" Brannigan shouted, his voice echoing off the cave walls.

Kate flinched at the clamor, but gave back as good as she got. "I didn't do it. The horses did."

He stared at her. He should have known this wouldn't last. Kate was becoming more resistible by the minute.

"Any fool knows to tether their horses."

"I did that," she announced proudly in self defense.

Brannigan strode to the cave entrance. "Kate, exactly what did you tie them to?"

"Why, to the bush."

"What bush?"

She pointed to the newly barren spot where the bush obviously used to be. Now only the displaced clump of dirt remained as evidence. "There." Her voice came out meek for once.

Brannigan forced back the rest of what he'd been about to say. It wouldn't do any good to tell her that they were stranded, or to inform her of the dangers they now faced. Or to tell her that the chances were they might not make it back alive.

He rubbed the persistent ache at the back of his neck. It was beginning to hurt worse than his side.

"Kate—"

She raised her hands and stepped away from him. "Not another word. I'll take care of it."

"Kate—"

With a defiant toss of her head, she entered the cave and crossed to the saddlebags. She grabbed up a handful of money from the pouch and stormed back out of the cave before he could stop her.

Brannigan started to run after her, but a sharp pain in his side reminded him it was better if he didn't. She wouldn't go far, he reasoned. Knowing Kate, he knew she'd be back within minutes. All he had to do was give her time to cool off.

Within half an hour, Kate was hot, dusty, and she'd emptied her slippers of dirt and sand more times than she could count. She longed for the cool shade of the cave. And for Brannigan, she admitted.

Keeping to the trail, she plodded on. After another thirty minutes of walking, she'd about given up of finding anything but more dust. Then, she saw it.

It couldn't be. She shaded her eyes against the blazing sun and stared in open-mouthed amazement at the apparition before her. She couldn't believe it.

Why, if she hadn't read in Mrs. Parker's imported San Francisco paper back home about this experiment taking place in the Nevada Territory, she would question her sanity at what she beheld spread out before her. Thank heavens her finishing school instructor had insisted that all her young ladies be well read.

Kate still found this sight hard to believe.

She continued to stare at the procession of eleven— she counted them twice to be certain— eleven huge, awkward-looking, humpbacked beasts plodding across the sand. No, she wasn't crazed. They were real. A smile of disbelief mixed with elation spread across her lips. A camel train loaded with goods was coming towards her!

She let out a very unladylike whoop of joy. They were saved.

She curled her fingers around the roll of money in her pocket. All she had to do was to convince the man in charge to rent her and Brannigan a camel for the return trip to Deadrange.

Convincing the camel train leader to rent her a camel for what she was certain had been an exorbitant amount had been the easy part. However, convincing Brannigan of the wisdom of her decision was another matter entirely.

As soon as she entered the cave, he proceeded to yell at her for disappearing. She noted the concern that was all but hidden with his words, but she was too tired to give a whit.

"Hell and damnation, where have you been?" he shouted at her for the third time.

"Dammit, I found us transportation!" she yelled back.

She didn't bother to mention that by the time she'd ridden this particular transportation ten minutes, she disliked it worse than she did a horse. In fact, she was rapidly coming to hate it. Not only had the creature tried to bite her at every opportunity, it had horrible breath which smelled like dead broccoli. She repressed a shiver of revulsion.

"What? You found the horses?" He shook his head in disbelief. "I figured they were long gone."

"Not exactly."

"Not exactly what?"

"I said I'd take care of things, and I did. But it's not exactly a horse," she hedged.

"Kate, you didn't get a burro, did you?"

"Not exactly."

Brannigan sent her a suspicious look and strode past her. Once outside, he stopped dead still. Kate was following right on his heels and careened into his back, shoving him forward unintentionally. He stepped back, bumping her.

There, standing in the sunlight, tied to a huge rock, stood a camel. The animal's coat was brown with flecks of gray, and it turned its head to stare back at them, peaceably chewing its cud. The next instant, the camel spit, barely missing both Brannigan and Kate.

Brannigan jumped to the side, not willing to take one step nearer. "A camel. You bought a damn camel." His voice raised in shock.

"Of course not," she assured him. "I rented it."

"You got us a damn camel?"

"Yes." Kate sent him a false smile of self-confidence.

Of course the beast would choose now to spit at them. Not that it hadn't done it to her numerable times on the trip here. However it could most assuredly have waited, couldn't it?

She closed her eyes and waited for the coming explosion from Brannigan. She didn't have long to wait.

"Hell and damnation. Whatever possessed you to do this?" he charged.

"I suppose you had a better idea," she snapped back at him, hurt by his reaction and not willing to admit that she'd had a few reservations about the brilliance of her inspiration during the ride. She refused to confess that she may possibly have made a mistake.

"Yes. One hell of a lot better one." Brannigan rubbed the back of his neck, never taking his eyes off the camel.

"What?" Kate demanded to know his idea.

He paused and blinked at her rapid-fire question and chanced glancing away from the camel for a minute.

"Well? What is your idea?" she prompted, with her hands balled into fists and planted firmly on her hips. "A horse?" she offered the suggestion, her voice dripping with sarcasm.

Glancing to her left, then her right, she leaned forward and asked directly in his ear, "Tell me, do you see any horses around here?"

"No—"

"Would you suggest we walk to Deadrange?" She stepped around him and continued talking.

"No, I—"

"Sorry, but I don't see any buggies here either, do you?" She gestured to the wide open space around them.

"Dammit, Kate, will you let me get a word in?"

"Do you have one worth listening to?" She crossed her arms over her chest and proceeded to tap her foot.

"All right," he surrendered. "You took care of things."

"I—"

This time he cut her off, "But did you have to find a camel?"

Kate opened her mouth, then snapped it shut. Finally, she admitted only one thing in a low mutter, "It was all I could find."

Brannigan sighed and clamped his hand on her shoulder. "Like I said, you did take care of things," he offered in slight apology. "Well, then, shall we mount up and get going?"

Kate cringed at his suggestion. In truth, the last thing she ever wanted to do was get back on the camel. She was convinced the thing hated her, but there was no way that she could admit this to Brannigan. No way whatsoever.

She gulped and answered. "After you."

"I'll get our gear." He turned on his booted heel and strode back into the cave. Within minutes, he returned to her side with the saddlebags and bedroll.

Staring at the camel in distrust, Brannigan took a step forward, then stopped. "What is that thing supposed to be?"

Kate barely stopped herself from flinching at the question. She blinked and pretended innocent misunderstanding. She'd hoped he wouldn't notice the saddle, or at the least that he wouldn't question it. "What are you talking about? It's a camel."

He muttered something and pointed at the contraption sitting atop the large hump. "What is that?"

She raised her chin a notch in defiance and said calmly, "It's a saddle."

Brannigan narrowed his eyes and sent her a look that clearly said he wasn't buying her explanation for a single moment.

Under his intense scrutiny, she added, "Take my word for it, that's the best camel saddle that money can buy."

She wasn't about to admit to him the thing was a makeshift saddle the camel driver had hastily put together with scattered bits of leather and canvas. Or that he'd charged her dearly for it.

Why, she bet she could have likely bought a whole horse— saddle, bridle, oats, and all for less money. But she'd been desperate. Obviously, the camel driver had heard of her papa's favorite phrase about desperate times and desperate measures.

Brannigan stood his ground, staring at the saddle. He didn't appear any more eager than her to climb on the beast. Kate bit back her smile. Good.

A moment later, Brannigan stepped forward with a resigned sigh and pulled down on the hackamore. The camel obediently bent down, doubling its long legs underneath it and settled down on the ground.

Kate's mouth dropped open in disbelief. The

animal had never done that for her. Now it waited most docilely as Brannigan secured their gear and climbed on the calmly waiting animal.

Kate knew the impression was entirely false. The camel had proven to be far from docile.

Brannigan leaned over and held out his hand to Kate. "Ready?"

She knew he was grinning at her, even if she couldn't catch him at it. Watching Brannigan as she was, she didn't see the camel's mouth until it caught the edge of her sleeve firmly between its teeth.

Kate jumped away from the creature, and a loud rip sounded. She caught back the scream on her lips and whirled on Brannigan. "He snapped at me."

She glared at the camel as it chewed peaceably on the bit of lavender now dangling from its mouth. At the rate her clothing was being used up, she'd be lucky to have a stitch left on her when they reached Deadrange, she thought in disgust.

"Kate, come on and climb up," Brannigan ordered. "And hurry, before she does it again."

"But he—"

"It's a she."

"It is? How do you know?"

He looked uncomfortable for a moment. "I noticed."

"Never mind, I don't want to know any more. But it tried to bite me."

"That's what camels do," he informed her.

"If it's a she, why did the camel driver tell me her name was Sheik?" Kate crossed her arms over her chest and waited for his answer.

"How the hell should I know? Maybe the owner

had a sense of humor. Now get your pretty behind—"

Kate's yelp rent the air, ringing in Brannigan's
ears.

She swiped a hand over her cheek and shivered.
"She spit on me."

"Kate, get on the damn camel."

"So much for what that newspaper article had
said about the camels being docile and tractable
creatures," she grumbled under her breath.

Not by a long shot.

"Why, they're mean-spirited and downright vicious," she added, stalling for more time.

"Kate."

"Oh, all right. I'm coming."

She inched forward one courageous step at a
time, keeping both of her eyes firmly fixed on the
camel's head. They locked gazes and the camel
growled at her.

"Did you hear that?" she asked Brannigan.

He bit back a chuckle without much success.
"This was your idea," he reminded her.

"I didn't see you getting us any transportation,"
she shot back at him.

"Well, I sure as hell wouldn't have gotten a
camel," he muttered under his breath. "Get up
here," he added with a low growl of his own.

Kate glared back at Brannigan a moment before
she climbed up to land in front of him with a
thud. The camel promptly rose from her knees
and set off with a strange, rocking gait.

The movement was completely unlike anything
Brannigan had ever experienced before. He realized immediately it was nothing like the smooth
gait of a horse. The beast swayed from side to side
like a ship instead of an animal.

Over the course of the afternoon, the side to side movement of Kate's body pressing back against his did unusual things to Brannigan's anger. The longer they rode, the more his anger with her melted away under the heat. He tried to blame his uncomfortable warmth on the sun, but knew the source was much closer. In truth, it was pressing tightly against him from chest to thighs, and went by the name of Kate.

He shifted and attempted to focus his attention elsewhere. Anywhere, but on the pleasurable feel of Kate's sweet curves fitting so well against him.

It didn't do a bit of good. His desire for her was growing with each step of the camel and the resulting sway of Kate against him.

Why couldn't she sit ramrod straight the way she did on a horse! he asked himself. Instead it seemed the rocking of the camel's movement relaxed her, and she leaned back comfortable between his legs.

Hell and damnation, he should be avoiding any contact with her, Brannigan told himself. He should be keeping his mind free of any thoughts of her sweet body, and instead concentrate on the area around them. He should be watching for any possible dangers.

The hell with should. What he wanted to do was stop the camel and make passionate love to Kate right here and now. But what he was going to do was protect her. From any and all danger, including him.

He intended to keep his feelings for her under control and hidden as far away from her as possible. He would not let anything happen to Kate, and he'd come to the conclusion that Nevada provided entirely too much danger for a city lady like Kate.

As soon as they reached Deadrange, he was going to put her safely aboard the very next stage headed East himself and send her straight back to her precious Boston. And safety.

Kate sensed the change in Brannigan even before they stopped for the day. He'd become distant and polite. And irritating as could be.

He responded to her conversation in as short of sentences as possible, sometimes with only an aggravating "yup" as an answer.

What in heaven had caused this change to come over him? An uneasy feeling traced its way down her back like a sharp fingernail.

What was going on? She fully intended to find out and do something about it. She longed to have back the same Brannigan who had made such tender love to her the night before.

Tonight he'd chosen another cave for them to make camp in. Kate wrinkled up her nose. While she had to admit that a cave had proven to be better than the ground, she still didn't have to like it. She could hardly wait until they reached Deadrange and a real bed.

When the recalcitrant camel refused to kneel down for him, Kate took one glance at the long distance down to the ground and pointed out a large rock nearby.

"That's how I climbed up on your horse, why shouldn't it work for a camel?" she suggested.

Brannigan guided the animal alongside the large rock and then dismounted. He helped Kate down, but she noticed that he carefully kept just enough distance between them so that their bodies didn't touch.

What in heaven's name was going on with the man?

Right now, she was almost too uncomfortable to care. She felt as if a layer of dust covered every square inch of her body, and what the dust missed, the camel smell surely made up for, she was certain of it.

"What I wouldn't give for a bath." She looked up at Brannigan and sighed loudly, then wrinkled up her nose. "I smell like a camel."

The tiniest of smiles pulled at his lips before he answered. "There's a hot spring that runs through this area. After we make camp, I'll see if I can find it for you."

Kate reached out and hugged him. "Oh, yes. Yes. Yes."

Brannigan couldn't help but chuckle at her exuberance. "If only you'd show that much enthusiasm for setting up camp."

Kate promptly stuck her tongue out at him. "Just for that remark, I'll make dinner, and you can do the rest."

She turned and sauntered away from him and the camel who'd been eyeing her sleeve again.

Brannigan watched her leave, and the ache in his body increased tenfold, until he remembered that the only provisions they had for her to work with were more jerky and hard biscuits. The only portion of work she had to do was set out the food.

"Dammit, Kate," he muttered.

Her soft laughter was his only answer.

Once he'd unloaded the camel and staked the animal so it couldn't wander off, he checked out the cave. It had a nice sized opening and an even larger room inside. A fire would make it cozy, and tonight, he'd make the coffee— no matter if Kate had offered. His stomach still knotted each time he recalled the taste of her first attempt at brewing coffee.

As he'd promised, he set off to check and see if he could find Kate a pool of water safe for bathing. Luck followed him, and he discovered a hot spring running through the other chamber of the cavern. The steamy, gurgling water tempted him, but he made himself agree to wait until after Kate had bathed. Then his turn would come.

"Kate, I found your water," he announced as he returned to the entrance.

"Where?" She gazed at him as if he had just performed a feat of magic.

He pointed over his shoulder with his thumb. "In the next chamber— "

Kate hugged him so hard, she knocked the breath out of him.

"Kate," he coughed once.

She drew back and stared at her toes. "Yes?" Her smile peeked out at him.

"You need to watch— "

"Bears, I knew it." She propped her hands on her hips. "I'm going to have to share my bath with a smelly bear now. I— "

"No, Kate. There aren't any bears in the cave. I've checked it out. The only ones here are you and me."

This brought a strange smile to her face that made him decidedly uneasy.

"What you need to watch out for is the water temperature."

He felt like telling her that what she needed to beware of was him, if she kept smiling that way. It was pure invitation. And mighty hard for a man to resist.

"The closer you are to the source, the hotter the water," he explained. "You got that?"

She nodded in agreement. "The closer I get, the hotter things get," she repeated in a complete twisting of his explanation.

Brannigan swallowed around the lump that had formed in his throat in response to her words. Damn, what was the woman trying to do to him?

At his silence, Kate swept up her skirts and strolled further into the cave. He watched her until she was out of sight. Only then did he realize that the cave had gotten unusually warm.

"Be careful, Kate," he called out, unable to resist at least saying something to her.

Looking back over her shoulder, Kate wondered what had come over Brannigan. He was back to blowing hot then cool, like an early spring that couldn't decide if it was time to warm up yet or not.

She sighed, pondering the problem and took another step forward. The next instant, her right foot met air and she tumbled. Right into the pool of water with a resounding splash.

Kate's scream sent Brannigan racing for the next chamber. As his boot heels met the splashed puddle of water, he slid into a skid. Flailing his arms to regain his balance, he landed right in the pool of water beside Kate.

They both came up sputtering at the same time. Kate shoved her hair back out of her eyes and blew out a mouthful of water.

"Why did you scream?" Brannigan demanded, wiping water from his face.

"I fell in."

Brannigan shook his head in amazement, sending a fine spray of water splattering over her. "Only you could fall in."

"Oh?" She cocked her head at him in challenge. "And exactly what do you call what you did?"

"I . . ." He fell silent a moment. Only Kate could manage to turn the tables on him.

"Yes?" she prompted, scooping up a handful of the warm water and throwing it at him.

He responded by slapping the water in front of him, sending up a small wall of water. It hit Kate squarely in the face.

She sputtered and immediately splashed back, catching him off guard and pelting him with water.

"I'll get you for that." He advanced a step.

"At least it wasn't ice cold," she remarked with a grin that was pure temptation, splashing him again.

That smile did strange things to his body. It made him ignore the little voice in the back of his mind that was saying no. He allowed his gaze to travel down, past the water dripping off her chin to where the droplets were landing on her breasts. Her wet gown clung to her like a second skin, outlining and emphasizing her breasts.

Brannigan swallowed, but something caught at his throat.

"Kate, I'd better go."

Her gaze met his, and he was held spellbound as if by a force of magic.

Her softly whispered, "Why?" hit him like a punch to the gut.

He ground the words out, "Dammit, Kate, I'm trying to be noble."

"Why?" she whispered again.

Right then, he couldn't for the life of him remember the answer.

The flickering light from the campfire reflected
off the walls, lighting the chamber with a warm,
seductive glow. It turned Kate's silken skin the
color of golden honey, and turned his resolve into
the consistency of overheated butter.

In one swift move, he swept her into his arms,
covering her mouth with his. She tasted wet, and
inviting, and like pure heaven. He groaned against
her lips, his reasoning fleeing as if defeated in a
fierce battle.

The water swirled around them, enclosing them
in a cocoon of warmth. The currents caught at
Kate's skirt, tugging. Brannigan reached up and
assisted. Within moments, he tossed the dress over
the side of the pool. It fell into a pile of silken
color.

At the far end of the pool, near the source, wisps
of steam floated upward to disappear into the dim
firelight. Their clothes disappeared just as quickly
until nothing separated them but the warm, caressing water pluming around and between them.

Brannigan's gaze met hers, pulling at her with
more force than the water possessed. Without saying a word, he commanded her attention, demanded her surrender, begged for her love.

Kate gave all to him willingly, lovingly, totally.
She knew that no matter what else had happened
between them or could happen in the future, she
loved him more than life itself.

Looking into his loving gaze, Kate decided then
and there that she no longer wanted to leave. She
had no intention of returning to Boston.

In the next instant, all thought of anything but
his touch fled her mind as surely as the wisps of

steam floating away. Brannigan drew her to him, until nothing separated them.

Over the next two days of travel, Brannigan developed a new respect for Kate. He learned she was far from the useless city woman he'd believed her to be. Kate Danville of Deadrange was far from being a helpless bit of fluff that she appeared to be on the surface. She could take care of herself, as well as take care of him when the need had arisen.

However, everything changed when they rode into Deadrange. The peace between them was shattered.

The moment Kate and Brannigan reached the main street of the town, pandemonium erupted. A team of horses bolted down the street, dragging the wagon behind them as the team careened out of control. The wagon tilted, dumping Frank Jones's new shipment of liquor.

Before Kate could do more than blink, a dog ran out into the street, barking and snapping at the camel's heels. The camel promptly blew its cud at Miss Sally as she stood openmouthed on the boardwalk in front of Peabody's General Store.

In sharp contrast, Sheik, the camel, lowered her head and stood calmly in place, paying absolutely no attention to the commotion around her.

Kate ducked her head and closed her eyes as she heard Brannigan swear. Nearby a woman screamed. Things couldn't get worse.

The second Kate opened her eyes, she knew she was wrong. Half the town stood around, staring at her and Brannigan. She could feel him stiffen. Not only could things get worse—they had!

"Katherine!" a familiar voice called out.

Kate cringed. She'd recognize that voice anywhere. No one said her name in that particular tone except William Danville.

She turned her head to see her papa striding towards her. In his wake trotted Richard Hale.

"Kate, my dear!" Richard shouted.

"Hell and damnation," she muttered.

The camel growled, and a nearby horse reared and threw its rider into the dirt. Kate watched in continuing horror as Deputy Tom Avery stood to his feet and brushed himself off. His horse reared again and raced off through town as if his very life was being threatened. The deputy swore in a low tight voice.

Kate closed her eyes again. Oh, ginger.

"Folks," Deputy Avery raised his voice and shouted over the din that was erupting.

Calm through all the ruckus, the camel chose now to change her mind. The animal took two quick steps away from the deputy.

"Now, stop right there. Dammit, Marshal, don't you know it's against the law to bring a camel through town in daytime?"

Behind her, Brannigan swore under his breath.

Deputy Avery strode up to them. "Sorry, Marshal. I hate to do this, but it's the law. You're both under arrest."

Twenty

"Dagnamit!" Buck called out from the safety of the raised boardwalk. "Kate done found herself a camel." He slapped his thigh and burst into gruff laughter.

Deputy Avery shifted uncomfortably. "Will you stay quiet, Buck. I got a big enough problem without you adding to it any."

"Well, dagnamit Tom, if Kate's camel is your problem, I can lead or corral anything that walks on four legs." He winked at Kate. "And some things on two legs, too."

"It's not *my* camel," Kate injected into the conversation, but no one paid her any attention.

She noticed that Brannigan was remaining strangely quiet, and she could almost feel the tension coiled up in him. Oh, ginger.

The deputy ignored them both and sent Buck a scorching look that had little or no effect on the older man.

"Hey, Tom," Buck paused to rub the whiskers on his chin. "Supposing that Kate's camel weren't in town, there wouldn't be anything wrong then, would there?"

"It's not my camel," Kate repeated.

"As long as I don't see a camel in town, there's

nothing to arrest anybody for," Deputy Avery admitted with a grin.

Buck stepped down off the wooden boardwalk and in practically no time at all, he took charge of the bedlam surrounding their arrival, bringing calm in its place. He coaxed Sheik into kneeling, shooed off the barking dog, and calmed Miss Sally.

The last Kate saw of Sheik, the camel, was Buck leading it away with one arm. He had his other arm firmly around Miss Sally's rotund waist.

Brannigan helped Kate down from the animal's back. He remained silent and stiff to her.

"Katherine?" her papa called out.

"Papa!" Kate raced the few steps separating them, and threw herself into her father's arms.

He straightened his suit coat and cleared his throat. "Katherine, dear girl, we're in public."

Kate closed her eyes on the sudden rush of tears his words brought. How could she have forgotten how much importance her father placed on appearances? Blinking back the moisture behind her eyes, she stepped away. She could feel Brannigan's searching gaze on her, but couldn't meet his eyes yet.

"Of course, Papa. I'm sorry," she said the expected words.

"I can't believe whatever has come over you." Her papa stepped back and observed her. "Why, look at your clothing."

Kate raised her chin. Things were most assuredly returning back to normal with a vengeance.

"Yes, Papa," she answered in a soft voice that didn't reveal any of the hurt feelings underneath. She silently assured herself that her father cared;

he had a difficult time showing it. And she had a difficult time believing her own assurances.

The disapproving silence stretched between them, snaking out to envelop those standing around.

Deputy Avery cleared his throat and stepped up to Brannigan's side. "Darn it all, Marshal. Did you have to bring that critter into town in daytime?" He scratched his head.

Brannigan sent the departing camel a look of pure disgust.

"Let's just say I had my mind on something else." There was little doubt that the something else behind his words had been Kate.

He couldn't believe that he had managed to completely forget all about the law against camels being in town during daylight hours. He rubbed the growing ache at the back of his neck. The damned woman had made him, a sworn lawman, break the law. It was past belief.

Kate crossed over to him and tapped his arm tentatively. "Brannigan," she whispered, "are we really under arrest?"

Before he could answer, Kate's father stepped between them. "Now, see here. I'm certain this can be taken care of quickly," he decreed.

Brannigan stiffened even further. "It's already being handled."

William Danville gave Brannigan a look of dismissal and turned his attention to the deputy. "Now, see here, sir."

Kate cringed at her father's patronizing tone. Of all times for her dear papa to intervene, now was most assuredly not the time she would have chosen.

As he proceeded to automatically issue orders,

she realized that she'd never before noticed how commanding and arrogant her dear father sounded.

Then to her horror, right there in front of half the town, her father pulled out a large wad of bills. He began peeling them off.

Kate wished the dirt-packed street would open up and swallow her then and there.

"Don't you worry one little bit, Kate, my darling girl. I'll take care of everything," William Danville announced, pulling her back away from the dusty man at her side.

"Well, ah, ah," Deputy Avery stammered, at a loss of what to say or do. He turned to Brannigan. "Marshal? What do I do now?"

"I'm the one addressing you, young man," William Danville cut in. "How much is the fine?"

The deputy automatically rattled off the amount. In the next instant, several bills were shoved into his hand.

"I believe that will more than cover it." Kate's father winked broadly at the deputy, then turned away, dismissing him as if the man never existed.

"Papa?"

"Now, dear, I'm certain that's enough money."

Kate gulped in embarrassment. Did her father think he could buy everything?

Before she could utter another word, her father held out a bill to Brannigan as if he were tipping a hotel clerk.

She'd never seen Brannigan tense so stiffly in her life. He ignored the proffered money, and when he spoke his voice was every bit as tight as his lips. "Sir, I believe you should see to your daughter."

"Very well. Come along, Kate." He turned away, dismissing Brannigan as of no importance.

"Papa— ," she sputtered, as her anger rose.

"I've reserved the finest room in the hotel, if you can call it that, had to offer." He tucked her hand in the crook of his arm.

Kate jerked back and stomped her foot. "Dammit, Papa, Brannigan saved my life."

Her father looked at her in shock. "Katherine." He straightened his tie. "I'm certain the man performed his job admirably, and— "

"Papa," Kate's voice failed her.

Had her father always been like this? She'd never noticed him behaving like this in Boston. But then, she hadn't noticed a lot of things about life before she'd come to Deadrange.

She turned back to Brannigan, but he was halfway down the street, deep in conversation with Deputy Avery. Not that she blamed him for leaving. Papa and Richard, both together, were a bit much to take. Especially on a near empty stomach.

"Kate, my dear girl, we will make plans to leave here first thing in the morning," her father announced.

"Like hell," she said in shock.

"Katherine!"

"Papa, I'm staying in Deadrange," she informed him in a calm voice.

"You'll do nothing of the kind." He patted her hand in an obviously uncomfortable gesture. "You must be exhausted. I'll take care of everything for you."

"Papa, I've been taking care of myself." And liking it, she added to herself.

"Oh, but all that is over now. I'm here."

"Papa— "

"Come along, Kate. A bath and bed await you shortly. We'll discuss the matter later." He turned away and strode toward the hotel, not looking back to see if she was following.

"Yes, we most certainly will," she muttered to his departing back.

She had no intention of meekly following her father and Richard Hale back to Boston. Furthermore, she had no intention of leaving Deadrange or Brannigan.

Richard, who had been standing quietly on the sidelines, stepped forward and clasped her hand in his. He raised her hand to his lips and placed a cool kiss on her knuckles.

"Kate, my dear. I have been so worried about you. Why, I— "

Without even thinking about what she was doing, Kate wiped her hand on her skirt.

"Shut up, Richard."

She turned with a sigh of resignation and followed her father's lead to the hotel. Right now, a hot bath and a soft feather bed sounded like a small bit of heaven. It would also delay the endless questions she knew her papa was waiting to ask her. And the ensuing arguments.

At a knock on her door long after dark, Kate jumped to her feet. Brannigan. She knew it was him.

Rushing to throw open the door, she stared in disbelief at Richard Hale.

"Good evening, Kate, my dear." He sidled his way inside the open door before she could do more than gape at him.

He looked so out of place to her. His pale skin

and blond hair made her long for Brannigan's tanned firm arms and dark hair beneath her fingers. She brought her wayward thoughts up short.

"What are you doing— ?"

"Here, my dear," Richard eased her back a step farther into the room and held out a bouquet of flowers to her. "I've brought you flowers, but they can't equal your beauty. Can you ever forgive my horrid behavior?"

The scent of the blossoms was overly sweet to her, as well as his voice. Did he really expect her to kiss and make up?

Richard continued to explain in a teary voice what a mistake he'd made, confessed that he'd gotten as far as the Rustin ranch and stopped, but been too ashamed to come back to town.

Kate promptly tossed both him and his flowers out the door.

By the following afternoon, Kate was convinced that both Richard and her father believed she was a fool. She didn't know how much more of their smothering concern she could stand. She knew if she didn't escape the hotel room soon, she would surely scream the hotel down around her.

She had obediently tolerated about all the suggestions on ladylike behavior from her father that she could handle. He absolutely refused to believe she was serious about not returning with him to Boston. However, he had delayed his trip for another day.

She paced the length of her room repeatedly, sure that she'd wear a path in the wood before she was finished. While the room was much larger than the one she'd occupied previously, she still chafed to escape outside. If she could survive a little bit longer, her father would lie down for his nap, and she could get out before the walls closed in on her.

Odd, she thought, she'd never been claustrophobic before. However, she'd never had to deal with her father and Richard Hale in constant proximity before either. When had her father and Richard struck up their truce? It was more than a mite suspicious to her.

It would be just like her overly concerned father to pay Richard to try and woo her back to Boston and away from Brannigan.

They didn't have a prayer of succeeding.

Crossing to the mirror to check her appearance, she admired her soft green dress, then touched her perfectly coiffed hair. The fancy curls looked so out of place to her now. She was actually coming to like her hair simply tied back with a ribbon instead of pinned up in intricate curls.

However, that was one argument her father had won yesterday— she'd finally agreed to allow him to hire a maid to "care for her." The woman proved friendly enough, but the instant her father was out of sight, she had slipped the woman an extra bit of money to keep her secret and shooed the woman out the door.

Kate hadn't been able to stand the prodding and pampering a second longer. It was ridiculous to think that she was incapable of picking out her own clothes or dressing herself.

Smiling at the absurd thought, she scooped up her reticule and sneaked out the door. She intended to pay a visit to one Marshal Lucas Brannigan.

This time her walk took considerably longer

than ever before. It seemed that half the town of
Deadrange wanted to stop and chat with her. She
was stunned by the honest caring and concern she
felt from these people.

A memory of Miss Sally's unexpected visit came
to mind. The woman had knocked on her hotel
room door yesterday evening, handed her a basket
filled to the brim with crisp fried chicken, fluffy
biscuits, and a hot apple pie. Wiping away the first
tear that Kate had ever seen the gruff woman shed,
she'd suddenly hugged Kate close, practically
smothering her.

When Kate had dared make the mistake of gaping at the woman in disbelief, Miss Sally had
stated, "Hell's fire, gal, you saved my life. I think
it's time I made you a peace offering."

Miss Sally had certainly proven to be a surprising
woman. Why, she'd even offered Kate her job back.
Although, she had appeared a mite relieved when
Kate politely refused. However, next thing, she
had asked Kate to think about staying on in Deadrange.

The answer to that was easy. Yes, she was definitely staying in Deadrange.

Kate could scarcely wait to see the expression on
Brannigan's face when she told him the news. Perhaps it would be best to reveal it to him in private,
she thought. Perhaps on the outskirts of town, after a nice horseback ride— to escape her father and
Richard.

After the time spent with Sheik, the camel, Kate
had developed a different view of horses. They
had become an acceptable creature to her— when
compared with a camel. Yes, camels were most assuredly crossed off her list as future modes of
transportation. Forever.

She was actually beginning to look forward to her planned horseback ride with Brannigan. Alone.

Catching up her skirt in one hand, she stepped up onto the boardwalk fronting Brannigan's office. She could scarcely contain her anticipation at seeing him again. As she neared the door to the jail, she paused to place a hand over her suddenly racing heart.

What if he didn't want to go with her?

She'd drag him away from work if she had to. Why, today was a perfect day for a ride . . .

Her steps halted at the sound of her father's voice coming from within the jail building. Whatever was he doing here? Unashamed, she stepped closer, cocked her head, and listened to the conversation going on between her father and Brannigan.

"I had to come out here to see what kind of a man turned down honest money."

"Honest money?" Sarcasm coated Brannigan's question.

"The money I'm paying you to keep an eye on Kate," her father explained in an overly patient voice.

Kate stood outside the door, her feet rooted to the wooden boardwalk. Shock had rendered her speechless as well as motionless. She couldn't have uttered a single sound even if her life had depended on it.

What did her father think he was doing?

"You're forgetting something," Brannigan answered.

"What? I was certain my telegram covered everything you needed to know." Her father's voice shifted into his best banker's negotiating tone, and

Kate knew that he was shifting from one foot to
the other as well. "I may have forgotten to mention
that Kate can, ah, be rather ah . . . ," he paused.

Kate gritted her teeth, waiting for him to continue. *Rather what, Papa?* she ground out silently.

"Headstrong," he finally completed his assess-
ment.

"Is that what you call it?" Brannigan asked. "I'd
say spoiled was a bit more accurate."

Kate sucked in a sharp breath. What they said
about an eavesdropper never hearing good about
themselves was most assuredly true.

"Well, that may be valid," her father admitted.
"She can be difficult."

Stung by the words, Kate raised her chin in injured pride. How could they talk about her that
way? Why, she should walk right in there and . . .

Brannigan's next words stopped her in mid-step,
knocking the very breath from her lungs as well.

"I never agreed to take your money, Mr. Danville."

Brannigan hadn't been doing a job for her father? The true realization hit her full force, and
Kate's lips turned up in a smile of wonder. He
didn't care about the money. He truly didn't.

Kate smiled a heartfelt grin of joy. Brannigan
loved her for herself, not her father's money.

Holding her joy close, she leaned against the
wall of the building. An instant later, her father's
harsh laughter cut through her joy like a jagged-
edged knife.

"I checked on you, Marshal. You're nothing but
a lawman. You don't have the kind of money to
turn down the amount I was offering."

"My finances are none of your business."

"Everything about you is my business where my daughter is concerned. What are you up to?"

Kate heard the snap of fingers and recognized her father's usual ploy to make a point.

"That's it, isn't it? You turned down my money so that you could acquire my entire fortune by fooling Kate into marrying you."

"Mr. Danville—"

Kate scarcely recognized Brannigan's voice it was so filled with icy disdain.

"I don't give a damn about your money."

Kate grinned. Wouldn't that surprise her papa?

"Everybody cares about money."

Kate wondered how many times she'd heard that phrase while she was growing up. She'd never questioned it until she'd met Brannigan and the people of Deadrange.

"How much will it take?" her father asked in resignation.

"Take?" Brannigan repeated.

"Yes, take for you to break off this foolishness with my daughter."

Kate knew her heart had surely stopped beating as she waited for Brannigan's answer.

"Let me get this straight. You are offering to pay me to stay away from Kate?"

"Name your price, Marshal."

"Forget it." Brannigan's voice was as icy as a cold stream.

"Surely you aren't going to continue with this farce of attempting to marry her? Think about what would happen if I disowned her and left her to you. How long do you think you could afford to keep my daughter in the luxuries she's accustomed to? The luxuries she demands."

Kate opened her mouth, and barely stopped

herself in time to keep from charging into the
room. Reluctantly, she had to admit that she had
been as her father described— once. But not now.

Love meant far more than money to her now.
Far more.

"Well, if you persist in this, I won't be paying
you a thing, do you hear me?" her father suddenly
shouted. "Fine care you took of my Kate. You almost got her killed," he accused.

"I'm not asking Kate to marry me." Brannigan's
voice had a funny sounding edge to it.

Kate swallowed, and felt her earlier feelings of
joy fly away like a butterfly escaping from an open
net.

She couldn't believe what she was hearing. Brannigan didn't want to marry her. He had no intention of marrying her.

She'd heard enough. Shaking her head, she
spun around and fled back down the boardwalk
as far and as fast away from the two men as she
could get.

"Hell and damnation, Buck. The man offered
me money to stay away from Kate." Brannigan
stormed away from the window and crossed to the
chair.

"So?" his friend scratched his whiskers and
asked.

Brannigan paced back to the window and gazed
out without seeing anything outside the glass.

"Well, I'm sure as hell not taking his money."

"And you're not leaving that little gal alone
either," Buck proclaimed with a wide grin. "I
knew it. Why, you and her are— "

"No, Buck. I am."

"What?"

Brannigan leaned his forehead against the glass pane. A ragged sigh shook his shoulders. "Don't you see? I almost got her killed."

"It appears to me that you were the one who rode after her and rescued her from that band of outlaws. You brought back Kate and the town's money."

"If I'd protected her better, Joe Crocker would never had been able to get to her to kidnap her."

"Like I said, you saved her."

"Hell," Brannigan muttered, "Kate saved herself from Crocker."

Buck chortled. "Told you that gal was sturdy. She ain't gonna die easy like, no siree."

"I almost got her killed," Brannigan repeated.

"Dagnamit. If that ain't a bunch of horse—"

"No, it's the truth. Do you know how close she came to dying the same way as Elizabeth?"

Buck fell silent a moment. "Boy, don't blame yourself. I've heard the whole story. It weren't nothing the same."

"Buck, Kate almost landed in that rattlesnake pit along with Joe Crocker. She almost died from snakebite just like Elizabeth."

"Dagnamit, boy. Let the past stay buried. Elizabeth chose to light out of here in the middle of the night. She made her own death. And I'm sick and tired of listening to you keep blaming yourself just because you happened to be the one that found her dead."

Buck paused to rub his chin, then gentled his voice. "Boy, what happened is over and done with. Things was meant to be. Elizabeth weren't for you or this town. Accept it and get on with your life. Take Kate and have a life together."

"I can't."

"Humph."

"Buck, I can't ask her to give up everything to live here in Deadrange—"

"Did you ever think that maybe she might want to do just that?"

"I won't give her the opportunity. She's going to return safely to Boston. I'll see to it." He rubbed the back of his neck. "The life of a lawman and his family is too dangerous, even here in Deadrange something could happen."

"Dagnamit," Buck bellowed. "And something could happen in Boston. Ever think of that?"

Brannigan left the room as convinced as before that he had to do what was best for Kate.

By the next afternoon, Kate was furious with everyone presuming that they knew what was best for her. Why, her father had even resorted to laying out her clothes for her.

She had to admit that what was bothering her the most was Brannigan. Or rather the lack of him. He appeared to be giving her a wide berth. And she was fed up with it.

However, if Brannigan was avoiding her, Richard was doing everything in his power to regain his way back into her good graces. Nothing she said had any affect on him. Her papa must be paying him very well indeed.

Kate picked up the pillow from the bed and flung it across the room. What she wanted to do was scream— loud and long.

Frustration ate at her. She eyed the pitcher and bowl on the washstand, but couldn't bring herself to throw them and break the pretty pottery. Instead, she kicked off her slippers and threw them against the wall. They bounced to the floor with a very unsatisfying soft thump.

Kate was miserable. Brannigan no longer wanted her, and once again her father was taking over every aspect of her life, even down to choosing the color of her gowns. Things surely couldn't get much worse than this, she thought in disgust.

How had everything gone so wrong?

Back on the trail with Brannigan those days, she'd been so sure that he loved her. Their love-making together those times had been a piece of heaven on earth to her. She'd known she could be happy here in Deadrange. What went wrong?

She determined to get to the bottom of this. One person in Deadrange would know the truth of what was really going on. Buck.

Shoving her feet back into her slippers, she grabbed up her reticule and stormed out the door.

After ten minutes of talking with Buck, Kate was no closer to the answer than when she'd left the hotel. She'd hinted and cajoled without results.

"Buck, what has gotten into Brannigan?" She jumped out of the chair as if she'd been shot. "He refuses to have anything to do with me. What do you know about this?" she demanded.

"Me? Why, gal, you know I could never betray a confidence. I sure did miss your visits while the two of you was gone. Had to make do with Miss Sally's company," he informed her.

Kate's eyebrows raised at this.

"Don't you go looking at me that way," Buck ordered her gruffly. "She was a mite lonesome was all."

"Umm."

"Dagnamit, gal, don't go hearing no wedding bells for us."

Kate smiled. "You seem to be protesting awfully loud, if I do say so."

"Well, don't. I thought you wanted to know about Brannigan." He changed the subject abruptly.

"So you do know what's going on with him." She leaned forward. "You know what is going on with Brannigan. I know you do. So, tell me."

Buck rubbed his hand back and forth over his whiskers, hiding his smile. Yup, things were going exactly according to his plan. He'd have the two of them together again in no time at all.

"Why, this is a fine howdy do for your wounded old friend," he feigned insult, goading her on.

Kate leaned forward and smiled at him sweetly. "Hah! You are as healthy as that ornery camel."

Buck grinned. He had the gal right where he wanted her. He remained silent, making her speak first.

Kate spun away and paced the room like a caged cougar. "Brannigan doesn't want me. And do you know that this morning, Papa had the nerve to forbid me to marry Brannigan." Kate strode back to him in a swirl of emerald green ruffles.

"So?" Buck challenged. "Doesn't appear that your father forbidding you something has ever stopped you in the past."

"But Brannigan is as cold as ice to me. He's— "

"The fool boy's giving you what he thinks will make you happy," Buck informed her in disgust.

"What?" Kate whirled about to face him.

"He thinks you need the safety some Eastern town is gonna give you."

"That's ridiculous. Why— "

"And he has this fool idea that you need all kinds of fancy things to make you happy." He spit the last word out.

"Oh, he does, does he?" Kate planted her hands on her hips.

"Yup. So, gal, what are you going to do about it?"

Kate narrowed her eyes, deep in thought for several minutes. Finally, a wicked smile teased her lips.

"I'm going to make him change his mind."

"That a gal."

She had a foolproof plan.

Twenty-one

Kate pounded on Richard's hotel room door. The instant he opened it, she strode inside.

"My dear, you've come—"

She held up her hand to silence him.

"Richard, I've come to offer you a business proposition."

His pale eyebrows almost disappeared into his hairline.

"How would you like to earn back the money you stole from me?" She patted her reticule, then withdrew the bills, showing him only the edge of the money.

"You haven't forgiven me, have you?"

"Richard, there's nothing to forgive. You did me a favor. If you hadn't abandoned me, I would never have fallen in love with Brannigan."

He took a startled step backwards.

"Now are you going to help me marry him or not?" she demanded, waving the money in his face.

"What do I have to do?" Richard asked in resignation. After all, between the money he'd received from her father and the money Kate was offering, he wouldn't be leaving with nothing.

"Pretend to be my adoring fiancé for the next week," she announced.

When he stared at her in shock, she added, "Or get out of my sight without a single bit of this money."

"What do we do?" he asked.

Kate proceeded to outline her plan.

Over the next three days, every time Brannigan saw Kate she was with Richard Hale. The man appeared to hang on her every word. And, even worse, Kate couldn't seem to take her eyes or her hands off the man.

As Brannigan watched the two of them stroll past his office that evening, arm in arm, his gut clenched into a knot. He balled his fists, reminding himself that he was doing this for Kate's own good.

"Hell and damnation," he muttered, turning away from the disturbing sight of Richard's hand on Kate's arm.

That should be *his* hand on her arm. His lips on her cheek.

Richard Hale didn't love Kate. All the fool loved was her father's money. Kate deserved better.

He couldn't stand it any longer. Grabbing up his hat, he stormed out the door. He wasn't going to stand idly by and allow Kate to ruin her life.

Brannigan paused only long enough to yank up a bunch of purple wildflowers he spotted blooming in the cracks of the boardwalk. Flowers in hand, he followed the couple down the street and into Miss Sally's Restaurant.

Without even stopping to remove his hat, he strode up to the table. Kate sniffed at him in disdain and turned her head away.

"Kate, we need to talk," Brannigan informed

her, dropping the flowers onto the table in front of her.

"It will have to be later. I'm busy having dinner with my fiancé." She stressed the last word.

"The hell you are."

Brannigan caught her by the hand and drew her to her feet. "You're coming with me."

Kate made a delicate show of surprise, hiding her smile of glee. She lagged behind him just enough so that he'd believe he was the one doing the leading.

Brannigan led her straight to the jail building, slamming the door behind them.

"What do you want?" she finally asked, her heart lodged in her throat as she waited for his answer. "Richard is waiting for me."

"The hell with Richard."

Brannigan tugged her after him to an empty cell. He positioned himself between Kate and the door.

"I can't let you do it, Kate."

He slammed the cell door closed behind him with a well-placed kick. The door clanged loudly in the empty jail.

"Do what?" she asked, her voice perfectly toned innocence.

It took every bit of her finishing school training to keep her expression calm and distant, and her voice even. Mrs. Parker would be proud of her.

"Live *our* life with *him.*" Brannigan pushed himself away from the cell bars.

"I don't know what you're talking about," she denied, crossing her fingers as she lied through her teeth, and smiled sweetly up at him.

Brannigan dragged his hand through his hair. "I can't stand the thought of you marrying him.

Of you having children with him." He stepped away from the bars. "Of you sharing your life with him."

"But he's asked me to marry him," she lied.

"He doesn't love you."

Kate resisted the almost overwhelming urge to throw herself in his arms. She knew she was pushing him, but she had to do it. She raised her chin and sent him a defiant look that dared him to act.

He took the invitation and took one long stride forward. Kate swallowed and inched back a step farther into the small jail cell.

"Hell and damnation." Brannigan took another stride closer to her. "I won't let you do it," he announced. "Not even if I have to keep you locked up in here until hell freezes over."

Kate opened her mouth, took one look at his hard, set face, and quickly closed her mouth again.

"That's our marriage." He punctuated it with another step. "Our children." And yet another step. "Our life." He stopped mere inches from her.

Kate felt her heart melt right then and there. It turned into a ball of warm liquid in her chest. She couldn't continue her charade. She couldn't deny him.

"You are not marrying him."

"No, Brannigan, I'm not," she said softly, the love for him shining forth.

"You're going to marry me."

"Yes, Brannigan."

He swept her into his arms, kissing her as if he'd never stop. Kate sighed in total surrender.

When he paused and gazed down at her, she whispered, "Love me, Brannigan."

He took her lips again in a kiss to seal their love. Brannigan knew he'd spend the rest of his life loving Kate.

Epilogue

"Hell's fire! What's taking so long?" Miss Sally twisted around to look back over her shoulder where Kate knelt on the floor adjusting the hem to her ivory silk gown.

"I'll only be another moment. Hold still," Kate ordered, mumbling around the pins clamped between her teeth.

Miss Sally shifted from one foot to the other. "This is worse than waiting on a room full of hungry ranchhands."

"Stand still," Kate ordered. "I don't want to hear you yelling if you get stuck with one of these pins. I'm almost finished."

"Do you think Buck will like it?" Miss Sally asked in an uncharacteristically hesitant voice.

"He will love it. It's a beautiful wedding dress," Kate rushed to assure her. "What are you worrying about? He already loves you."

The gruff older woman turned a most becoming shade of pink.

"Never thought I'd live to see the day you'd blush like a school girl," a husky voice called from the doorway moments before Belle Wilson pushed open the door to the shop and sauntered into the room.

A little bell tinkled merrily beneath the sign pro-
claiming "Kate's Courtier Fashions."

Miss Sally turned back around to face the newest
occupant of the fashionably decorated shop. "What
do you think you're grinning at, Belle?"

Belle gave a firm effort to restrain her smile and
failed. A soft chuckle flowed from her lips. "I do
declare, Miss Sally, I'd have never believed this day
would come— "

"Don't you dare give me any of your lip." Miss
Sally planted her fists on her hips and took a step
forward. "If you don't behave yourself, I'll unin-
vite you to me and Buck's wedding."

Belle raised her hands palms up in surrender.
"I wouldn't miss tomorrow's festivities for anything
in this world."

Kate sat back on her heels and watched the interchange with a rush of pure happiness. So much
had changed in Deadrange over the last year. Belle
was being courted openly by Howard Peabody,
Buck had proposed to Miss Sally, and the town's
population was growing. Rumor had it that the
next mayor would likely be Marshal Lucas Brannigan.

Mayor Lucas Brannigan. The words carried such
a nice ring to them.

"Hell's fire. How much longer do I got to stand
here?" Miss Sally grumbled.

"Finished," Kate announced, attempting to push
herself to her feet.

Belle was at her side in a flash, helping her up.
"Don't you know better than to be— "

"I'm perfectly fine." Kate brushed off her
friend's motherly concern. "Ginger! I'm only preg-
nant, not an invalid." She rubbed her hand back
and forth across her rounded stomach.

"Well, how's it look? Hell's fire, I feel like a trussed-up turkey." Miss Sally humphed, but ran a hand lovingly down the skirt of the fancy silk gown.

"But a pretty one." Belle tempered the words with laughter. "I'd have never guessed that my dressing gown could look so dang good." She tilted her head to admire the gown. "You did a good job, Kate. Remind me to order another dress from you."

Kate hid her smile behind her palm as she removed the pins from between her lips. Belle and Miss Sally had finally buried the animosity between them by the gesture of Belle supplying the fabric for Sally's wedding dress.

She dropped the pins into a crystal dish and looked around her shop with pride. It was prospering. Why even Mrs. Parker would be proud.

Spotting the lace parasol propped in the corner, she crossed over and scooped it up. "Here, don't forget this. Something borrowed."

Miss Sally blushed again and took the frilly object. Caressing the lace edge, she asked, "Are you sure?"

"It brought me luck, why not you?" Kate said, with a smile.

Her smile widened into a happy grin of pleasure as the bell of her shop tinkled again and Brannigan strode into the room.

"Excuse me, ladies." He tipped his black Stetson to them and turned his loving gaze to Kate. "If you'll pardon us, it's time for my wife's afternoon nap."

"Brannigan," Kate objected in a low voice.

"Coming?" he asked.

"I'm not finished here yet—"

"Oh, yes you are." He reached out and scooped her up into his arms.

"Brannigan!" Kate yelled.

Nodding goodbye to the other women, he turned and strode out the door with Kate held close in his arms.

"Brannigan," she murmured against his neck, clasping her arms around him.

"Yes, wife?"

"Am I under arrest?"

"Yup. And consider this a life sentence."

He bent his head and lowered his lips over hers. Kate tilted her head back, kissing him thoroughly in return.

A lifetime of love. Definitely a sentence worth serving.

Dear Reader,

I hope you enjoyed *Loving Kate,* and that Kate and Brannigan will live on in your hearts as they will in mine. *Loving Kate* was a very special book for me. For one thing, it allowed me to indulge my love of the Old West. I'm certain I was destined to love the Old West— I grew up watching every episode of Gunsmoke and Bonanza with my dad.

My next book will be another western. *Tempting Tess* takes place in San Francisco where Tess Fontana is on the run with a wanted man— her father. And Texas Ranger Zack Mackinzie is hot on their trail. Look for it next October.

While my dad gave me a love of the Old West, my mother taught me to believe in love. I still do. I'm happily married to the man I met and fell in love with way back in high school. Natives of Missouri, we now live in northern California with our cocker spaniel puppy.

I believe in love and laughter, and my wish for you is that *Loving Kate* has brought a little bit of both into your life.

I want to thank each of you for your support and your letters. Those letters hold a special place in my heart, for I believe the highest compliment an author can receive is such a letter from a reader. Once again, thank you. If you ever see me at a conference, please come up and say hi, because I love to meet readers.

I'd love to hear from you. If you would like to write to me or to receive a bookmark, send your letter along with a stamped, self-addressed envelope to me in care of Zebra Books, 850 Third Avenue, New York, NY 10022.

— Joyce Adams

PUT SOME PASSION INTO YOUR
LIFE . . . WITH THIS STEAMY SELECTION OF
ZEBRA *LOVEGRAMS!*

SEA FIRES   (3899, $4.50/$5.50)
by Christine Dorsey

Spirited, impetuous Miranda Chadwick arrives in the untamed New
World prepared for any peril. But when the notorious pirate Gentleman
Jack Blackstone kidnaps her in order to fulfill his secret plans, she can't
help but surrender — to the shameless desires and raging hunger that his
bronzed, lean body and demanding caresses ignite within her!

TEXAS MAGIC   (3898, $4.50/$5.50)
by Wanda Owen

After being ambushed by bandits and saved by a ranchhand, headstrong
Texas belle Bianca Moreno hires her gorgeous rescuer as a protective es-
cort. But Rick Larkin does more than guard her body — he kisses away her
maidenly inhibitions, and teaches her the secrets of wild, reckless love!

SEDUCTIVE CARESS   (3767, $4.50/$5.50)
by Carla Simpson

Determined to find her missing sister, brave beauty Jessamyn Forsythe
disguises herself as a simple working girl and follows her only clues to
Whitechapel's darkest alleys . . . and the disturbingly handsome Inspec-
tor Devlin Burke. Burke, on the trail of a killer, becomes intrigued with
the ebon-haired lass and discovers the secrets of her silken lips and the
hidden promise of her sweet flesh.

SILVER SURRENDER   (3769, $4.50/$5.50)
by Vivian Vaughan

When Mexican beauty Aurelia Mazón saves a handsome stranger from
death, she finds herself on the run from the Federales with the most dangerous man she's ever met. And when Texas Ranger Carson Jarrett steals
her heart with his intimate kisses and seductive caresses, she yields to an
all-consuming passion from which she hopes to never escape!

ENDLESS SEDUCTION   (3793, $4.50/$5.50)
by Rosalyn Alsobrook

Caught in the middle of a dangerous shoot-out, lovely Leona Stegall falls
unconscious and awakens to the gentle touch of a handsome doctor.
When her rescuer's caresses turn passionate, Leona surrenders to his fiery
embrace and savors a night of soaring ecstasy!

*Available wherever paperbacks are sold, or order direct from the
Publisher. Send cover price plus 50¢ per copy for mailing and
handling to Penguin USA, P.O. Box 999, c/o Dept. 17109,
Bergenfield, NJ 07621. Residents of New York and Tennessee
must include sales tax. DO NOT SEND CASH.*

THE FIERY PASSION, EARTHY SENSUALITY, AND THRILLING ADVENTURES OF THE McLOUGHLIN CLAN

Book I, CARESS OF FIRE (3718, $4.50/$5.50)
by Martha Hix

Lisette Keller wanted out of Texas. The stubborn beauty was willing to work her way north, but first she needed a job. Why not hire on as trail cook with the McLoughlin outfit? To virile rancher Gil McLoughlin, a cattle drive was no place for a lady. Soon, he not only hired her, he also vowed to find out if her lips were as sweet as her cooking . . .

Book II, LONE STAR LOVING (4029, $4.50/$5.50)
by Martha Hix

The law at her heels, smuggler Charity McLoughlin had enough trouble without getting abducted by a black-haired savage called Hawk. When he fired her passion, were her fortunes looking up or down? But she wouldn't try to get away just yet, even though he would deliver her to a fate worse than death. For one night, she'd surrender to those dark eyes and his every desire . . .

Book III, WILD SIERRA ROGUE (4256, $4.50/$5.50)
by Martha Hix

Sparks flew when Rafe Delgado teamed with starchy and absolutely desperate Margaret McLoughlin on a rescue mission to save her mother. It irked Margaret, depending on the very rogue who'd wronged the family to lead her to the legendary Copper Canyon of Chihuahua. She condemned the rake's lack of redeeming values, while he meant to take the starch out of her drawers. They didn't count on falling in love . . .